Ten for Dying

Books by Mary Reed and Eric Mayer

Ten for Dying

A John the Lord Chamberlain Mystery

Mary Reed and Eric Mayer

Poisoned Pen Press

Library of Congress Catalog Card Number: 2013941455

ISBN: 9781464202278   Hardcover
      9781464202292   Trade Paperback

Poisoned Pen Press
6962 E. First Ave., Ste. 103
Scottsdale, AZ 85251
www.poisonedpenpress.com
info@poisonedpenpress.com

Printed in the United States of America

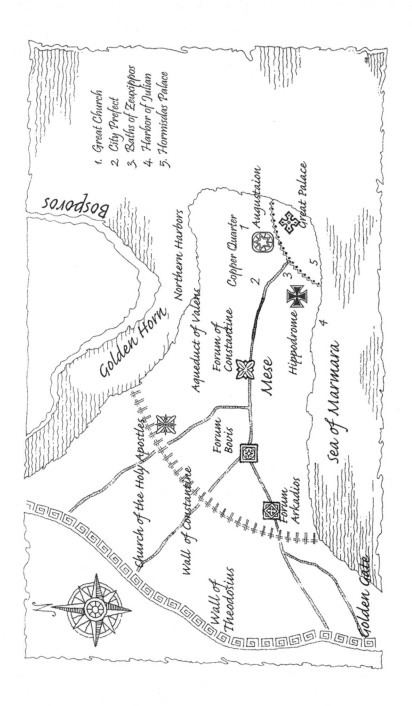

Bosporos

Golden Horn

Northern Harbors

1. Great Church
2. City Prefect
3. Baths of Zeuxippos
4. Harbor of Julian
5. Hormisdas Palace

Aqueduct of Valens

Copper Quarter

Augustaion

1

Great Palace

2

3

5

Forum of Constantine

Mese

Hippodrome

4

Sea of Marmara

Church of the Holy Apostles

Forum Boris

Wall of Constantine

Forum Arkadios

Wall of Theodosius

Golden Gate

Prologue

At the deadest hour of a warm summer night, the door to the mausoleum behind the Church of the Holy Apostles opened with a creak resembling the short cry of a sleeper disturbed by a nightmare.

The door closed, barely stirring the humid air in which the sharp odor of incense overpowered the faint, fading perfume of flowers left to wither at the base of the sides of the sarcophagus. Again the brooding silence was broken, this time by the throaty croaking of frogs and the shuffle of feet across the moon-washed marble floor.

A pause. Then a babble in a strange tongue emanated from the deep shadows, gathered like death at the head of the sarcophagus.

"Beloved wife of Petrus Sabbatius, I summon you back from the hall of judgment! Return from the embrace of Anubis, god of the dead! As the sacred scarab brings forth the sun from night each morning, I command you with words of power to come back from the darkness!"

A hand, small as a child's, leathery as an old man's, laid a carved scarab inside one of the olive wreathes carved into the reddish Sardian sandstone lid of the tomb.

"Hear the song of frogs, sacred to Heqt, giver of life to the returned dead! When I name you, you will answer and obey me!"

The diminutive speaker paused, turned, and listened.

Was that a noise outside?

Was his magickal ceremony working?

Would the door swing open and his former employer glide into the chamber rather than materializing next to her tomb?

There was no sound but the croaking of the frogs.

What if she did not appear?

What if he was caught desecrating a holy place?

He laid trembling hands on the sarcophagus, bent forward to whisper in the ear of its occupant, and continued in desperate tones.

"I summon you! You must return!"

Another pause.

"I served you well and now I need your protection," he pleaded.

There! A noise outside!

She had obeyed his summons. Or was he discovered?

The thought took him to a narrow window. In his haste he trod on one of dozens of frogs hopping everywhere. His foot slid and he clamped a hand on the windowsill to keep himself from falling.

Moonlight turned the gnarled hand to unpainted marble.

He pulled himself up, standing on tiptoe to see outside.

The cry of horror he could not stifle reverberated around the mausoleum.

What had he done? What dreadful gates had he inadvertently opened?

Two figures, one clutching an object as pale as the uncaring moon to its chest, loped away from the illuminated doorway at the back of the church.

Demons!

DAY ONE

Chapter One

Felix came awake staring into a pair of shining eyes, mirrors in a hallway to the fires of Hell.

No, that had been his nightmare, or his memory of the Anastasia of the darkness. He was captain of the excubitors, responsible for guarding Emperor Justinian, but the past few days and nights he had not been doing a good job.

"What are you thinking?" Anastasia murmured.

"That you're an angel."

She pressed herself against him and nestled her face in his beard. "You're lying. Naughty bear."

He had no answer to that. He had not had any answers to Anastasia since he'd first seen her. Had it only been a week before? He could hardly believe he had had a life before Anastasia. He always felt like that at this stage of an affair. He never remembered how badly his liaisons invariably ended. Never asked himself exactly how badly and in what way this particular fling would end.

He saw Anastasia's slim body pressed against his bulk. Why had he never noticed the disgusting middle-aged paunch he'd developed? Anastasia wasn't that much younger, was she? Ten years younger, but appearing more. He hadn't asked. In the first, hesitant light of morning her skin looked so white one would have thought it as cool as marble to the touch. Quite wrongly, Felix knew. He would need to spend more time at the gymnasium.

"You're feeling guilty about us," she said. He felt her fingers tiptoeing through the tangled hair on his chest.

"No. Not a bit."

"Is it because you were supposed to be finding Theodora's murderer rather than falling in love?"

"That has all been resolved. Why should I feel guilty?"

"What's wrong then? I can tell something's bothering you."

"No. Nothing. What could be bothering me, lying here beside you?"

Felix wasn't sure what worried him. He looked at the ceiling. At the fluffy clouds and birds painted up there at great expense for a woman whose name he couldn't recall immediately. Thin light coming in past the open shutters showed the early hour. The already humid air filling the bedroom held the tang of the sea, the odor of Constantinople—overripe, on the verge of going bad—and the smell of love, mingled scents of wine, perfume, and perspiration.

"You're thinking about politics again, aren't you?" Anastasia's expression verged on a pout.

"No," he said. Which had been true until she mentioned the subject. Political maneuverings at the palace in the wake of the death of the empress had been about the only thing on his mind recently, aside from Anastasia's charms.

She twisted a tuft of his chest hair around her finger. "You were wise to ally yourself with General Germanus, my love. Don't doubt your decision. Theodora's gone. The fact that Belisarius is married to the best friend of the empress can't help the poor bungling cuckold any longer. The emperor is sure to come to his senses and turn the army over to his cousin Germanus where it should have rested in the first place. "

"Maybe."

She gave his coiled hair a sharp, painful tug. "Not maybe, Felix, dear. You shall soon have your military command. You can trade captain for general. I know what goes on at the palace."

She probably told the truth. Felix had encountered Anastasia during his tedious interviews with Theodora's huge entourage following the empress' long illness and suspicious death. Theodora's vast private apartments were packed with ladies-in-waiting, courtiers, servants, decorative young pages, and anyone who amused her, from acrobats and dwarfs to dancers and clerics. She had been hiding the heretical and supposedly exiled Patriarch Anthimus for twelve years.

Talking to them all was daunting. As soon as Felix ascertained a person had not been near Theodora during her final days he moved on quickly.

Except in the case of Anastasia. He had found an excuse to seek her out again. He thought he detected an invitation in the manner of the attendant with aristocratic looks. He had not been mistaken. Since then he had wondered whether she was attracted to him or to his potential for advancement. But he hadn't thought about it very often or very hard. Did it matter?

"Let's not fret about politics." Her words came to him on the warm, winy breeze of her breath. "A little honey will get the bear's mind off palace intrigue." Her fingers left the heavy growth of his chest and started to climb the overly steep slope of his belly.

The door of the bedroom burst open.

Felix's servant Nikomachos stood there, his shoulder to the door. "My apologies, lady." The young man bowed deferentially but for a little too long toward Anastasia. "I didn't realize…I would have knocked, However…" He held up in his right hand a silver tray bearing a sealed scroll. His gaze flickered in the direction of where his left hand should have been but was not. His entire left arm was missing.

Felix got out of bed, pulling a sheet around his middle, and took the scroll. He slammed the door shut as his servant retreated, then returned to bed, broke the wax seal, and unrolled the parchment. Anastasia was sitting up, face half buried in her hands, giggling like a child.

Felix read the message and grimaced. He looked up, groaned, and threw his sheet across Anastasia's inviting nakedness. "A relic's been stolen from the Church of the Holy Apostles. Must be important. The excubitors are ordered to look into it along with the urban watch. There's no time for honey when the emperor calls."

Chapter Two

Felix clumped disconsolately past the excubitor barracks and across the cobbled square fronting the brick-walled house where his friend John, Lord Chamberlain to Emperor Justinian, lived. His head throbbed from too much wine and not enough sleep and he could still smell Anastasia's perfume in his beard.

Two months ago Justinian would have summoned his Lord Chamberlain to order him to look into the theft of an important relic. John would have been receiving orders in the emperor's chilly reception hall and Felix would still be in Anastasia's warm arms. But since Theodora's passing, things had changed in Constantinople. John's investigation of her death had resulted in his dismissal.

It was one of Justinian's transitory whims, no doubt. No successor to the post had been appointed. In the meantime, Felix hoped John would help him even if he was temporarily in disfavor.

He was surprised to see a laden ox cart outside the house.

"Peter! Is your master at home?"

The old servant looked up from the crate he was tying to the back of the cart. "The master will be out shortly, but I fear he has no time for visitors."

"Why the gloomy look, Peter? Isn't your new marriage agreeing with you?"

Felix's jocular tone failed to brighten the wrinkled visage. "Life's joys are always accompanied by sorrow, sir. Our lot is to run with patience the race that is set before us, as the holy book says."

Felix thought a man of Peter's years should be happy to run the race with a new bride half his age. He reflected that it must be a platonic relationship as a tawny-skinned and raven-haired Egyptian woman emerged from the house. In Felix's opinion she more resembled the parchment-skinned man's daughter or granddaughter than his wife.

Then he saw with a shock that Hypatia cradled a swaddled figure. Before he could say a word, she lifted a corner of the blanket.

A shriveled head with enormous whiskers stared up glassy-eyed.

"Cheops, our poor little mummified cat," Hypatia explained. "A souvenir of Peter's travels with the master."

"Ah…well…congratulations to you and Peter. On your marriage, I mean. But what's all this about?" Felix gestured toward the cart.

"You must know that the master has been exiled, sir. The whole city knows."

"This is home no longer, Captain Felix." Peter added.

"Yes, I know the emperor was displeased, but Justinian always comes to his senses before—"

"Not this time, my friend." As John stepped out of the house into the sunlight Felix couldn't help noticing his face looked more gaunt than usual and there was, hard to believe, a hint of a stoop in the tall frame. Cornelia emerged and stood beside her husband. Her eyes were red-rimmed.

"You aren't really going away?" Felix blurted.

"Our ship leaves for Greece this morning," John replied. "I hoped to have a chance to talk with you before we departed."

Felix realized the quartet—master, mistress, and servants alike—all wore rough traveling cloaks. "I would have come to see you, John, but I never imagined…and I've been…well… very busy…important business."

Cornelia walked over to the cart. Her nostrils flared. "Busy, indeed! That's an expensive scent you're wearing! Everyone at the palace knows about your important business, even those of us in disfavor."

Felix felt his face flush.

Cornelia glared at him. "Anatolius has been exceptionally busy in his legal endeavors lately, what with all the uncertainties everyone faces with Theodora gone, but he managed to tear himself away from the charms of the magistrates to pay his respects. Even Isis visited and cried the whole time."

"Isis left the refuge?" He was surprised the brothel owner, now head of a sanctuary for reformed prostitutes, would have dared to visit a disgraced Lord Chamberlain.

"Why not? She's known John for years. She had several girls in tow. To protect her reputation I suppose. Very proper they look now in their plain garments. Quite a contrast to the old days."

"As usual Isis wanted to reminisce about when we knew each other in Egypt although in reality our paths never crossed there. Not that I recall." John pulled the heavy nail-studded wooden door shut and locked it. "However, speaking of Egypt, there's still an ample stock of Egyptian wine left in the house." He handed the key to Felix. "Help yourself to anything else left behind before the emperor does."

The key was a massive weight in Felix's hand. "Why didn't you warn me you were about to go?"

The former Lord Chamberlain answered only with a faint smile.

"I realize you don't like farewells, John, but—"

"And you didn't come to say farewell. What is it then?"

Felix's head seemed to be filled with cobwebs. Perhaps he wasn't as sober as he had imagined after the night's excesses. "A relic's been stolen," he said, realizing that he shouldn't be burdening John under the circumstances, but too befuddled to change course. He pulled the emperor's message from his cloak. "It's all explained here. Very strange. I was hoping you'd accompany me to the Church of the Holy Apostles."

Cornelia's eyes gleamed, resembling the edge of a newly honed sword. "Felix, you know very well Justinian made it plain nothing happening in Constantinople is of interest to John any longer. Not to mention our ship sails in an hour or two."

John put his hand on her arm. "We'll take a couple of the excubitors' horses. You and the others go on to the docks. I'll be there before the cart's unloaded."

"Master, if I may ask, could we leave now?" Peter put in. "That big man lounging against the barracks has been taking quite an interest in us ever since we came outside."

"No wonder. It's not often you see a former high-ranking official being sent away in disgrace," Cornelia snapped. "He's no doubt one of Justinian's spies, making certain the emperor's orders are obeyed."

"John's fortunate," Felix pointed out. "Usually those who fall from favor disappear permanently."

The glare Cornelia gave him made Felix wish he could vanish. She climbed up onto the seat of the cart beside her two servants. "Are you certain you aren't going to get John involved in anything dangerous?"

Felix shook his head. "Hardly, unless you consider frogs dangerous."

"Frogs?"

Felix opened the scroll and glanced at it. "So it says. The new mausoleum at the back of the church was overrun with frogs."

Hypatia suddenly leaned around Peter, who had taken up the reins. "Are you certain, sir?"

"At least thirty of them."

Peter glanced at Hypatia. "You look distressed, my dear. What is it?"

Hypatia bit her lip.

"There is something you wish to say?" John asked.

"If I may, master," Hypatia replied hesitantly, "in Egypt frogs are sacred to the goddess associated with resurrection. That so many appeared overnight in a place of the dead seems a great wonder. Where could they all have come from?"

Felix ran a hand through his beard. "Strange you should mention Egypt. A carved scarab was left behind."

John looked thoughtful. "Frogs and a scarab are an unusually suggestive pairing. Was someone trying to raise the dead?"

Felix didn't answer immediately. He hoped John was joking. But his friend didn't smile. "It could be," Felix finally said, reluctantly. The implications of John's observation made him shudder. "The scarab was found lying on top of Theodora's sarcophagus."

Chapter Three

Theodora's shade was not waiting for Felix and John at the entrance to the Church of the Holy Apostles.

Not that Felix had truly expected her, although, he had to admit, his imagination had bedeviled him during their ride along the Mese.

Leaving their horses with one of the excubitors arrayed around the church, he and John made their way upstream against a flood of worshippers pouring out into the sunshine after morning prayer. In the nave, where they found the priest Basilius, beams of sunlight dropped through wisps of pungent incense, sparkling here off a silver lamp, there from jewels set in a gilded reliquary.

Christian ostentation had never impressed Felix like John, a secret follower of the soldier's austere god Mithra. But recently, battered by the changes at the palace, he had felt a guilty appreciation, an attraction, not to the gold and gems and fine marbles in the churches, but to their solidity. Theodora was dead, John would soon be in exile, his own life had careened past with shocking speed, but these monuments to the Christian god were ever-present, in every street. Wherever you stood in Constantinople you could see a glittering dome, a cross. Endlessly built and replaced, the churches, and perhaps what they represented, would forever be here.

Basilius did not appear to be taking any comfort from his surroundings. Short and slight, of indeterminate age, he looked distraught as he spoke to a shabbily dressed man and woman beside the marble-columned templon guarding the sanctuary beyond. Lingering worshippers, Felix guessed.

He strode up to Basilius, accompanied by John. Both men towered above the priest, whose robes were disheveled.

"Ah, Captain. Thank you for coming. I've already spoken to one of the City Prefect's men. I was told the emperor would be sending someone as well." Basilius offered John a nervous glance, started to address him, then, instead, handed Felix a green stone, carved into the shape of a beetle. "Here is the scarab found on Theodora's tomb. The frogs have been removed from the mausoleum." He absently wiped his hand on his vestments.

Felix peered at the scarab, turned it over, looking for what, he couldn't say. The ancient talisman, crude and dull, seemed profoundly out of place amid the magnificent trappings of Christianity. "Do you have any idea who might be responsible for this?"

Basilius shook his head.

Felix gave John an inquiring glance, but John said nothing.

"We'll need to examine the mausoleum," Felix said. "But what about the relic that was stolen?"

Basilius appeared ready to burst into tears. "One of the empire's most sacred and powerful relics, the fragment of the burial cloth of our Lord's mother!"

The words took the air out of Felix like a blow to the stomach. Surely not the Virgin's shroud? He knew of it, of course. Who in the city did not? Constantinople was said to be under its protection. A fine thing if it couldn't even protect itself from thieves.

"You saw the theft?"

"No. I have witnesses." Basilius indicated the poorly dressed couple whom Felix had taken for worshippers. "This is Mada, who serves the Lord in the capacity of church cleaner, and Peteiros, her husband, who takes care of lighting the lamps and polishing the holy vessels."

The couple gave feeble smiles, bowed, and moved forward a few paces. They were of late middle age, sturdy but pallid-skinned, suggesting farmers who hadn't seen the sun in years.

"Please tell the captain and his companion what you told me," Basilius instructed them.

Felix noted the priest's description of John as merely the captain's companion. Two weeks ago he had been the feared and respected Lord Chamberlain. Now the whole city knew of his fall from imperial grace. It was obvious John's presence made Basilius uneasy. People kept their distance from Justinian's enemies if they knew what was good for them.

Mada clasped her red and knobby hands together and began in a faltering voice. "We came here early this morning to attend to our duties, sir. My husband was refilling the lamps. They were burning low and the church was full of shadows. And it seemed wrong, somehow. We got to work…"

The woman spoke with a faint, rough accent Felix could not place.

She shivered and looked around fearfully. "But after a while the church felt different. There was a strange smell, a bad smell, overpowering the incense, and suddenly the walls began to move."

"Move?" Felix asked.

The woman wrung her clasped hands. "Yes. The Lord is my witness. It was as if the stone had turned to water. Like a waterfall. Yet my mouth felt as dry as the desert. And then my husband fell down."

"That is true, sir," Peteiros confirmed. "I know how a fly must feel when a man brings his hand down on it. One moment I was standing here and the next—"

"Oh, Peteiros, you do go on," scolded his wife.

"But it is true, sirs. All turned black and I went straight to the floor." He pointed to a large bruise on his forehead. "Does this mark lie?"

Felix looked to John, who did not appear inclined to assist in the questioning. "So what happened then?"

"I was helping him get up as best I could," Mada said. "I was feeling very unwell myself, and then I heard the sound of running feet. I looked around. There were two of them, keeping to the shadows, they were. It was hard to see, what with the walls bubbling and trembling, but it seemed—"

"Demons, sirs." Interrupted Peteiros. "Hideous demons!"

Felix thought the priest looked faint. "Demons? My orders mentioned frogs and a scarab. Nothing was said about demons."

"I only caught a glimpse of them," Mada admitted, "between the shadows and my head spinning and helping my husband, but they had to be demons. There was that smell I mentioned, surely it was the smell of demons?"

"That's right," her husband confirmed. "The unholy stink of them is still in my nostrils."

Felix sniffed the air but discerned only incense, predominately frankincense. He had noticed that the breath of the cleaning woman and her husband was particularly foul. He suspected they had both been drinking the night before. "Are you sure this dreadful odor is in your nose and not just in your head?"

"I wish it were only in my head, sir."

"And then? What did these demons do?"

Mada waved a claw-like hand in the direction of several elaborate reliquaries sitting on a table in front of the templon. "They ran over there. To where the holy objects are kept. When they raced away one of them carried something that glowed white in the shadows."

"Like a halo," added Peteiros.

Felix had seen the shroud when it was displayed during holy days. In truth it was merely a piece of the shroud, a stained scrap of cloth.

Basilius walked over to the reliquary. Felix managed to compose himself and followed.

The priest's hand shook as he pointed out how the lock on the dome of a miniature, gem-encrusted Great Church had been forced.

To Felix's consternation John remained adamantly silent. "What do you think, John?" he hinted.

"A very small lock to secure such a great treasure," John replied.

Basilius shook his head. "The shroud is usually housed at the Church of the Virgin and well-guarded indeed. But it was brought here temporarily for the empress' funeral. Who could have guessed anyone would engage in such desecration? I sent one of my younger assistants out to find a patrol but by the time he brought someone back it was far too late."

"It's obvious someone decided to take advantage of the shroud being kept here without adequate security," Felix observed. He lifted the golden dome and peered down into the reliquary's interior. A thread lay coiled there. Did even a minute bit of a sacred object hold divine power? If the Christian god was all powerful, why not? But if that god was present everywhere, as the Christians claimed, what was the point of relics anyway?

He shut the dome with a click. Felix well knew the only point that mattered to him right now was that the emperor valued this peculiar old scrap of cloth more than the head of his excubitor captain. If Felix didn't find the relic he would soon be joining John in exile, or a worse fate, given Justinian's apparent derangement since Theodora's death. But how was he supposed to accomplish that? To believers, the shroud was holier than the Great Church. The Great Church, however, could not be folded up like a child's tunic for hiding.

There was no use pondering the problem now. He forced his attention to the matter of Theodora's tomb. "You'd better show me where the frogs were," he told Basilius.

The mausoleum's elderly doorkeeper was half dozing on a stool by an outside entrance. A stout stick leaning across the inside of the door frame provided an attempt at a barrier. As Basilius, Felix, and John approached, he blinked and grabbed the stick, and attempted to stand.

"Remain seated," Basilius told him.

Felix was dumbfounded. "This ancient is who you have guarding the mausoleum?"

"Timothy is perfectly dependable, sir."

The sight of the stick caused Felix to raise his eyebrows. "You mean he's too crippled to want to stroll about during the night?"

Timothy turned a watery gaze on Felix. "There's not a soul in the city wants to go creeping around a tomb in the middle of the night, sir. Especially Theodora's tomb. It makes my hairs prickle just sitting in the doorway. More than once I've felt the hand of the empress this close to the back of my neck." He showed Felix his thumb and forefinger, the space between them the thickness of a coin. He looked toward the priest. "It's then I mutter a prayer, and she goes back where she came from."

"You shouldn't speak of our blessed empress that way," chided Basilius.

"Last night someone wanted to creep around and did," Felix reminded the doorkeeper.

"Not men. Demons."

"So you saw these demons, too?"

"That's right. Two of them. They came running out of the church."

"I have already questioned Timothy," Basilius put in. "He confirmed everything Mada and Peteiros said about them."

"And in which direction did they run?" Felix supposed Timothy had not been able to pursue them further than the seat of his stool.

The old man must have guessed his thoughts because he planted his stick on the ground and pulled himself upright. "There was no way to pursue them, sir. I leapt to my feet, just as I did now. But as I was about to give chase they vanished!"

Felix stared around the courtyard behind the church. There were several fountains and shrines, along with a few small trees. "Vanished? Behind what?"

"Into the air, sir. Into the darkness. It was as if Satan opened his mouth and gulped them down."

◇◇◇

"I wonder if Satan had as bad a bellyache as I do," Felix complained.

He and John were riding slowly to the docks as their horses picked their way around pedestrians, carriages, and litters crowding the streets between the colonnades.

"What's made your stomach hurt?"

"You, John. I hoped you'd assist me."

"When there's nothing to say, it is better to say nothing. Besides, you'd better get used to undertaking investigations like this. It may be that Justinian is going to turn to you now that I'm leaving."

The suggestion horrified Felix. "I hope not!"

"He can count on you, can't he?"

"You need to ask?"

"I'm not certain. Do I?"

Felix wondered whether John knew something of his recent activities. Not that it mattered now. He could see the waters of the Golden Horn glistening beyond the seawall on the other side of the open square where the descending street ended. John's ship would be there, Cornelia, Peter, and Hypatia awaiting him.

"But at least tell me what you make of it all, John. What about the frogs?"

"Just frogs, judging by the bloodstains left by those that were trodden on. Not to mention the leftover legs. I saw nothing that supported these claims of malignant fiends running about."

"You mean Timothy imagined or dreamed of seeing them and it improved in the telling?"

"Perhaps."

"Perhaps? You have no opinion? You didn't ask any questions, John. I can't understand why you weren't paying attention."

"Mada and her husband were from somewhere around the Euxine Sea. They had lost much of their accents, so I suspect they probably came to Constantinople when they were young."

"All right, so you were paying attention after all, my friend. But didn't you learn anything of use to me now?"

"I don't know yet." John dismounted, handed the reins to Felix, and with a quiet "Mithra guard you" walked quickly toward one of the archways giving access to the docks.

Felix let him go. As he watched John's receding back, now as straight as if he had thrown off a burden, he wondered why John hadn't mentioned the stolen relic.

It was the relic that worried Felix the most.

Chapter Four

"When they told me to be ready to receive a valuable item I never guessed they meant a relic as important as the Virgin's shroud!"

Felix had been pacing the bedroom, pouring out his worries to Anastasia who sat on the bed. She had put back on the blue silk gown she wore when she arrived the night before. It was crumpled and she hadn't finished applying her makeup. Her powdered cheeks belonged to a girl. Her untouched eyes looked older.

Felix dropped down beside her, cursing under his breath.

"So you have been using your office for financial gain?" Anastasia stared at him. He tried to read her expression. Condemnation? Admiration? Fear? Anger? He could not fathom what she was thinking.

"Using my office…that's not a very pleasant way to put it."

"And how else can I put it? You receive goods and then order excubitors to transport them safely under imperial seal."

"But neither I nor my men have any idea what we're delivering."

"Which makes it better?"

"I've seen enough to have a notion of what's going on. It's miraculous how saints' bones resemble those of the unsaintly. It's nothing but forgeries. What's the harm?"

"Indeed. Forgers are being taxed for delivery of their fraudulent goods and those hoping to buy real relics illegally are penalized by being cheated. You're practically doing the empire a service!"

"Did I say I was proud of myself? I've already explained my difficulties."

"But how can you be in debt? You're the captain of the excubitors. Don't tell me Justinian doesn't reward you handsomely."

"He does but—"

"He'd better. Your men could pull him off the throne as easily as guard him."

Felix raised his hand, gesturing her to be silent. "Please don't say such a thing, even in a whisper, even in private."

"I see you looking at the door. Do you think that impertinent servant of yours is eavesdropping?"

"No. Well, I don't know. Any of the household could be passing by."

Anastasia briefly pressed her lips together in annoyance before speaking. "How large can these debts be? You must own a fair amount of property."

"Certainly I have properties. They cost me more than they bring in."

"What kind of useless properties are these?"

"Vineyards, farms. I can hardly keep track. The only thing that seems to grow on them is debt. It's amazing how well debt thrives in rocky soil."

"Are you certain?"

"Do I look like a farmer? I only know what my stewards tell me. Last month a hailstorm destroyed most of my grapes."

"Did you inspect the damage?"

Felix shrugged. "Why? I know nothing about grapes."

"Except when they are in your wine cups. Oh, Felix, you may not be a farmer but you can be a perfect chickpea."

"You don't think my stewards lie to me, do you?"

"Everybody lies. How would people live without lying? It would be impossible. You are going to be a general soon, my love. You have to stop thinking like a soldier and start thinking like a general."

"I suppose you're right."

She leaned over to kiss him lightly. "Of course I'm right." Her breath felt hot against the side of his face. He had a sudden urge to pull her down onto the bed and forget his finances.

As if reading his mind she straightened up and crossed her arms over her breasts. "You must have put your money into something other than land, Felix."

He forced himself to look away from her. He stared at the door, half wondering if someone might indeed be lurking behind it. "What's wrong with land?" he muttered. "Land is what wars are fought over. I've seen colleagues bleeding to death on the battlefield over a piece of ground smaller than the Augustaion."

"Don't you have investments?"

"Investments! Yes. I almost forgot. Another excellent way to diminish one's fortune."

"Let's see. Your business partners advise you that they encountered unforeseen circumstances. Just a little more money is all it will take to overcome them. Enough to hang on until conditions change, and then the gold will start to rain down."

"Exactly! How did you know?"

Anastasia gave one of her pretty little laughs. "Oh, my poor dear…"

Realizing she was making fun of him, Felix felt his face flush. "I'm not so stupid that I don't know people take advantage of me. I detest business. I hate the smell of ink and lawyers. I try to choose advisers I can trust, then forget about them. But as you say, everyone lies, so I'm always disappointed. I'm not a fool, you know."

Anastasia tried to look chastened. She didn't do a good job of it, but the attempt mollified Felix.

"But how much money can you make smuggling relics?" she asked.

"Enough to pay certain of my debts. Gambling debts, if you have to know. The charioteers I've backed lately have served me as well as my vineyards. Every time they take to the track, their horses are struck down by a hailstorm of bad fortune."

"Why not sell a vineyard to pay the debts?"

"It wouldn't look good. People at court would wonder why I was selling off land, and they'd ferret out the reason. Besides, land is land, even if it isn't sprouting gold. I've fought hard for that land."

"So then tell the gamblers to consider their loans to you as gifts to Justinian's soon-to-be general, and hint at benefits to come."

"Those men aren't generous. They want payment now."

"Tell them to get into the habit of giving or go to Hell."

"They'll all be in Hell soon enough. I doubt they're in any rush to get there."

"Have them arrested for threatening you. Whatever they say, accuse them of lying."

"It isn't that easy. I'm not the only one caught in their web. They've spun their sticky strings from the palace to the dome of the Great Church. Too many high-ranking officials would be eager to flay me alive to save their own skins."

"What a strange turn of phrase. Do spiders skin flies before they eat them?"

"I apologize for not being a poet!"

Anastasia put her arms around his shoulders. "Now, now, my big bear. I don't want any poets poking around me with their nasty little pens. I was only trying to make you smile."

Felix apologized for his apology.

"What a repentant bear you are this morning."

"You do understand I would never agree to help smuggle the Virgin's shroud?"

"Who says you'll be asked? Perhaps the robbery was a coincidence. No one brought anything to your doorstep last night. I know. I was here."

"Yes. How could I forget?" He reached out to paw at her but she squirmed away.

"Not now, Felix. What are we going to do about this? Why don't you tell these people dealing in relics that you've found out about their scheme—if it turns out you're right—and you won't help them any longer?"

"Because they'll go to my creditors and complain that I refuse to work to pay off my obligations."

"You think the smugglers and gamblers are working together?"

"For all intents and purposes. And my financial difficulties could prove more dangerous than smuggling. The knowledge could easily be used against me. An ambitious underling might point to the possibility of my being bribed. After all, I'm the man who guards the emperor…you can see how it would seem to Justinian. He'd have my head, especially given his state of mind right now."

"So you're afraid of losing your head as well as your skin. You'll be little more than those relics you're smuggling. Yet you have just confessed your debts to me."

Felix found himself gazing at her speculatively. Why should he trust this woman he barely knew? Weren't there dozens like her swarming around the palace, attending to their superiors, hoping to catch an aristocrat of their own? Dressed in expensive silks, her face expertly painted, Anastasia resembled an empress. But didn't they all? Most likely she was the daughter of an ambitious petty official. Or, given her age, the widow of such a man.

"You can't sit here and brood, Felix. You need to do something about this. Time flies."

Who was this woman to order him about? He started to protest, then stopped himself. She was right.

Besides, she wasn't just any woman. There was something different about Anastasia.

Chapter Five

As Felix passed the doorway to a boarded-up shop he felt the edge of his cloak being grabbed. He went for his sword, then saw the feminine hand belonged to a skinny young girl who reeked of perfume. She simpered at him with crookedly painted lips and used her free hand to yank down the top of her tunic, displaying an undeveloped breast.

He pried her fingers from his cloak and continued on.

"Eunuch!" she spat after him.

Felix couldn't help wishing John were here. The Lord Chamberlain would know better how to extricate him from a delicate situation like the one in which he was embroiled. But John and his family must be on the Marmara by now, gazing back at the dome of the Great Church for the last time as it dwindled and finally sank from sight.

Felix could see sunlight flashing off the dome between gaps in the ramshackle wooden tenements along both sides of the street, a vision of heaven even as he passed archways from which the heat of metal forges issued, akin to the fiery breath from gateways to the Christians' Hell. At the edge of the Copper Quarter, the air smelled of smoke. The buildings, coated with soot, looked diseased. People in the street glanced at him furtively, suspicious of someone in a helmet and cuirass. It was the sort of area where its inhabitants made their livings by robbing one another.

He had never understood why the man he needed to see, his contact with the smuggling ring, chose to live in such an insalubrious place. But then Julian—the Jingler, as everyone called him—was a most uncommon man.

Felix entered the doorway of a five-story wooden building indistinguishable from its neighbors, and climbed the stairs to the top floor. Worn slick, canted at odd angles, the boards sank alarming beneath his boots. A sickening miasma of boiled onions and fish filled the building.

He rapped on Julian's door. There was no answer.

"I know you're in there, Julian," he shouted. "It's Felix."

There was a scuffling noise, like a rat in the walls, from the other side of the planks, then a tight, high-pitched voice. "Please. I'm not prepared. You'll have to come back later."

"I have to speak to you now! Shall I see if I can kick this door down?"

"No. No. Please! Give me a little time…"

Felix waited, trying not to choke on the stench in the hallway. There was silence for a long while. Somewhere below a baby howled as if it were being tortured. Finally he heard a faint ringing, as of small bells, then bolts sliding, locks clicking, chains rattling. The door sagged open with a groan.

He had hardly stepped inside before Julian slammed the door behind him and, muttering to himself, immediately refastened an array of security devices that resembled a display in a locksmith's shop.

It occurred to Felix he could use a few of the devices on his bedroom door to keep Nikomachos out when it was necessary to do so.

There was a rattling and chinking as the man known as the Jingler finished his task and turned toward his unexpected and unwelcome visitor. Julian's narrow, lined face bore its usual expression of extreme anxiety. His plain garments were virtually concealed beneath amulets and talismans dangling from short golden chains sewn to the cloth.

"You hardly gave me time to recite the imprecations, Felix. For all I know there could be a devil under your cloak."

"I'm sure I'd feel its claws biting into my shoulder."

"You weren't followed?"

"No?"

"You're certain?"

"Yes. I'm positive."

The Jingler shuddered and his protective decorations rattled faintly. The room was stifling. The shutters were all closed and numerous lamps produced more smoke than light.

"They're sly, you know," the Jingler said. "They can conceal themselves in a wisp of shadow, or cling to the belly of a cat. If anything did get in, it could hide anywhere." He gestured vaguely toward the jumble filling the room. Crates and sacks were stacked between and on top of expensive furniture. Vases, amphorae sat in corners. Painted icon panels leaned against the walls where there was space. Felix had never decided whether these were goods destined for sale or the Jingler's own possessions.

The Jingler walked around Felix, keeping his distance. He was jingling loudly today. That meant he was worried and wearing extra charms. Felix didn't like what he was hearing and he hadn't even questioned the man.

He noticed two or three new amulets, including a tunic roundel depicting a mounted soldier spearing a monstrous creature, and a small bronze disc incised with what were no doubt protective incantations. A green gemstone carved in the shape of a scarab hung from one shoulder.

"Felix, I do not think it wise for you to visit me here." The Jingler's tone verged on panic.

"I learned about a disturbing matter today connected with our business. It would have been even more unwise to commit it to parchment and a messenger."

"You are right. Continue."

Felix rapidly outlined the events of the morning. He couldn't tell whether his story was affecting the Jingler since the man looked uniformly terrified all the time. "You advised me to be on the alert for an important shipment. Assure me it isn't this shroud of the Virgin that's been stolen."

The Jingler made a dismissive gesture, causing talismans on his arm to clash together. "I know nothing about that. I'm only one link in the enterprise, and a small one. I receive wrapped packages and instructions and pass them on to you, with payment. I know nothing further. I don't even know what the packages contain. Nor do I wish to."

"So you claim. How do I know you're taking orders from anyone? Who is this person?"

"Even if I knew I wouldn't dare tell you." Julian's expression resembled that of a frightened rabbit.

"I should think mere human beings would hold no terrors for a man who spends his days stalked by demons."

The Jingler shook his arms clamorously. "I can protect myself from devils, not from sharp swords."

"That armor of charms looks as if it would stop a lance. Think, will you? We're not talking about some old saint's tooth that spent life chewing the cud. A relic like this is far too dangerous. The emperor and Patriarch will both want it back."

"I'm afraid I don't know any more than you do."

"I believe you when you say you're afraid. At least tell me when I can expect this new delivery, whatever it is?"

"Soon, as I told you already."

Felix could almost feel the man trembling. In fact, his own hand started to shake, as if in sympathy."Try to calm down. I need your help and you need mine. Give me some hint of assistance. Where do you receive the goods you send me? Here? Some other place where I might happen to linger, just by chance you understand? No one needs to know you told me anything."

"They'd kill us both. I can't—" The Jingler gave an agonized cry and shot a shaking forefinger toward a corner of the room. "Something moved! Didn't you see it?"

Felix shook his head. "Probably just a shadow from the lamps."

"They love shadows!"

"I assure you, I saw nothing."

"You might have missed it!"

"I've spent nights at the empire's border watching for Persians crossing moonless deserts. If there was anything in this room besides the two of us I'd know it."

"Other people can't see the devils the way I do!"

"Yes, you're probably right."

The Jingler waved both arms in a frantic fashion. "Leave now! I am going to have to perform rituals expelling fiendish creatures for the rest of the day, thanks to your intrusion."

Felix had to stop himself from pulling out his sword. John had told him often enough that it was a good habit for a soldier on campaign but a dangerous one in the vicinity of the palace. "What about this delivery?"

"What about it? Do your job and don't ask any more questions. That's what's best for both of us." The Jingler's voice rose into a strangled shriek. With his wild expression, flailing arms, and maddening jingling, he resembled a demon himself.

Felix shuddered.

"Very well. I'll leave. If you manage to calm yourself and change your mind about what you can tell me, let me know."

As he hurried downstairs Felix was shivering. He hoped Anastasia was still lounging in the bedroom.

Chapter Six

Nibbling a sweetmeat, Anastasia sank back into a nest of couch cushions and studied the garden beyond the window painted on one wall. There was a yellow bird caught in the jaws of a lion almost concealed in a thicket. She licked her sticky fingers and wondered whether Felix would be back from his mission yet and how he had fared.

The heat lying honey-like over the city did not penetrate into the reception room of the mansion owned by Antonina and her husband General Belisarius. Here, the air was heavy with the fragrance of lilies and roses spilling from enormous floor vases.

Anastasia looked away from the fresco and toward that of the late Empress Theodora and her attendants, which took up the entire back wall. Surely Theodora would have known exactly how to coax forth any information she wanted without rousing suspicion. However, this afternoon she was not offering advice. The dead empress' dark eyes stared fixedly into the room.

"Antonina, a question." Anastasia patted the knee of the woman perched at the end of the couch.

"Yes, my dear?" Antonina's garment was the same shade of yellow as the poor painted bird. It complemented her shockingly blue eyes. Her hair was the color of the moon, her chin strong. To an onlooker she would appear to be Anastasia's age, but in fact she was much older.

Anastasia pointed to the life-size portrait. "Doesn't it upset you to sit in here and see Theodora watching even though she's been dead for almost two weeks?"

"Not particularly. You know how close we were. I greet her every morning. I envy her. Our dear Theodora will never age, whereas we…well…"

"Aging is the price of living."

"And every wrinkle is more costly to me than a sack of gold."

"What wrinkles? You keep them at bay with those herbal potions of yours." And, it was whispered though not too loudly, with the same magick she used to keep Belisarius to heel. It was common knowledge the general was besotted with her and overlooked, or simply failed to see, that his wife was a woman of less-than-impeccable morals.

"You should see me when I awake in the morning! Sometimes I'm tempted to have all my ladies-in-waiting put to death every week or two so they can't betray what they've seen," Antonina chuckled.

"Oh, I wouldn't worry. People will see what's best for them to see." Anastasia was thinking of Belisarius. She admired the sway Antonina held over him. Nothing a woman could possess was more precious than a powerful man. "I was sorry you were not able to say goodbye to Theodora."

"It was difficult. I arrived in the city in time. Then she refused to let me visit. I cried bitterly."

Anastasia could not picture Antonina shedding bitter tears, except possibly from frustration. "She didn't want you to see how she looked. Her illness made her ugly. No amount of cosmetics helped. She looked like a painted skull at the end, and she always was vain."

"Her vanity served her well. Unfortunately you can turn a man's head but not Fate's."

"What about your fate? I suppose you're worried about Belisarius' prospects? General Germanus is Justinian's cousin, after all. Justinian is likely to favor his relative's advancement now that Theodora can't interfere."

"Germanus!" Antonina wrinkled her nose as if the room were filled with dead fish rather than lilies and roses. "What accomplishments does he have to brag about? Theodora championed my husband for good reason. Consider all the victories he handed to the emperor in Persia and Africa. He is in Italy now, ready to drive the Goths out, but even a brilliant general needs an army."

"Yes, he can hardly fight the Goths single-handed. It must be distressing."

"I rushed back from Italy thinking I might persuade Justinian not to be so parsimonious. My poor husband will be waiting for funds, camped out in Crotone, a town about as interesting as a rut in the Mese and not much larger. With nothing to do but build walls to protect himself. And everyone at court knows it. It's humiliating. They laugh. He's expecting support but what he'll get is an order relieving him of his command, they say."

Anastasia patted her friend's knee again. "Yes. It's a terrible injustice. Word of Theodora's death will have reached him by now and he'll know what that portends. It won't be a shock if he were replaced."

"We'll see. He may receive some encouragement after all."

"Never mind. Italy must become tedious. All that fighting, nothing but ruins. You'd be able to spend more time together in the capital."

Antonina's grim expression conveyed her opinion of the possibility.

Anastasia clucked at her. "Is it possible you do not want to spend more time with your husband? Perhaps there's something other than fallen ruins in Italy? Something younger and better-looking, whose column remains standing? You may have brought a souvenir of Italy back with you?"

"You are referring to Belisarius' aide?"

"Karpos, isn't it? A handsome young man."

"Sent to assist me in my negotiations. He is better versed in my husband's military affairs than I am."

"I am sure he has been of great assistance."

Antonina smiled cooly. "At least he is young and handsome. Unlike some men of your acquaintance."

Anastasia felt her face redden. "Oh, Felix…well…"

Antonina's eyes glittered as coldly as stars in a winter sky. "You know Felix has aligned himself with Germanus?"

"He's mentioned hopes of fighting in Italy. He thinks Germanus might give him a command there."

"But has it not occurred to you that your grizzled lover could be working against my husband? He knows Belisarius won't favor him because of that little misunderstanding years and years ago."

"When you seduced Felix in the Hall of Nineteen Couches, you mean?"

"Men can be so unforgiving about mere trifles and life is so short. I do so enjoy talking with you, my dear. You should visit more often. You could keep me informed about Felix. Tell me if anything is said that Belisarius and I should know about."

"I came to make just such an offer, but then we got to gossiping."

"I should have guessed! Why, I almost suspected that you might have come here to see what you could learn from me for Felix's benefit."

The gaze from the vivid eyes was as steady as the gaze from Theodora's painted orbs. Anastasia felt her heart beating too fast. Could Antonina read her thoughts? She made herself laugh. "What an idea! Don't worry, I will report to you every day, if you wish. Not that Felix and I discuss military matters often, or very much of anything else."

"A love match, is it? With a man so much older than you?"

"Ten years older if that. Just because you prefer boys—"

"When the two of you are together, he might be mistaken for your father. If he needs assistance I have potions."

Anastasia sat up, away from the pillows. "Felix doesn't need a potion to please me, but he might be glad to have a talisman against the supernatural."

"He is troubled by the supernatural? How very interesting."

Anastasia explained what she knew about the theft from the church and how Justinian had ordered Felix to investigate.

"Oh, by supernatural you mean those demons. I've heard about them already."

"You have?"

"The story was all over the city by dawn, like a fog from the sea. And growing every hour. Mark my words, before nightfall the gossips will have it Satan himself emerged from a trap door to Hell and ripped the relic from the priest's very hands! I didn't know about Felix's involvement. The demon Felix has most to fear may be the emperor himself. What a shame his eunuch friend cannot assist him."

"You almost sound as if you wish Felix harm, Antonina."

"Certainly not. It's Germanus who concerns me, not his would-be subordinates." She stopped abruptly and laid her hand on Anastasia's shoulder. "I'm sorry, my dear. I know how it is between a man and woman. We can't help our feelings. But you can do better for a lover. You have in the past, and I'm certain you will do so again in the future."

Anastasia bit back numerous retorts that came to mind, including the lurid matter of Antonina and her adopted son. There was no point in arguing when her friend was trying to be kind. "This business at the church worries me," she finally said. "I always scoffed when Felix told me tales of strange beings lurking in the forests of Germania, but now I am not so certain."

"It's superstitious nonsense, Anastasia, but since you feel that way it's just as well you weren't here last night."

"Oh?"

"My women servants were hysterical this morning because one of them saw something she described as ever so small and strange lurking near the back of the house. Ever so small and strange, she said. Well, what kind of a description is that? It might have been a three-legged cat. Once it realized it had been seen it scuttled off."

"Could it have been one of those fiends?"

Antonina's gave a sour laugh. "Certainly not. Having frightened the servants today, the stupid girl finally admitted it resembled a man. She'd initially dismissed it as a beggar hoping for scraps but as soon as she got out of bed this morning and heard about demons being seen in the church, naturally her beggar grew horns. Now the household's in an uproar. My cook burnt my breakfast looking over her shoulder rather than at the brazier. I see I shall have to be severe with them."

Antonina's smile suggested that the task did not displease her.

Although a fierce sun was heating the path when Anastasia left Antonina's house, she crossed the street to avoid walking in the shadow of the Hippodrome. Did she catch a glimpse of a small unnatural figure as it dodged back into the dimness of a shadowed entrance way? Was it the demon her friend's servant had seen?

Don't be silly, she told herself. Imagining things out of nightmares in broad daylight! What was wrong with her?

But wasn't it true that the world teemed with demons? Hadn't Jesus cast out unclean spirits? If there had been that many roaming the sparsely populated wastes of the Holy Land how many more must infest overcrowded Constantinople?

She touched the cross that hung from a gold chain around her neck.

Yes, the Lord would protect her. But what about Felix, who clung to his pagan god Mithra?

Anastasia had pleaded with him to abandon his god. There was no future for pagans at Justinian's Christian court. And now it was even more important that he accept Christ, if only to avoid being carried off to Hell by whatever had carried off the shroud.

She was still musing about what strategies she might employ to convince Felix to change his beliefs when she entered the square of the Augustaion. She looked toward the Great Church, seeking inspiration, but the sun reflected off the dome was so blinding that she had to avert her gaze. The after-image lingered in her vision. Waves of heat rose from the square, distorting figures hurrying across it. The whole city seemed to be melting in the bright light.

Even the cross lying against her breast felt hot to her finger-tips now. She prayed that Felix had encountered no difficulties. What protection could he expect from his illusory Mithra?

Chapter Seven

Felix sat on a bench under the peristyle of his house, idly fingering the cross pendant Anastasia had given him and staring at the statue of Aphrodite set in a bed of rosebushes.

The last owner must have had strange humors or else been a philosopher. Love surrounded by thorns! What a sight for a military man to see every day. He should have the goddess replaced by a statue of Mars.

He squinted into the bright sky. Military man? What sort of military man was he, stationed at the palace? A servile bodyguard of perfumed courtiers. If only he were able to join the glorious fighting in Italy. But how could he? He had to obtain an appointment. It was the only way.

Germanus was the key. As soon as Justinian recovered from his grief he'd replace that fool Belisarius, and Germanus was a man who remembered who'd aided him when he was out of favor.

He turned at the sound of soft footsteps. His nascent smile of welcome died as he recognized his servant Nikomachos. He stuffed the cross back under his clothes. His shaggy beard concealed even the gold chain around his neck.

"At what hour do you wish the evening meal?" Nikomachos' tone was, as usual, peevish, if not quite to the degree of justifying a reprimand.

"The time of my guest's arrival being uncertain, lay out a few dishes that can be eaten cold. And wine. Not the everyday wine. Something fit for a banquet."

Felix remembered John and his disgusting Egyptian wine. Now Felix had inherited a large store of the stuff. Perhaps he would donate it to a church, if they would take it. That would make Anastasia happy.

How far had John traveled on his way to Greece by now? Would they meet again or not?

"Cheeses? Fruit?" Nikomachos was asking.

Felix nodded absentmindedly. His servant bowed, almost imperceptibly, and went indoors.

Would Nikomachos have been surprised if he knew how his master envied him? He had lost an arm on a battlefield near Rome. Felix would gladly give an arm, or his life, to go into battle again. He had employed Nikomachos chiefly because of the man's service to the empire. He often regretted it, being reminded every day by the sight of him of his own soft and unseemly post.

Felix got up with a grunt. He felt stiff and fat and lethargic, prematurely old. He walked slowly around the sunlit space. Flowers and bushes lay utterly still under a heavy blanket of heat. The only movement was when a bee lit on or took flight from a blossom. A gentle hum filled the hot air. The fragrance of roses overpowered other floral smells.

Anastasia liked having fresh flowers in the house. He picked a rose, which dug a thorn into his thumb. With a curse he tossed it into a bush and sucked the bleeding thumb.

Was it an omen?

How much longer would Anastasia be?

Staring in the direction of Aphrodite he found himself comparing the marble goddess to Anastasia. His lover was more mature, her figure more voluptuous. The sculptor had not had very good taste in women. A smile puckered Felix's lips. Anastasia was a lively partner, well skilled in the ways of Aphrodite. If only she would stop trying to persuade him to convert to Christianity! He was a besotted fool to have revealed his faith, but in bed after passion such confidences were exchanged and he felt unable to refuse her questions. At least he had not revealed too much about Mithraism. He was careful to wear the little cross she had given him whenever she visited. Women liked that sort of thing.

Yet he was leaning toward converting. Only ostensibly, he told himself. It made sense. It was a Christian court and if to appear to be Christian meant a better chance of advancement, would it not be wise to at least pretend to follow their gentle god? Certainly a soldierly god like Mithra understood the necessity of suiting one's tactics to the situation.

But he couldn't ponder that right now. The stolen relic presented an urgent problem. Had he been unwise in arranging for the onward passage of packages without inquiring about their contents? He had given the matter some thought after visiting the church and the uncooperative Jingler and decided his best move would be to hand the next package—the one he assumed would contain the stolen relic—over to the authorities. The action would surely bring a large reward of some kind.

He could even make up some story about having tracked down the relic. He'd deceived the smugglers into delivering it to him. Anastasia would be able to think up a convincing tale.

In any event it was better to run the risk of retaliation from the smugglers—whoever they were—than the anger of Justinian, whose spies were everywhere.

He paused in his perambulations.

Was it possible there was a spy in his household?

Felix knew nothing about the religious beliefs of his servants but they were almost certainly Christians. He kept nothing of Mithra in his house. However, he did not always check his tongue in private, so they might well know he was a pagan. If the servants guessed he was profiting from the illegal sale of objects they venerated, and especially such an important object as the Virgin's shroud, they might well decide to cause him trouble— extorting money to remain silent, for example.

Or betraying him to the authorities.

He scratched his sweaty neck nervously. He muttered a curse. What was the matter with him? He was starting to think like the Jingler.

Nevertheless, might a Christian baptism serve as a charm against exposure? The Lord was supposed to protect even the lowliest of His followers, although Felix had never seen evidence of it.

The baptism would need to be performed privately.

But he was a soldier of Mithra, like John and other friends. How could he abandon his faith? Abandon both his god and his friends?

He could imagine John's stinging rebuke. The Lord Chamberlain—the former Lord Chamberlain—was a man he greatly admired for his stoic acceptance of the terrible fate he had met at the hands of Persians. Surgery that had made him a eunuch.

Even as the excubitor captain continued pacing impatiently around his garden, his thoughts turned from an angry John to a friend in danger sailing further away from Constantinople at every passing hour. Going into exile and yet, in Felix's opinion, no safer than he had been when living on the palace grounds for years.

Justinian had a long memory. Imperial assassins, like imperial spies, were well-paid and numerous.

Imperial assassins had a way of catching the disfavored unawares.

The thought brought Felix back to his own dilemma.

He wished Anastasia would arrive.

Chapter Eight

Felix went inside and paced from room to room. He eyed the wine jug sitting on the table beside the bed. No. It would be better to do something constructive than start drinking. He and Anastasia had been doing a lot of drinking. He must keep a clear head.

Instead, he could have a word with General Germanus. It wouldn't hurt to remind Germanus of his loyalty. If there was going to be trouble, Germanus might be his strongest ally.

The general's doorkeeper informed Felix that Germanus had gone to an important poetry reading at the Baths of Zeuxippos. "Of course, you wouldn't have known about such a cultural event," the doorkeeper sniffed.

Luckily, from Felix's point of view, the reading had just ended when he arrived. The audience was leaving the semi-circular exedra off the main atrium of the bath complex, excitedly debating the merits of competing court poets as if the versifiers were charioteers and money was riding on the winner of a forthcoming literary debate.

A group of big, imposing men, all with an obvious military mien, lingered between the curved rows of seats and the speaker's platform.

Felix spotted Germanus among them.

In his early forties, the general was, like Justinian, a nephew of the late Emperor Justin. However, like Justin and unlike Justinian, he had retained the rugged look of the family's peasant origins, with a granite block of a face and powerful, sloping shoulders. He kept his dark hair and beard trimmed to a stubble.

This was a man who looked and acted like an emperor. Not a man who took orders from a woman, as Justinian had. And what would Justinian do now that Theodora was gone? Had it not been for her admonitions he would have fled the city like a frightened girl during the Nika riots years ago. And considering that Justinian's chief general Belisarius was likewise ruled by his wife Antonina…well, Felix feared for the fate of the empire. Whereas if Germanus replaced Belisarius he would soon restore things to their proper order.

As Felix approached he saw Germanus speaking to a swarthy, clean-shaven young man. "Excellent work, Florus. Your arrows go straight to their targets. I look forward to the next reading." He clapped the man on the shoulder so hard Felix was surprised the slight fellow remained standing.

The poet bowed and left the exedra, a large scroll thrust before him, a spear of words.

Felix caught Germanus' eye. "Captain Felix, you're late. Florus was reading from his *New Illiad*, the part where Belisarius retreats to his ship off the coast of Italy and sulks. I admit I offered a few suggestions. He says I inspire him."

"You inspire many of us," Felix said, wondering how much of Germanus' gold had watered the inspiration. Surely Germanus' Uncle Justin, whom Felix had served as a bodyguard, would not have bragged about inspiring poets. The old soldier-turned-emperor couldn't even read.

Felix read only history, such as Cassiodorus' *History of the Goths*, ever hopeful that he would one day be sent to Italy to help vanquish those bold warriors. And of course lately he had read a few biblical verses at Anastasia's behest.

Felix's expression must have betrayed his lack of enthusiasm.

"Florus is a real man's poet," Germanus added. "Cold steel and hot blood, none of these pitiful perfumed worms squealing like suckling pigs while they squirm under a woman's dainty thumb."

One of the general's looming entourage went so far as to clap Germanus on the back and laugh heartily. "You should write that down, sir. You're a better poet than Florus!"

Felix attempted a polite chuckle.

"Why are you here, Felix? Do you have information for me?" The general's tone was chillier than Felix would have liked.

"The Lord Chamberlain has departed for Greece. I saw him leaving this morning."

"Everyone in the city knows he's been sent into exile."

"True, but he has actually left now. Meaning Narses will now have Justinian's ear. There will be no one to challenge him."

"One eunuch is much like another."

"The emperor might, however, be inclined to listen more closely to his excubitor captain. I am after all in charge of palace security and the palace is even more dangerous than usual with Theodora gone and Justinian still reeling from his loss. Changes are coming, and changes always bring danger."

Germanus barked out a laugh. "Since Justinian's uncle was captain of the excubitors before he usurped the throne, the emperor might consider you dangerous."

"Am I dangerous to the emperor? Do you want me to be?" Felix asked softly.

Germanus smiled. It was the smile of a wolf baring its teeth. "I'm pleased to see you are so eager, my friend. But we must be careful."

"I am looking forward to fighting by your side in Italy. But if there is anything I can do immediately, I am at your service."

"I appreciate your support. But Constantinople is not Italy. We are not at war here."

"You and Belisarius are at war."

"Indeed." Germanus ran an enormous hand over his cropped hair. His colleagues stood silent, pretending not to listen although they could not have failed to hear every word. "It is not a war that can be fought with steel, however, which is where you excel."

"Nevertheless, if I can assist, I will. Whatever you need."

"What I need is something to fatally soil Belisarius' reputation, something that will make him a stench in the emperor's nostrils, something that will cause the emperor to distrust him."

It was the sort of information John would have been more likely to turn up, Felix thought. "I will keep my eyes and ears open," he said. "I have many contacts at the palace."

Possibly Anastasia knew something useful. He did not voice the thought.

"Very good." Germanus clapped him on the shoulder. "I like to see enthusiasm in my allies. But you must not seek me out. I will send for you if I need you. I will see you are invited to Florus' next reading."

Chapter Nine

When Felix got back home, Anastasia still had not returned. Felix ate by himself by lamplight.

He was more irritated than worried. She had her duties at the palace, although she had never specified what they were. Attending a doddering old matron who did not take notice of her frequent absences perhaps?

Nikomachos cleared the table with his typical maddening slowness. How else could a one-armed servant clear a table? If not for Felix he would be unemployable since he couldn't fight anymore. His service to the empire entitled him to live in dignity.

Felix went out into the back courtyard for a breath of air. Over the top of the wall he could see only vague shapes of buildings.

Sunset had bloodied the sky. Darkness, assassin of daylight, had fallen upon the city's cross-decorated roofs sheltering commoner and courtier alike. The dome of the Great Church spilled a radiant halo of light. The fires of furnaces in the copper smiths' quarter were banked down. Ill-lit narrow streets filled with humanity hurrying back to their homes. In darker areas under porticoes and in the angles of church walls the homeless settled down for another restless night. In the houses of the rich, guests began to arrive to pick at exotic dishes, over-indulge in wine, and complain about the state of the empire. The pious worshipped while the profane gathered in smoke-stained taverns, drank, and wagered on knucklebones.

Felix strolled toward the stable. It seemed unlikely now that Anastasia would appear and there had been no message to say what had detained her. Perhaps he should do his duty and consider the best way to continue his investigation into the theft of the holy shroud.

What did he have to go on? The witnesses claimed it had been stolen by two demons who in some fashion had worked evil magick incapacitating those within the church.

He could hear the horses moving about in their stalls and the skittering of a rat through straw. Laughter emerged from the servants' quarters at the rear of the house. The humid air lay unpleasantly against his skin, heavy with the odor of horses and the sour tang of garbage in the alley beyond the back gate.

A dark figure looked in through the bars of the gate.

Had the messenger Felix was anticipating with dread arrived so soon? Usually he called in the middle of the night.

Why was he skulking around the back, drawing attention to the house, rather than entering boldly by the front like any casual visitor?

Felix walked to the gate. As he approached, the figure whirled around and ran.

Someone was afraid of being caught!

In his haste Felix fumbled with the bolt. By the time he stepped into the alley the man was vanishing into the darkness.

Felix sprinted in pursuit. The winged feet of panic could only partly make up for lack of visits to the gymnasium. Luckily his prey ran like an injured crab, lurching wildly from side to side. He was small, perhaps only a child.

Puffing and wheezing, Felix caught the intruder at the mouth of the alley. He grabbed a wrist resembling a fleshless bone and yanked hard. The emaciated figure fell on its back with a gurgling whimper that barely sounded human. A torch in front of a closed shop across the way illuminated the end of the alley.

Felix could make out a hunched, hooded form.

The thing wriggled and gasped, a fish flopping on the dock.

Felix shook his prey fiercely. The hood fell back and Felix looked into a grotesque demonic face.

No. Not demonic

Worse!

He dropped the thing's arm.

"Please, master. I meant no harm," the monstrosity gurgled at him. "A bit of food for the love of Christ was all I wanted…"

The face before him was covered with lesions.

Felix backed away in horror.

He had just manhandled a leper.

Felix was still soaking when Anastasia came flying into the bath chamber without warning. She appeared agitated.

"Felix…" She faltered, then stopped.

He pushed stray wet hair back off his forehead and ran a hand through his dripping beard. "Has your husband become suspicious?"

"What? What husband? Certainly not. What makes you say such a thing?"

"Considering the disasters that have been seeking me out, it seemed a reasonable guess. What's scared you so badly?"

"Is it obvious?"

It was. Her face looked paler than usual despite the stifling heat in the cramped, circular room. Steam swirled up from the water in the basin that occupied most of the space. The fine silks Anastasia wore were already wilting.

"You wouldn't have burst in here unless there was something wrong. What is it?"

"I saw a demon as I was approaching the house. A dreadful, twisted thing, loping through the shadows under the colonnade. I got into the house as fast as I could."

"The city seems to be infested with demons. Everyone's seeing them."

"It's true. They're skulking about everywhere. The servants spotted them!"

"My servants?"

"No. Servants at the…palace…where I've been all day."

Felix let his head fall back against the edge of the basin and stared up into the foggy cloud gathered in the small dome overhead. "I can assure you that what you saw wasn't any sort of evil spirit. I encountered the creature myself earlier tonight. It was a leper."

"A leper!" Anastasia gasped. "How do you know?"

"By its disfigured face. Claimed to be looking for something to eat, but how often do honest beggars creep around in dark alleyways? No, they go to the house door and ask for charity and refuse to leave until they get it or the urban watch happens to go by on patrol. Then they scuttle off fast enough."

He heaved himself out of the water. "I'll make sure he's removed from the city tomorrow if he's still around."

Anastasia had her hands up to her face as if suppressing a scream.

"Don't worry, my little dove. I've had the garments I was wearing burnt and I've been scrubbing myself raw. You need not fear being close to me." He tried to smile.

He thought it best not to mention he had actually touched the leper, particularly since he was trying to forget that himself.

DAY TWO

Chapter Ten

John stood an arm's length from the rail at the stern of the *Leviathan*, his back to the captain's cabin, and watched sunrise over the Marmara.

As sky and sea lightened, clustered sails replaced twinkling constellations of shipboard lights. Vessels beyond counting streamed toward and away from Constantinople, now vanished into the distance. Long warships, oars churning the flashing water in mechanical unison, arrowed past ponderous merchants and flocks of smaller boats. The decrepit coastal trader carrying John and his companions groaned and complained, an old mariner trying to get out of bed.

The *Leviathan* was due to follow the Thracian coast of the Sea of Marmara, through the Hellespont strait southwest to the Aegean, calling at local ports. It would reach John's destination, Megara, near Athens and not far from where he had attended Plato's Academy, when the vagaries of commerce decreed. Not an ideal mode of travel but the best available given Justinian's impatience.

The ship had made two stops during the first day of sailing and then anchored for the night at the mouth of a tiny noisome bay where ancient walls had collapsed into the scummy water. John reckoned they had not traveled as far as he could have ridden.

Cornelia brushed by him to lean out over the rail.

"Be careful," he told her. He feared deep water. Long ago he had seen a colleague drown.

"How long have you been on deck, John?" Annoyed, she spoke without turning around. "Waking up alone gave me a start."

"I meant to be back before you were up but my mind wandered."

Also, he had not been able to descend again into the cramped cubicle the two well-paying passengers had been granted, away from crates and amphorae and the bunks of the crew where Peter and Hypatia had been relegated, so terribly near to that eternal night of the sea depths.

"You must stop fretting about Felix," Cornelia said sternly. "I'm sure he can take care of himself. How could he possibly get into trouble over the theft of a relic?"

"Perhaps you are right," John admitted.

Cornelia peered into the mist shrouding the shore. "Will we be able to catch a glimpse of Zeno's estate?"

"It's too late. We passed it during the night."

"I'm sorry we didn't have a chance to see Thomas and Europa and our grandson one last time before leaving. Still, they'll join us soon."

"I'm sure Thomas will be a capable estate manager for us."

Cornelia turned away from the sea. Concern softened her irritated expression. "Oh, John, I can tell you're brooding. Haven't we always talked about leaving the city and retiring to Greece? I know you wouldn't actually have done it. And now see how your sense of duty and loyalty to Justinian has been repaid!"

"He granted me my life and some of my land," John pointed out.

"Indeed! How generous! And he's also given you a well-earned retirement you would never have chosen for yourself. That's how I try to see it."

"Perhaps you are right." He didn't want Cornelia to be upset and he didn't want to argue. He was glad when she turned away again and silently surveyed the crowded sea. She looked less drawn and exhausted than she had of late, now they were doing what needed to be done rather than anxiously waiting to start. And, he supposed, it pleased her to be going somewhere—any-where—to be traveling again after years in Constantinople.

They had met on the road. He a young mercenary, she one of a troupe of entertainers, her specialty re-enacting the legendary acrobatics of Crete's ancient bull leapers. Then circumstances separated them for years, until they encountered each other again in Constantinople and John found he had a daughter he had never known.

Gray tinged Cornelia's hair and city life had dulled slightly the bronze to which foreign suns had darkened her skin. John knew well the tiny wrinkles around her eyes and at the corners of her mouth where formerly the flesh had been smooth. How-ever, she was as lithe as when he had met her. She looked as if she could still somersault safely from a running bull. He, on the other hand, was much changed.

Probably Cornelia felt caged in the city, like one of the accursed birds twittering ceaselessly below decks. Some type of songbirds, wicker cages full of them. John preferred the ragged cries of the seabirds soaring above.

A swell rocked the ship. John shifted his feet but made no effort to move forward to grasp the rail. He didn't want to be any closer to the water. The sun's rays already felt hot.

"I must speak with Hypatia," John said. "She knows about herbs. I had an idea, suddenly, about what might have happened at the church."

Cornelia smiled wearily. "You mean you were standing out here alone, agonizing over the mystery until you came up with a solution. I saw her with Peter as I left our little nest. He wanted to get the captain's permission to use the brazier in his cabin. Apparently he doesn't trust the ship's cook to prepare fit meals for us."

John stepped around the back of the cabin and looked down the length of the ship. Crewmen crowded the deck which steamed in spots as the sun burned away the night's dampness. During his solitary watch he had watched a sailor prodding at the waters with a long pole, making certain the ship didn't run aground as it moved away from the bay.

He found Peter looking cross. "Captain Theon is an obstinate man. It isn't right that the Lord Chamberlain should delay his meals until after the crew are fed."

"Were I still Lord Chamberlain it would not be the case, Peter."

"Imagine, a sailor insulting an imperial official," Peter fumed. "He said he had better things to worry about than who ate when. The way the birds were flying meant bad weather, he said."

John glanced at the cloudless sky where seabirds circled. "It looks like a fine day to me. And Hypatia…?"

"I asked her to see about getting fresh fish." He pointed to the prow, where John saw his Egyptian servant talking with several sailors who were preparing fishing lines.

John thanked Peter for his efforts and made way his forward, trying not to trip over the ropes strewn across the deck. None of the crew spoke to him. Passengers were just so many goods to be transported.

The day before, John had been taking inventory of the other travelers. There were two farmers, judging by their rough appearance and clothing. They may have been returning to their native soil after failing to find work in Constantinople. Then again, they might have gone to the city to petition the emperor over matters concerning land or taxation. An ancient woman by the name of Egina and her attendant occupied the makeshift room next to John and Cornelia's cubicle, almost certainly returning from a once-in-a-lifetime pilgrimage. They heard her reading scripture late into the night in a voice whispering like dry leaves in a winter wind. The last passenger was a young man who appeared to be staying with Captain Theon. Dressed a little too well for travel, John guessed he was a callow scion sent to inspect the family holdings.

Hypatia looked happier than Peter. She had arranged to purchase the pick of each day's catch, she told John, who couldn't help reflecting that women seemed better than men at handling life's unexpected vicissitudes.

When she screwed up her tawny-skinned face to consider the question he put to her, it struck him that she alone, of the travelers on board, looked as if she belonged amidst the sunburnt sailors. "Visions, master? You wish to know which plants could cause visions?"

"I have heard such exist, Hypatia."

"There is mandrake. Yes, mandrake would do it. But I'll have to ponder the question further."

"Could mandrake be prepared so that it could be burned?"

"I don't see why not, if it were properly dried. But I'm afraid I didn't bring any mandrake. I do have other herbs and preparations, in case you need something." She looked puzzled.

"No, I don't need anything right now, nor am I seeking a vision." Except, perhaps, for a vision of his uncertain future, John told himself as he returned thoughtfully to Cornelia, who still leaned precariously over the rail, breathing in the sea air.

He detailed his conclusions for her. "So mandrake, or a similar herb, could have been mixed with the incense smoldering in the church. Anyone inhaling the fumes might have seen the human thieves as fiends. Unfortunately I can't tell Felix now."

"Oh, John, you had other things to think about! Felix is bound to solve the mystery as soon as he puts his mind to it."

Chapter Eleven

Gray light fingered the shutters of Felix's bedroom when he woke from an uneasy sleep populated by dark monstrosities and dreamlike shapes of no particular outline but radiating an aura of dread.

He immediately recalled his encounter with the leper. It took him a moment to disentangle the memory from his nightmares. No, unfortunately, he had not dreamt it.

Anastasia slept on as he hastily dressed and went outside. In the inner garden birds had begun to address the dawn. The sky pearled to rose in the east and not far off the clang of hammers announced artisans had risen even earlier. The air was still and already warm, heralding another day of uncomfortable heat.

Felix raked his fingers through his hair and yawned. He wondered how John was faring. At least the weather was good for sea travel. How long would it take John's ship to reach Greece? Would the estate where he intended to take up residence be habitable? Perhaps John kept better track than Felix did of his holdings.

There was no point worrying. He couldn't help John at this point nor could John help him. He'd better concentrate on his own problems.

Suddenly realizing that he had been straightening his hair without thinking, Felix lowered his hand. He couldn't stop himself from examining the fingers. It was the hand with which he'd grabbed the leper. There was nothing to see. Why should there be? He'd hardly touched the creature. Still, he could almost feel his scalp tingling where he'd touched it.

He chided himself for overreacting as he continued on through the wing of the house housing the private bath where he'd cleansed himself so assiduously.

The noise of hammering was louder in the back courtyard and he could hear workmen shouting to one another. He suspected laborers often chose to make excessive noise in the vicinity of wealthy abodes, a safe way to exact a small revenge on those born luckier than themselves. Felix surveyed the deserted courtyard. He'd apparently beaten his servants out of bed. They had been getting lazy recently. Probably they realized that the master, being strenuously occupied most of the night, would not be expected to make an appearance until late morning.

He was making a mental note to speak to them about being at work at the proper time when he noticed the man lying near the stables, face turned to the back wall.

The leper.

That was his first thought. The leper had crept in. Why hadn't Nikomachos made certain the gate was secured? But as he forced himself to approach he saw the intruder wasn't dressed in beggar's rags. Far from it. The richly embroidered robes were those of a courtier.

Some aristocratic young carouser then, too intoxicated to get home, taking advantage of the first unlocked gate. Not that Felix hadn't bedded down in similar circumstances.

He didn't like being reminded of such follies—and not all of them youthful—so he gave the fellow a boot in the ribs. "Wake up, my friend. Time to let the devils in your head have their due."

The body shifted like a sack of wheat and the head lolled over far enough for Felix to recognize the anonymous courier who regularly delivered illicit packages to the house. The broad ruddy face was bluish now, the mouth no longer wore a sneer. The bruises circling his neck made it obvious he'd been strangled.

"Mithra!"

Felix's first thought was to regret that John was somewhere at sea now and unreachable. As a military man Felix was expert at creating corpses, not in handling ones that turned up unexpectedly. What about their mutual friend Anatolius, the lawyer? Lawyers were always dealing with inconvenient unpleasantries. True, he and the younger man had had their differences.

He stood there unable to move as if the corpse had grasped his ankle. He tried to calm himself down. What did the captain of the excubitors have to fear from the discovery of yet another murder in the city? He might well fear for his life if it was the captain himself who found the body of a smuggler in his own courtyard, particularly if the captain was working with smugglers and one of the most valuable relics in the empire was involved.

He commanded the excubitors, but not Justinian's spies.

Felix gave the body another kick, freeing his leg from an invisible grip. "Bastard! Why didn't I find out who you were?"

He could hear horses moving around uneasily in the stable. Was that a voice from the house? He looked around in a sudden panic. The courtyard remained deserted. But for how long? Nikomachos or one of the other servants was liable to appear any moment. Then what?

He had to get the body off his property.

Oddly, the gate was still bolted but there was no time to ponder that. Felix glanced up and down the narrow passage. To his horror two armed men came round the corner where the alley met the street.

The urban watch!

A routine patrol?

He couldn't take the chance. He slammed the gate shut and ran back to the corpse. He could drag it into the stable for concealment.

No, too accessible.

He grabbed at the corpse's garments, stiff with embroidery and jewels, and tugged. The courier had not been a small man. The body barely moved.

Cursing silently Felix managed to get the carcass over his shoulder. It was a skill he'd learned as a young man on the days after battles. Then he had been too glad to be among the survivors to feel the revulsion he now experienced as he staggered toward the house, the dead man's soft leather boots dangling against his thighs, limp hands flopping at his back.

He managed to reach the back hallway and leaned against the wall, catching his breath. His burden weighed as much as he did. It was as if he was carting a side of beef. He had no notion what to do next and he could clearly hear Nikomachos giving orders to the cook in the nearby kitchen.

The bath.

He forced himself a few painful steps further down the hallway and pushed the door open, keeping his load precariously in place. He felt the burden start to slither off his shoulder. Then the dead man's hair became tangled in the door latch.

"Mithra!" Felix muttered yet again. He twisted awkwardly and forced himself to tear the longish brown strands loose, animating the lifeless head, making it bob up and down as he tugged at its hair.

Finally the hair came away and the head lolled backwards.

By now Felix was half carrying the corpse in his arms. The glazed eyes stared at him. Just when he began to lower the body, the purpling lips emitted a last hideous sigh.

He let go and the corpse fell and slid down the three steps leading into the water. Felix was certain the splash was audible in the inner sanctums of the Great Palace. Wiping water from his face, he exited the chamber and rushed back to the bedroom.

Chapter Twelve

Anastasia sat up in bed as Felix raced into the room.

"What is it?" Her words were almost drowned by a thunderous knocking on the house door.

"Urban watch! And there's a dead man in the bath," Felix gasped. "Stay here. I'll get rid of them. We'll worry about the body later."

He raced out of the room and ran along the passage into the atrium where Nikomachos was arguing with a pair of the urban watch. Felix was certain they were not the same men he had glimpsed coming down the alley. Which meant there were guards at both the back and front.

He didn't like the implication.

Nikomachos blocked their path, gesticulating violently with his one arm. The two visitors, who were youthful and pink-faced, looked taken aback by the spectacle.

"What is it?" Felix snarled. "Why did you wake me up at this hour?"

The one apparently in command turned a startled face toward Felix. The skin which appeared pink from a distance was, up close, a mass of red blotches. The result of youth, not leprosy. "We...we have orders to search this house...sir."

"Search my house? Hasn't anyone explained to you boys that I am captain of Justinian's excubitors? What possible reason can there be to search?"

The blotchy guard licked his lips and stammered. "Trouble has been reported."

"Trouble? Do I look as if I need a pair of fools wet behind the ears to deal with trouble in my own house?"

It was probably not the best choice of words since Felix himself was still literally wet behind the ears from the bath water into which he'd dropped the body.

The guard banged the butt of his spear on the tiles. "Stand aside, sir. We must follow orders."

Nikomachos stepped over to Felix's side. "If I may speak to my master in private—"

The point of the spear immediately prodded his chest.

"No, you may not! Get back to your quarters." Blotches evidently found it easier to order a servant about than an excubitor captain. But just as obviously he intended to carry out his mission. He addressed Felix, his voice firmer than before. "The orders of the City Prefect take precedence in this situation, sir."

Nikomachos made a slow exit while Felix desperately tried to think of a way out of his dilemma. What would happen when they discovered the corpse? Was that what they were looking for? Or was it the stolen relic? Or hadn't they been given any hint of what they were supposed to find?

"You will allow me to accompany you," Felix said. "I have too many valuables here to allow strangers to wander around unobserved." It was easy enough to sound angry but putting a note of unconcern into his voice was more difficult.

Still, the house was large. The intruders might flag before covering every room or lose track of where they had looked if their host led them on a circuitous route, which he proceeded to do.

The guards showed little interest in his office, except to prod the wall hangings. They passed through the dining room with a quick glance under the table. In the garden they bent to peer beneath bushes or poked at them with their weapons. Apparently they were not looking for something small. They couldn't be searching for the relic.

The sun had surmounted the wall of the house and now blazed down. Dew steamed away in wispy tendrils. Felix took the guards in one direction, then another. He escorted them down a side corridor to the servants' quarters. Each room was the same, a chair, a chest, a bed, a cross on the wall, and little more. Only Nikomachos had anything approaching decoration in his space: some tattered wall hangings, a wood inlaid table with random bits of small crude statuary of the sort found at the edges of the empire, along with several rather ornate chests.

The servant stood in one corner and glared at the guards.

Blotches picked up what might have been a weathered clay frog covered with Egyptian hieroglyphs. No, Felix corrected himself. It didn't look anything like a frog. A cat, certainly. It was only the frogs in the mausoleum that had brought the image of a frog to mind.

"All the objects you see are tokens of military campaigns I served in," Nikomachos informed the guards stiffly. "In your line of work, you will never possess such things." The way he sniffed as he pronounced "your line of work" made employment in the urban watch sound several steps below cleaning the public toilets.

Blotches made no reply. Felix noticed he didn't bother to open any of the chests. Was he thinking that a body wouldn't have fit in any of them? He must have been told there would be a body here, Felix decided.

He directed the guards back into the garden and along a roundabout path, intending to return to the atrium. As they followed Felix through the peristyle, Blotches stopped. "We've seen the dining room already. What about that hall?"

"Oh, yes. I'm certain there's nothing hidden in any of the guest rooms, let alone my bedroom."

Felix was obliged to open the doors to a series of luxurious, seldom-used rooms which he never bothered to inspect for months on end. He was half-afraid there might have been something left in one of the rooms, given he'd already found a body in his courtyard. Momentarily he considered pretending there was a valuable object missing, blame the guards, claim they'd distracted him to allow an accomplice to sneak in, create a scene. At least he'd buy himself time. But for what?

"This is your bedroom, sir?" The quaver that had been evident in Blotches' voice upon his arrival had turned to a tone of mockery. The two youngsters leered at each other. And no wonder. The bed and its sheets resembled the site of an earthquake, the air was thick with Anastasia's exotic perfume, her cosmetics and a big silver comb were strewn on a bedside table.

However, as they examined the wall hangings, searching to see if they concealed anything Felix found nothing comical about the scene. Because it lacked one important thing.

Anastasia!

She must have fled.

Was it surprising? Why should a woman from the palace who'd only known him a few days let herself be implicated in who-knows-what?

But she did know what. Felix had blurted everything out to her. All about the smuggling and the missing relic. He'd even stupidly told her just now about the dead man.

If she tried to leave through the back gate, as she usually did, she'd be surprised to find her way blocked by a pair of guards.

Or would she?

Who had sent the authorities after him?

What was he thinking? He didn't suspect Anastasia, did he? After all she was…well…what was she? Except a tireless bed partner? Felix only knew she served at court.

Even if she wasn't involved in a plot against him, what would she do when the guards blocked her way? The easiest thing would be to tell them she had been going to report a crime.

To report a dead man. A murdered man.

"We're done here, I said. Aren't you listening?" It was Blotches.

"Yes. I know. I hope you're satisfied." Felix found himself looking frantically up and down the hall as he left the bedroom, expecting more guards to appear at a run. "You've seen the whole house now. My servants will be in an uproar all day. I'll accompany you back to the atrium."

Blotches looked down the hall.

"That side passage." He pointed his spear in the direction of the short passage to the bath. "We didn't check there."

"Of course you did," Felix snapped. "That was the first place I took you. Don't you remember? You don't think I have time to escort you around the entire house again, do you?"

But the two guards were already striding away.

"There's nothing there." Felix's voice came out in a croak. "Wait, I think the door's locked. I'll need to get the key."

They rounded the corner and came to a stop in front of the closed door to the bath. As soon as they opened the door and stepped inside to where they could see down to the water level, they'd spot the floating corpse.

Blotches tested the latch and gave Felix a meaningful look. "Unlocked. You have a bad memory this morning, sir."

Felix was certain the youngster was struggling to conceal a grin as he yanked at the latch. Out of inspiration, he could only look on in impotent horror.

As the door swung open there was a heart-stopping shriek that went on and on, echoing around the chamber behind.

The doorway was entirely blocked by Anastasia, who was entirely naked. Arms outspread, hands clutching the opposite sides of the door frame, she made no effort to cover herself but simply screamed and screamed with an effort that made her whole body quiver.

Blotches and his companion backed away in confusion, muttering apologies, faces as scarlet as a couple of abashed schoolboys.

Felix stepped forward, pushed the door shut, and as the screaming subsided turned a thunderous look on the two youths. "Well?"

Blotches licked his lips and swallowed. "Thank you for your cooperation, sir. I believe we've seen everything now."

Chapter Thirteen

Felix shook his fist at Anastasia.

"No!" She shoved the fist away. "No more micatio!"

He shook his fist again anyway, shouted "Three!" and opened his hand extending two fingers, just in case Anastasia relented and reciprocated.

She didn't. Instead she got up from the dining room table and stared out into the long twilight shadows creeping across the garden. "I can't bear to play that stupid game again. Besides, unless you're gambling on it, where's the interest?"

"There's the strategy. I noticed you kept showing one finger so I showed two and guessed the total would be three. I suppose you thought I was bound to guess you'd stop showing just the one eventually and—"

"I couldn't be bothered to lift more than one finger, Felix." She shook her hand. "My wrist is sore from micatio!"

Felix helped himself to some figs from a platter on the table. "Well, have some more to eat then. It isn't dark enough yet."

"I'm not hungry. After spending all that time in the bath, with that hideous thing…I may never feel like eating again."

"It's only a corpse, Anastasia. I'm still sorry you had to display yourself to those—"

She turned, her hands balled into fists. "Oh, Felix! I saved your life and you're fretting over me exposing myself to a couple of youngsters?"

Felix ran a hand through his beard. "Well…"

The grim line of her mouth suddenly softened into a smile. "It is rather touching, my big bear." Immediately her face fell again. "But you can't imagine what it was like half expecting to feel a cold, wet hand on my naked back."

After Felix had shown the flustered urban watchmen out, she had been waiting for him in bed, trembling. They had made love until Felix was worn out. Then they had made plans.

Felix had to dispose of the body, but it would have to wait until darkness, when there was less chance of being observed. Once they decided what to do they had to bide their time. They walked in the garden, Felix ate and tried to encourage Anastasia to do the same. They played micatio. They also listened for a knock on the house door, announcing the authorities had arrived to conduct a more thorough search.

"I often wish I had never come to this city," Felix said.

Anastasia gave a small lady-like snort of disapproval. "How often have you told me you were thrilled to escape that farm in Germania?"

"True enough. As soon as I could walk, my father had me patrolling the fields."

"As soon as you could walk?"

"Well, I may have been a little older. He had me protecting our borders from wolves. I was armed with a sharpened stick."

"What was your father thinking? What could a child with a sharp stick do against a wolf?"

Felix smiled, remembering. "Oh, there weren't any wolves. Our farm was part of a settlement around a Roman fort. Most of what we grew we sold to the army. My father wished he had led a more exciting life. He had entertained Roman officers at dinner from time to time and I listened to their stories. When I patrolled the fields I imagined I was guarding the Persian border."

"You did spend some time at the border, didn't you?"

"Yes, and during the middle of night, staring out over that desolate landscape, I remembered watching for wolves to emerge from the woods. The difference was, there really were Persians among the crags and ravines."

"You must have left home at an early age."

"As soon as I was old enough I walked into the local fort and joined the army. My mother cried. She had hoped I would be a farmer like my family had always been but my father had put other ideas into my head."

"Your father must have been happy. You certainly have led an exciting life."

"A farmer might think so. My mistake was excelling as a soldier. I was eventually sent to Constantinople and brought to the attention of Emperor Justin. I became one of his bodyguards."

"But soon you will be fighting in Italy."

"Provided the corpse in the bath doesn't end up blocking my way."

"Everything will turn out all right. Tell me more about Germania."

"But I've already told you about all that."

Felix felt the weight of his predicament pressing in on him and grew silent.

After a while Anastasia said, "I can't bear it, sitting here, waiting and waiting. I have things to attend to at the palace. I'll be missed. I'll come back before dark."

Felix had taken hold of her arm, gently but firmly. "Stay. Please."

She stared at him. "Do you think I'd betray you to the City Prefect?"

He looked away, ashamed. How could he doubt this woman who shared his bed? And yet a woman about whom he knew nothing? "Perhaps I should go for a stroll to calm my nerves."

She gave him a grim look. "No. I would prefer you didn't. It feels like rain. The breeze has a chill in it. I wouldn't want you to get wet. It's best that we both stay here."

So, they understood each other. Both feared the other, and with reason, given both might be found equally guilty. Those who unthinkingly trusted others, those who were never afraid, did not survive long at the palace.

Anastasia must have guessed what Felix was thinking. She grasped his hand and led him back to the bedroom.

The day passed slowly. There was time for speculation. The corpse remained a mystery. In death the courier had been empty-handed. If he had carried a package to the house someone had taken it. Had the man been robbed and killed in the courtyard upon his arrival or had he been left there? There was no way to tell. Anastasia did not recognize the dead man as anyone she had seen at court. The discolored and contorted face bore little semblance of humanity and she could barely bring herself to glance at it.

At some point Felix decided how to deal with his unwelcome visitor. He would not resort to lawyers or the authorities. Laws were unreliable allies. He would handle the matter himself.

After an eternity, when a single invisible bird sang from the darkness pooled in the garden, Felix instructed Nikomachos to order the servants to remain in their quarters for the night.

"I will summon you later to refresh the bath."

Nikomachos' face exhibited its usual vaguely supercilious expression.

How much had he observed apart from the obvious fact that two of the urban watch had searched the house? Had he seen the body? Had he overheard anything of their conversation?

"And you will remain at the house until I give you further orders," Felix added.

Nikomachos offered one of his bows, little more than a peevish twitch, and departed.

"He knows," Anastasia said.

"Why do you think so?"

"He's always hovering nearby, listening, peeping. And the other servants must know. They must have realized something illegal was going on, with this courier constantly arriving in the middle of the night."

"Not at all. I dropped hints to Nikomachos that I was buying silk at less than imperial prices. These days, who doesn't?"

He took the last fig, stuck it into his mouth, and wiped his fingers on his tunic. "But now I have work to do."

Chapter Fourteen

Less than an hour later Felix was cursing the narrowness of the alley behind his house.

He hadn't driven a donkey cart since he'd left the family farm in Germania to join the legions. He might have felt a pang of nostalgia under different circumstances, ones that didn't involve secretly disposing of a strangled corpse. The cart's wooden sides scraped brick walls as he urged the donkey through semi-liquid drifts of discarded vegetables and other slippery detritus better not investigated in the dark, or for that matter in such light as straggled down into the narrow way even in daytime. The stubborn beast refused to follow a straight line. Apparently donkeys were much stupider than they used to be.

Felix would have slung the body across the back of one of his horses but he feared drawing attention. Lying in the bottom of the cart, wrapped in a blanket, the corpse would pass for a sack of grain if anyone took any notice. Or so he hoped.

He kept expecting a contingent of urban watch to materialize in the alley mouth to block his way. When he had managed to maneuver the cart out of the alley and the wheels rattled over the street cobbles he began to feel easier. The further he could get from the house the better.

His relief lasted only a short time until he discovered the cart was too wide to be driven through the slit between the buildings opposite the mouth of the alley. He would have to travel in more public places than he had planned in order to reach the seawall, where his burden could be tossed into the water to become a plaything for Poseidon's children, as Anastasia had delicately put it.

He had left her behind. If she wanted to betray him this was her chance. He'd know whether she was loyal or not when he got back.

His house was located on a side street off the Mese, conveniently near to the Great Palace and not far from the water. Tugging clumsily at the reins, he convinced the donkey to turn down the thoroughfare. The beast continued to plod slowly but erratically, veering from side to side. Torches outside shops shut for the night intermittently illuminated the street. A gust of wind blew grit into Felix's face. Moon-silvered clouds raced through the sky.

The cart rolled into an oblong of light spilling from a doorway.

"Felix! Stop!"

What the voice stopped was Felix's heart. Discovered? Already?

He raised his whip, ready to urge his reluctant animal forward, then he saw a familiar figure reeling out of the tavern, one Felix too often frequented. Or had until he met Anastasia.

"Felix, my friend, come and share a cup with me! How long has it been since we've saluted Bacchus together? You've been away as long as Odysseus."

"I regret I'm off on urgent official business, Bato."

To Felix's chagrin the donkey decided to halt dead in its tracks, allowing Bato to stroll over to the side of the cart and lie against it.

"Official business, is it? That's why you're taking the imperial carriage?" Bato looked bleary-eyed into the cart.

"It's a matter that calls for discretion."

"Ah." Bato exhaled pungently, leering up at Felix. "You are off to see a lady, aren't you? Come my friend, are we not men? There is no need for prevarication. You have fallen under Circe's spell."

"Mithra!" Felix muttered under his breath. "I admit it," he said loudly, "I'm on way to visit a woman, who is waiting impatiently."

Bato made no effort to push himself away from the cart. Instead he banged the side. "And with such a conveyance? Do you expect to be so exhausted you'll have to be carted home?"

"Hardly. I just decided to...to show her how things were back in Germania when I was growing up."

Bato ignored his excuse. "I have it. You're going to pretend to be bringing the cart back after repairing it, so her husband will be misled if he hears of your visit."

Felix sighed, winked, tapped his nose, and flapped the reins. He didn't like the way Bato was staring into the cart. The donkey started to trot with a jerk, almost jarring Felix from his seat.

Relieved of his support, Bato crumpled to the cobbles and sat there in the tavern light, waving after Felix. "Go sail the wine dark seas into the arms of your sorceress, Felix! When she grows bored, you know where to find your loyal old friend Bato."

Glancing back over his shoulder Felix saw his inebriated friend shooing away a dog which had come to investigate the interesting offal in the gutter. Fortunately the street was otherwise deserted.

He had to get off this wide street. There were bound to be people about, not to mention occasional patrols.

With difficulty, Felix convinced the beast—or it convinced itself—to enter what was little more than a noisome crevice between tenements. Dark shapes swarmed around the cart and the wheels went over bumps that let out piercing shrieks.

The panicked donkey moved faster. Felix shouted orders, futilely. It didn't respond to any of the curses he tried.

The cart careened through various gradations of almost total darkness, banging walls, splashing through blessedly invisible filth, turning corners when the way ahead seemed blocked. Not that the route mattered. Felix was not familiar with the back ways here. As long as he continued downhill, as seemed to be the case, he would reach the water, which was all that was necessary.

Constantinople was a long, narrow peninsula. He couldn't help but find the water eventually.

When the cart reached more level ground and emerged from its dark narrow passage into what seemed by comparison a blaze of light, he discovered he had been optimistic, not to mention badly disoriented. Instead of the sea wall he had expected, he faced a thoroughfare broader than the one he had fled and more brightly lit.

It could only be the Mese.

Felix looked back into the cart. His dark, shapeless burden still lay there. Had he expected it to get up and walk away?

Considering everything that had happened lately he wouldn't have been surprised.

Now what? He hadn't calculated on having so much difficulty navigating or driving. Craning his neck, he was able to spot the glow from the dome of the Great Church rising toward the moon, now visible, surrounded by a misty halo, in a gap in the gathering clouds.

Perhaps he had better brave the Mese. If he simply continued straight on, he could dump the body in one of the cemeteries outside the city's inner walls. The worst risk of his being discovered had been near to his house, hadn't it?

He ordered the donkey forward.

Few pedestrians were abroad and mostly in the noisy vicinity of taverns. Horses trotted by, thankfully none carrying military men.

Despite the muggy air, Felix kept getting chills. He couldn't help recalling Anastasia telling him she'd been afraid the dead courier would reach up from the bath and put its cold hand against her back.

He resisted the urge to twist around to peer into the cart.

The eerie feeling that there was something there, reaching out, behind him, grew stronger. He could almost sense a hovering presence a finger's breadth from his neck.

"Don't be a fool," he growled. He didn't like the uneasy note in his voice. The courier was as dead as a grilled fish. No, Felix wouldn't turn. Wouldn't give in to irrational fear. He stared straight down the street.

He could hear the voices of those he'd interviewed at the church, describing the supernatural thieves they'd glimpsed fleeing, recalled the strange spectacle in the mausoleum, the dead frogs, the scarab on Theodora's sarcophagus.

Who could say for certain what might be out here in the night?

Where was he?

Wasn't that the fork, where the Mese split into a northern and eastern branch? The northern way led past the Church of the Holy Apostles.

"South, then!" Felix told himself, yanking at the donkey's reins. The beast resisted, slowed. Exasperated Felix swung his whip. Too hard.

"Gently, gently, my boy. The whip is only to direct the animal," he heard his father telling him.

The donkey leapt forward in its traces, jerking the cart. Felix grabbed his seat to avoid falling into the street.

The terrified beast would have tired itself out quickly but it didn't get the chance. A gaping rut spared it the effort.

Felix saw the jagged hole looming an instant before the cart hit with a bone-shaking jolt. There was a sickening crack from below and the cart tipped over sideways as one wheel flew off onto the nearby colonnade.

His precious cargo slid out, hit the ground, and lay there in the bright illumination of a nearby torch, looking exactly like a dead body wrapped in a blanket.

Chapter Fifteen

Dedi, desecrater of Theodora's tomb, lurked in night shadows, watching the mansion across the street with growing impatience.

During his pursuit he would have been happy to stand still, as he had now been doing hour after hour. With his short legs it had taken all his strength to keep the fleet-footed, demonic creatures in sight.

His first thought when he saw them burst from the Church of the Holy Apostles was that the spells intended to bring Theodora back to life had gone awry and called forth two monsters from the depths instead. But if so, what were they carrying away from the church?

On impulse, he decided to pursue them. At the back of the church grounds they cut behind a looming cliff of inky buildings and raced downhill to where the Valens Aqueduct emerged from the hillside to span the valley there. They kept to the base of the aqueduct, gliding in and out of the thick shadows cast by archways in the moonlight. For an instant Dedi would see two ghostly, silvered shapes, then they would vanish into utter blackness, only to reappear as if by magick. So he ran after two flickering phantoms, until they veered off into labyrinthine alleyways.

Dedi's snaggle-toothed mouth worked like a bellows as he sucked in the thick unwholesome atmosphere of the city night. There was a devilish air about him. He had always been able to make Theodora laugh. Perhaps his call had not gone unheeded.

The empress may have heard it while chatting with the two loping creatures in front of him. "Go and see what Dedi wants," she might have ordered.

Luckily their route continued to descend, which made running easier, or Dedi would have lost them. They avoided the main streets and open spaces. Dedi had no idea where he was. He began to fear that in their strange zigzagging flight they had traced an arcane symbol which had dropped them all into a maze leading to the anteroom of the underworld. Then they crossed the Mese in a band of moonlight and Dedi would have breathed a sigh of relief if his burning lungs had allowed it.

They plunged down toward the Harbor of Julian. Were they bearing whatever they had stolen to a waiting ship? Why would evil spirits do that when they could simply take to the skies, or sink down into the earth? But instead of continuing to the docks they ran along the periphery of the harbor in the direction of the Hippodrome and the Great Palace. The moon threw a shaft of icy light across the basalt sea. Dedi raced on until his legs began to cramp, but the moon remained always at his one shoulder and the reflection at the other so he seemed to be churning along in place, as in a nightmare.

As they came into sight of the curved end of the Hippodrome one of the creatures suddenly vanished. They had run into a pool of shadow but only a single one emerged, the other having apparently dissolved into the darkness from where it had come. Or, perhaps, cut abruptly into an alley.

Dedi forced his legs to move faster, determined not to lose the remaining demon, the one that was carrying whatever had been pilfered from the church.

He was not surprised when, at last, the creature ended its flight by slipping through a side door into a mansion Dedi recognized as belonging to General Belisarius and his wife Antonina. The magician had entertained there so often he knew many of the staff by name. He knew that the fortress-like granite exterior, adorned only by a wide marble staircase, concealed an interior as luxurious as that of the Great Palace.

He remembered too how uneasy Antonina made him. Her stare seemed to penetrate his heart, making him shiver with fear. It was not merely that she was ruthless, she was also widely rumored to practice magick, and not the harmless kind Dedi performed. Antonina's magick was malignant and self-serving. Thus had Belisarius been assisted in his rise to generalship, or so it was claimed by chattering courtiers.

Could Antonina be involved in the theft from the church?

He would rather wrestle with a denizen of hell than be caught looking at her askance. Suddenly he felt a presence at his back. Something infinitely cold with menace. He staggered around, heart leaping, but there was nothing to see except the icy moon hanging high up in the sky, beyond the grasp of the countless crosses reaching up from the rooftops of the Christian capital.

Nevertheless, he fled, peering this way and that, fearful of being observed.

Dawn and a nap had cleared away the black cobwebs of Dedi's fears. Having been frustrated in his attempts to revive his employer, he began to consider other schemes. It hadn't taken long to discover that the object clutched by the demon had been the shroud of the Virgin. News spread fast. Half the city had probably learned about the theft while Dedi pursued the perpetrators. Both Justinian and the church would be grateful if he were able to restore the relic to its rightful place. Could he steal it back?

He wasn't certain what he might learn, but he would soon be out on the streets and idle anyway.

So now a shriveled face peered out from behind a statue of Virgil. Although looted from Rome, the statue was not, in truth, a very good example of classical art, barely good enough to fill one of the many niches needing residents in the nether walls of the Hippodrome. Dedi had no interest in either sculpture or poetry, but only in the concealment offered by Virgil's voluminous marble toga.

Invisible though he was from the street and the mansion, his terror returned. However, his fear of demonic forces and

Antonina were outweighed by his fear for his future. He might have taken consolation in being free of Theodora's whims, for nobody could have shielded him from her wrath if he had offended her, even if the offense arose, as a storm on the Sea of Marmara, for no other reason than that she was bored. But the fact was, with Theodora gone, he no longer had a place at court.

The empress had delighted in his magick. Dedi's talking, human-headed snake might be an obvious fraud, but its often obscene repartee always made the empress laugh. Not that her laughter was a pleasant sound. Thus did the jackal cough over the dead and crows croak over their carrion. Still, coaxing that hellish noise out of her earned him a comfortable place to live, and the jingle of coins in his purse pleased him.

"Send for Dedi of Egypt," Theodora would order, and he had never failed to make her scimitar smile appear.

It didn't hurt that his shrunken stature almost qualified him as one of the dwarfs on which she doted. He puffed out his sunken chest with pride at the recollection. His elation did not last long. For she and her scarlet smile were gone forever and he had made enemies who sneered at him and whispered of unholy practices as he passed by in the frescoed halls of the Great Palace. And it was true, not all of his tricks were as patently fraudulent as the talking snake. Ironically, the courtiers were afraid of him. Afraid his magick would do them harm. But now, without Theodora's protection, his reputation was going to harm him.

During his solitary hours behind Virgil's toga, Dedi had reached a frightening conclusion. The desecration of the mausoleum was sure to be identified as his handiwork and by extension he would be accused of stealing the sacred icon on the same night.

Dedi wished he hadn't forgotten the Egyptian talisman in his panic. Still, he could never have caught all the frogs, and they were equally damning. It was unfair. He had only wanted to bring Theodora back from the halls of the dead, or at least within earshot of the emperor. Who could fault him for that? He had nothing to do with the theft of the holy relic. The Christians did not understand that the magick he practiced was not the same as their magick. What use would their holy charm have been to an Egyptian magician?

Except now he desperately needed it to save his own ugly little head.

And how did he plan to regain the shroud of the Virgin? It was one thing to trick the empress into laughing and quite another to do battle with forces of evil. Would the malign spirits he needed to overcome be as powerful as Shezmu, slaughterer of wicked souls in the underworld? He recalled tales he and his childhood friends had used to scare each other. Shezmu employed a press and the heads of such souls to make wine for the virtuous dead.

Movement at the side of the mansion caught his attention. A figure emerged from the side door, just visible in the light from an open window, and slunk away.

Things were becoming clearer. But what, exactly, was he going to do now he knew the demon had disguised itself as Antonina's servant Tychon?

Chapter Sixteen

Felix picked himself up off the street, cursing rut-splintered axles, overturned carts, dead bodies, Fate, and skittish donkeys. He took a few tentative steps, making certain he hadn't broken anything. Fat droplets of rain began beating down on his head, so he cursed the heavens too.

His cargo lay sprawled at the edge of the colonnade, clearly illuminated by the torch left burning in front of a shuttered butcher's shop. The blanket had become slightly undone. One hand stuck out, signaling for help.

Felix looked up and down the street. At present it was deserted. The rain increased, stirring up a smell of dust where it hit. A gust of wind groaned through the colonnade. Lightning flashed repeatedly. The flickering light made the dead hand look as if it were waving frantically. The noise of the accident may have alerted someone. For all he knew the urban watch could be on the way.

Even if he could push the cart upright it wasn't going anywhere with a broken axle.

Did he hear voices? The sound of rain drowned everything out.

He grasped the blanket-wrapped corpse and lifted it with a grunt, feeling a sharp twinge in his side. Perhaps he'd broken something after all. As he staggered over to the donkey the whole length of an arm freed itself and slapped against his leg.

He flung the horrid load over the donkey's back, undid the traces leaving the bit and a length of rein in place, and urged the animal onward. Forget the cemeteries. He couldn't be too far from the sea. Judging from the driving rain, blowing straight into his face, the sea was coming to him. He was moving downhill. Water rushed along the street, splashing around his ankles. All he needed to do was follow the gurgling rivulets.

Soon man, beast, and dead man were soaked. The corpse kept slipping and sliding further out of the blanket until both arms and an elegantly booted foot dangled in plain view. Luckily no sensible person would be abroad in such a torrent, and beggars sheltering in doorways or vacant shops had problems enough of their own without worrying about what others might be doing.

Thunder reverberated, the ground vibrated. Lightning flashes revealed a city devoid of color, a bas relief in pure white marble. The roar of the rain numbed the senses. Felix was hardly aware of his beard dripping or his saturated clothes. He might have been accompanying his lifeless companion into the land of the dead. The warm bedroom he had so recently shared with Anastasia existed in another world.

Then he saw an orange light in the thickening mist. A lantern, surely, to be shining in the midst of the downpour.

The urban watch sometimes carried lanterns.

Felix froze and pulled awkwardly at his reins, forcing the donkey to stop.

The light bobbed in the middle of the street. The rain and mist obscured whoever was holding it. A whole contingent of armed men might be staring at him, wondering what sort of madman would be leading a donkey along in weather like this. A madman whose actions required investigating.

The light moved, crossed the street, and vanished under the colonnade.

Felix began to breath again.

The donkey snorted uneasily.

A lightning bolt struck close enough to make Felix's ears ring and shook his bones. The donkey let out a bray of terror and ran.

Felix clamped his hand shut but there was nothing there but a raw welt where the reins had been. The donkey might have been ridden by Satan himself so quickly did it vanish into the storm.

There would have been plenty of room on its back for a rider because the courier's body had returned to the street, one hand resting against the toe of Felix's boot.

Felix kicked it off in revulsion.

"Mithra!"

Just his luck, the street here was brightly illuminated, this time by a torch in front of a perfumer's shop. The light reflected from the opaque eyes of the ashen face which had been uncovered in its most recent fall.

Would he never be rid of the cursed corpse? It pursued him like one of the Furies.

As the thought crossed his mind, the corpse laughed rudely.

No, Felix told himself, just noxious gases escaping as the thing started to decay.

He felt a sudden impulse to simply run, leave the corpse where it was. But that would be like fleeing the battlefield. Felix refused to flee. He must finish what he had begun, somehow.

He wiped rain out of his own eyes with a shaking hand and looked around. His attention was drawn by the perfumer's statue of Aphrodite, an exceptionally inept copy of a classical Greek work. The legs were too short. The breasts were almost those of a child's, but even though the amateur sculptor had apparently whittled first one then the other, he had never got them anywhere near the same size.

Nevertheless, at that moment, she was the most beautiful woman Felix had ever seen thanks to the recess behind her, large enough to conceal a body.

Why hadn't he thought of it before? He dragged the courier under the colonnade. The roaring rush of rain turned into a hollow thudding on the sheltering roof.

"Let's get you ready for the goddess!" Felix began stripping off the dead man's soaked garments. Beggars who died on the streets were invariably found naked, picked clean. And with no garments, the body would probably not be identified quickly, if at all. There was nothing remarkable about it that he could see. A well fed young man whose muscles had not been taxed with labor. The packages he had delivered had never been very heavy.

Just another man murdered in the street. How could anyone link the captain of the excubitors with a naked corpse discovered far away from the palace?

He carried the man's garments back to the public lavatory he remembered passing. The foul weather had kept people off the streets and the long marble bench was deserted. A beggar jumped up from a corner and fled, perhaps mistaking Felix for the urban watch.

Felix stuffed the garments down a hole then relieved himself after them, thoughtfully.

John might have come up with a better plan. But he wasn't here—for the time being.

Given Justinian's whims, his friend would doubtless be returned to favor soon. It wasn't as if John were dead.

DAY THREE

Chapter Seventeen

John knew what it felt like to drown.

The gusting wind whipped rain and blinding, stinging sheets of salt spray across his face. Opening his mouth to gulp in air, he inhaled water instead. He gasped and choked. His boots slid on slick planks as the deck tilted. He grabbed blindly at the rail to avoid falling. A splinter dug into his palm. He didn't loosen his grip. The *Leviathan* continued to roll.

It was going to capsize this time.

But again, at what seemed the last moment, the ship righted itself.

He kept a death grip on the rail and stared out into a chaotic, nacreous twilight of roiling fog and rain. It was past dawn but the storm which had kept him awake all night had not abated. The wind had picked up and the waves increased.

In summer the winds usually came from the northwest, assisting the prevailing currents to hurry ships out of the Sea of Marmara, but the night before they had shifted to the south. It was peculiar, almost inexplicable, as if the hand of evil were upon them. Or so John had been told by one of the rustic fellow travelers he had taken to be a farmer.

Even farmers knew more about sailing than John. He knew only that he dreaded traveling across the bottomless pit of the sea.

Why the captain had decided to leave their overnight mooring was a total mystery.

John had passed the night pressed against Cornelia's back, listening to rain clattering against the deck above, hearing the mingled moans and cries of the *Leviathan* and her restlessly dreaming passengers. Cornelia's even breathing told of the calm oblivion he only wished for. How could she sleep when he could not? In the time they had been together, wounded though he was, she had come to seem a part of him and he part of her.

In the dark sour-smelling hold, battered by the sea, John found himself staring into the abyss he had confronted so often as a younger man during his first years in Constantinople, when he had still been a slave.

He was on a voyage to nowhere. An estate in Greece? He couldn't imagine it. He had lived on the move, on the borders of the empire as a mercenary, had existed as a captive in Persian encampments, and lived in Constantinople as both a slave and a high official in turn. Through all the years he had fought to survive, battled steel and political intrigue to go on living. Was there truly anything else?

He had dreamt often enough of settling down in the country but now he realized if he did he would be no better than a shade, wandering Hades without purpose.

When the rain and wind let up for a time, John could here the occasional nightmare-induced cry or groan from a fellow passenger and the low prayers of the aged pilgrim on the other side of the thin partition. She mumbled on tirelessly to her god and the mother of her god. To some of these Christians prayer came as easily as breathing.

The pilgrim was convinced—or trying to convince herself, judging from the way she kept repeating her prayers—that the Lord would save her, as he had saved Saint Paul. She counted on her Lord's steadfast love. Or so she said repeatedly.

So far as John had observed there was no steadfast love in this world except between two human beings and that was rare. To throw oneself on the mercy of some imagined, invisible god of love was nothing more than surrender. Mithra demanded His followers battle the darkness, not meekly await salvation from it.

And wasn't John battling the darkness by working for Justinian, who imposed law and justice on the empire? Wasn't Justinian on the side of the light? Or was the emperor part of the forces of darkness, as many supposed?

Would John ever be certain?

Finally he had risen quietly, letting Cornelia sleep, and gone out on deck.

Captain Theon, a short, rotund man with a fiery red face, was speaking to a sailor who was taking soundings. John overheard bits of the conversation.

"I expected this to blow over by now," the captain was saying.

The other made what must have been a disparaging remark, judging from the captain's scowl.

"I'm not throwing out the anchors. If we can't see the shore we're not in the shallows. Keep testing the depth."

The rattle of wind-driven rain obscured most of the sailor's reply.

"...besides we're well past...Yes, I know when the wind shifted. That's why...you think I'm a fool? Who's captain on this ship?"

John told himself to be calm. Theon obviously did not consider their situation to be as dire as it seemed. This was a normal squall, terrifying only to a person unfamiliar with sailing.

The crew were doing whatever needed to be done, whatever that might be. It made John furious to be rendered helpless by his ignorance, dependent on these strangers.

The sea, vast and mindless, was not amenable to reason nor could it be vanquished by steel.

The deck shook as a wall of water smashed into the hull.

John knew he should return to Cornelia below, protected from the sea only by fragile timbers.

He hesitated to take his hand off the rail. He had been squeezing it so tightly his fingers were white, except where they were stained with red. He was bleeding freely from the splinter in his palm.

He paused, allowing a gust to die before releasing his grip.

Then he was hurtling forward, smashing into the back of the cabin. There was a shrieking, grinding noise and the ringing snap of splintering wood, a sound he had heard long ago when his company had battered down the gates of a besieged town.

He tried to brace himself against the cabin as the *Leviathan* began to swing around abruptly, as if trying to shake off the crew. Shouts and curses rang out over the groaning of the hull.

John had to reach Cornelia.

Another jarring crash vibrated through the ship and he found himself on his hands and knees, crawling up a tilting deck. Up and up the deck rose, a wooden cliff rearing itself in front of him.

Disoriented, he glanced around. He appeared to be suspended over the black water.

A wave hit him like a giant's hand and he felt himself sliding down the impossibly tilted deck.

Cornelia woke from a nightmare.

No, not a nightmare. The jolt and the deafening crack of breaking wood had been real. Passengers shouted and screamed.

She turned toward John as the ship rolled.

She felt his absence before she saw he was gone.

There was another crash and the ship rolled again and settled back down with a concussion so jarring Cornelia was surprised the hull didn't disintegrate immediately. It was in the process of doing so, to judge by the tortured grating and creaking filling the dark cavern below deck.

John must have gone up on deck while she slept.

She scrambled from the compartment and climbed out into the gray rain that rattled onto the deck with a noise resembling thousands of games of knucklebones.

The captain was bawling orders to the crew.

Cornelia scanned the deck in a panic.

Only strange faces, not the face she sought.

"John!"

There was no answer.

Chapter Eighteen

In the morning as Felix rode to the Church of the Holy Apostles, the naked corpse he had hidden behind the statue of Aphrodite kept threatening to leap into his path. He couldn't put the dead man's specter out of his mind. The pallid revenant kept flickering into view, only to turn into a foraging cat or a slinking dog.

Anastasia, Felix's personal Aphrodite, had found his solution amusing. Or at any rate she had laughed hysterically when he related his misfortunes with the cart and the eventual disposal of their unwanted visitor. A release of tension or a manifestation of horror. She had been drinking by the time he'd arrived home. He couldn't blame her. He was shaking himself and not merely with the cold and wet.

Well, that was over now, he told himself.

Had the body been discovered yet?

Probably not. The streets were still nearly empty. The storm had passed but the morning remained dark. Ragged black clouds torn to shreds against the rooftops raced away across a slate-colored sky. Mist rose from puddles. From everywhere came the sounds of water, gurgling in gutters, dripping from colonnades.

The sound of something that should have been dead shuffling noisily through the standing water at the mouth of an alley.

No, Felix reminded himself. The victim—the intruder in his courtyard—had been perfectly and completely dead.

Inside the church it was as bright as a sunny midday. Felix blinked. Reliquaries glittered in the illumination of countless lamps, their gold decorations glowing. Felix's vague speculations on why the Virgin's relic had been taken and by whom, meant to banish thoughts of the dead man, were interrupted by rapid footsteps ticking across the marble floor.

"Captain!" Basilius appeared at his elbow. The priest looked ill, pale with red-rimmed eyes. "Have you brought good news?"

Felix shook his head. "I've only just begun my investigation."

The priest gave a long sigh of despair. "By this time the thieves will have escaped far away. Already this morning I've been visited by the head of the urban watch and he thinks the same."

"Justinian is extremely anxious that the shroud be recovered, wherever it is."

"He would be, yes. The relic protects the city. Its theft is not only blasphemous, but involves a military matter, the defense of Constantinople."

Felix nodded politely. The Virgin's shroud might repel an enemy—as many believed—so long as it was accompanied by a thousand soldiers armed with steel. But then, he was a Mithran. Christians obviously felt differently. The emperor himself was anxious to have the shroud returned and he was a practical man notwithstanding his theological ruminations. If Justinian considered the relic a useless piece of cloth he wouldn't have ordered Felix to investigate.

"I see you agree with me, captain." Basilius gestured toward an emerald-studded reliquary. "We have many treasures, rich enough to tempt men to imperil their immortal souls. They would sell jewels wrenched from such beautiful works fashioned by the faithful, melt down the gold they are made from. Jewels can be replaced, but the holy shroud cannot. To think of it in evil hands!" Tears glistened on his cheeks.

It made Felix uncomfortable to see the man weeping like a woman who finds one of her best robes ruined by careless servants. "Would anyone buy such a famous relic?" He snapped. "Would it have any value? Who could want it?"

Basilius wiped his tears. "How would I know? I have nothing to do with affairs of the empire. Enemies of Constantinople might want to take it away."

"You really believe it protects the city as people say?"

Basilius looked at Felix uncomprehendingly. "It is the shroud of the Virgin. How could it not protect us?"

"What evidence is there for it? Do you suppose we would be knee-deep in Goths or Persians if the shroud hadn't been here all these years?"

"It is said that Emperor Anastasius carried it with him into victorious battle against the heretical rebels, many years ago."

"I wasn't aware Anastasius was a fighter."

"With the protection of the Virgin it was not necessary."

What did the priest mean? That one could fight the enemy from the comfort of one's bedroom by simply holding onto a bit of cloth? There was no point pursuing the matter. If enough people thought an object was valuable, it was. "Does someone think he has a claim to the relic?"

"How could anyone? The church here has been in undisputed possession for almost a century. A pilgrim brought it back from the Holy Land."

Stole it more likely, Felix thought.

"Could it really have been demons that took it? You heard what Mada and Peteiros said."

"Have they remembered anything more? Do they still insist they saw these things out of a nightmare?"

"You sound skeptical? You don't suspect them? They've always been faithful servants. Good Christians, both."

"Gold answers prayers the gods ignore."

Basilius looked shocked.

"As to these supernatural robbers they talked about," Felix continued, "it strikes me as too much of a marvel to be true. Then there's the matter of the frogs and the scarab. Is the mausoleum doorkeeper here?"

"Timothy? Yes. He hasn't gone off duty yet."

Felix was surprised to find the ancient down on his knees, washing the mausoleum floor.

"Don't want any trace of them dirty frogs remaining, sir." Timothy began to struggle to his feet, bracing himself against the sarcophagus.

Felix gave him a hand. "You remember me? The captain of the excubitors?"

Recognition came into the old man's face. He dropped his scrubbing rag. Felix saw he was trembling. "Are you going to arrest me? How did you find out?"

Had the fellow been drinking or was he mad? "Find out what? About the demons?"

"You do know then! I was afraid, sir. Have mercy on an old man. I didn't want to tell the truth when Basilius asked me if I had seen anything. It's true, I only pretended I'd seen the demons the other two were talking about. I need this job to get by."

"Go on."

"To tell the truth I was asleep until the uproar in the church woke me. Then I saw an ape leaving the grounds."

"An ape?"

"It looked like the ape that danced for its master at the shows at the Hippodrome. Like a man, yet not like a man. But I only got a glimpse."

"Are you sure you didn't dream this?"

"No, sir. I may doze, but I always keep one eye open."

Felix cursed silently. As if demons and frogs and scarabs weren't bad enough, along comes an ape. "Did the ape jump out from the mouth of a wine jug by chance?"

"Not so, sir. Not so!"

Felix's malignant glare caused Timothy to cower backwards, as if he wanted to climb into Theodora's sarcophagus with her. "I suppose I am under arrest now?"

"Not yet. But I may wish to speak to you again in case you remember anything else you've lied about."

Felix stalked out deep in thought. There must be some connection between whatever had happened in the mausoleum and the theft which had taken place at the same time. If only he could discover what it was, the mystery would be solved. Wasn't that how John would look at it?

As Felix rode away from the Church of the Holy Apostles the sky finally began to brighten. Light glinted off puddles and wet marble and further away in the cityscape stretched out below the hill upon which the church stood, the sun illuminated the gilded domes of other churches and mansions.

Was the shroud hidden in one of those mansions? Was a wealthy merchant gloating over his newly found power? With a relic potent enough to protect an entire city, what would any man need to fear?

He considered visiting the Jingler again. After all, Julian had acquired a new amulet in the form of the roundel on his garment. How much greater protection the missing relic would offer! But was it likely a man petrified of devils would even consider raising them so they could steal it for him?

Your humors are deranged, Felix chided himself. Demons are for terrifying children. If someone wants to steal anything they don't need assistance from demons.

The Jingler might very well have been ordered by his superior to steal the shroud. If indeed he had a superior as he claimed. Whoever was involved with the theft of the relic would be in extreme danger, including an excubitor captain who had unwittingly agreed to assist in its delivery to its buyer.

And what was Felix supposed to say if the Jingler's superior demanded to know whether the package had been passed along by excubitors as usual?

"No. I found the courier dead and disposed of the body."

The next question would be: What had Felix done with the relic after killing the courier?

Chapter Nineteen

"You can't be serious, Felix! A collection of thugs…smugglers…threatening the captain of the excubitors?" Anastasia used her knife to spear the last olive on her plate and raised it to her lips. "I should hope you'd have them arrested on the spot."

"It's more complicated than that. I've already explained the situation." Felix didn't like the irritation he heard in his voice. He had never spoken harshly to Anastasia. But Mithra! Was the woman really so slow to grasp the implications or just pretending? "Quite apart from my debts and all the problems those entail, there's also the small matter that Justinian has ordered me to investigate a theft in which I am involved."

"Not knowingly."

"Convince the emperor of that."

"The only link to you is the dead courier, but what could there possibly be about a naked corpse abandoned in the street that would connect it with you?"

"I can't think of anything, true, but I can't keep myself from wondering if there's something I've overlooked."

Anastasia's face clouded. "Wait! What about your donkey and cart?"

"It was just a work cart. I didn't have my name emblazoned on the side. It was probably gone by the time the sun rose anyway, scavenged for parts and firewood."

"And the poor donkey?"

"Would I bother marking a donkey as if it were the imperial plate? If he belonged to Theodora he probably would have worn jeweled earrings."

Anastasia set her fork down noisily. "Don't be stupid. Theodora wouldn't have done something that foolish, despite the tall tales people tell about her."

"Ah, well, you would know better than me. You're from the palace."

"And what if the donkey comes back?"

Felix started to bark out his reply but caught himself, closed his eyes for a moment, and only then spoke. "Donkeys are not trained to return home. Although it would be a fine thing, wouldn't it, to find him braying at the gate like an avenging Fury?"

"You've been a swine ever since you got back," Anastasia pouted.

"I can't imagine why! I keep waiting for something to happen, or not happen."

"That makes no sense, Felix!"

"It does. The best thing that can happen is nothing at all. But nothing happening isn't very reassuring. It doesn't put an end to worrying, doesn't insure something might not happen."

Nikomachos appeared in the dining room and began to clear the remains of the midday meal, slowly, methodically, and clumsily.

"Get on with it, will you?" Felix snapped.

Anastasia clucked, scolding. "If you insist on employing one-armed servants what do you expect?"

"Normally he has only one person to wait on!"

Nikomachos stacked the empty plates, his expression bored, the frozen face on a coin.

"It's all very exciting, isn't it?" Anastasia said. "Your investigation, I mean."

"You seem remarkably unconcerned, but then it isn't your neck in the noose, is it?"

"Oh, you are such a grumpy bear today. I'm concerned, but it's an adventure, can't you see that?"

An adventure compared to the pampered life at court she was used to living, Felix thought. An adventure compared to searching for an earring her mistress had lost. He managed to keep his tongue quiet. Why should Anastasia be concerned, anyway? She did not know Felix well, despite their intimacy, and she wasn't involved in the robbery.

"Look how easily you relieved us of our unwelcome visitor," Anastasia pointed out.

"You call it easy, but it wasn't you roaming the streets in the rain."

A silver knife clattered against a plate as Nikomachos continued collecting the remains of their meal. Was he eavesdropping? He was always eavesdropping, wasn't he? "Finish your task," Felix ordered.

The servant managed to look hurt and contemptuous at the same time. With one hand, he lifted the perfectly arranged pile of platters, cutlery balanced on the top plate, and strode off.

Turning his glare away from Nikomachos' ramrod straight back, Felix was startled to see Anastasia dabbing away tears.

"Did I upset you?" he asked. "I'm sorry I snapped. I shouldn't be worrying you with my problems. I'll think of a solution."

Anastasia snuffled mournfully. "I was just thinking about the poor donkey. Whatever will happen to him, left out on the streets all alone with nothing to eat?"

A short time and many barbed words later Felix found himself stalking along the Mese in a foul humor, wondering why he had left his own house. It was his house, wasn't it? Not Anastasia's.

He had listened to all he could bear about his lack of common human feelings for donkeys. Probably he should not have said he didn't give a fig if starving beggars were roasting the animal on a spit, although it was true. However, it was she who had said a beast like him should have some compassion for its own flesh and blood.

How had she survived service at court with such a poisonous tongue?

She made him furious and all the more because he was afraid she might not cool down by bedtime.

By the time his own fury had begun to subside, Felix realized he was halfway to the Church of the Holy Apostles. It occurred to him he should ask around in the vicinity of the church, in case anyone had noticed anything the night of the robbery.

How exactly should he go about it?

He couldn't very well ask did you happen to see two demons the other night? Or an ape? Perhaps a large number of frogs?

Obviously he would need to be circumspect.

He marched along the crowded colonnade without pause, past shops full of lamps, olive oil, fabrics. Puddles lingered in the street. A fierce afternoon sun turned the humid air into a noxious soup smelling of the dung of cart animals, exotic spices and fragrances, overripe fruit, and the sour reek of sweating humanity.

The long walk and heat had made him thirsty. He found himself in front of a tavern. Perhaps a drink before he got started?

Chapter Twenty

Felix sat in the corner of a reeking tavern somewhere near the Aqueduct of Valens as best he could recall. Or had that been the last place he'd been in, or the one before? He watched patrons staggering and reeling past his table, up and down the stairs to the lavatory. He lifted his wine cup. Hesitated, stricken with guilt.

Before he met Anastasia he had been drinking too much. Half the imperial court knew about it. Half the court always knew everyone's personal business. He had promised her he would give up Bacchus for her, as she put it. He was uncomfortably aware he had broken the promise.

"Well," he muttered, "you deserve it. You drove me to it." He took a long gulp of wine, punishing her for being unreasonable. It was her fault.

Besides, taverns were the only places where he might find witnesses willing to talk. Or so he had surmised after futilely questioning close-mouthed shopkeepers and wary beggars. Late-drinking tavern patrons would also have been the most likely to witness suspicious happenings in the night.

He emptied his cup and wiped his beard. "There. Are you happy now? See what you've done to me!"

An old man at a nearby table was eying him curiously. Felix took it as an invitation. He got up, his sword clanking against the side of the table, and clumped over to where the man was seated.

"Imperial business," Felix said. "There have been reports of strange happenings. Demons and apes." He went on to elaborate, having long since abandoned his efforts to remain circumspect.

The fellow had studied the bottom of his empty cup and after Felix paid to have it refilled he sipped reflectively and noisily. "Apes and demons you say? Now that you mention it I did see a pair of demons meeting that description the other night, being chased by an ape. Unless it was a hairy demon with a tail."

Felix eyed the man hopefully.

"Yes," he continued, "I remember it now. Seeing Theodora's shade flapping round and round the dome of the Great Church afterward put them demons and apes right out of my head."

"Should have grilled the old devil like Saint Lawrence," Felix muttered as he reeled away from the tavern, recalling what palace wits liked to say about a courtier, another Lawrence, notorious for his taciturnity. Then again in Constantinople it was wise to cultivate not only silence but also selective blindness, especially when a man from the palace came calling, asking awkward questions.

It was as well he was the questioner and not the questioned. He wasn't certain how he might stand up to interrogation by certain persons employed by Justinian to obtain answers with the aid of extremely unpleasant instruments. Well, at present he could barely stand up, torturers or not, he admitted to himself as he veered into a pillar of the colonnade. Still, he truly hoped he never made the acquaintance of those inquisitive men.

He had sent plenty of malefactors to be introduced to them. How could he have avoided it? That's the way things were done.

He navigated a courtyard and passed through an archway into a street. A sign on the archway identified the establishment he had just visited as the Inn of the Centaurs, not merely a tavern. Had he come in this way?

In the back of his mind he understood it was unwise to be drinking, given his uneasiness and sense of approaching disaster. When he drank he was carried aloft on the wings of the grape, as John's friend Anatolius had written in one of his execrable poems. Once up there Felix's problems always looked tiny and insignificant. Unfortunately the grape inevitably let go and he plummeted into the stygian pit of infinite despair.

Another snippet from one of Anatolius' poems?

Felix guessed he was about ready for the fall. Why else would he be worrying about the imperial torturers?

Anastasia would torture him if he returned in this state. Would she still be at his house? Did he dare return? Shadows were beginning to creep in from the west as night drew on.

Somehow or other he had made his way to the Hippodrome.

He ducked into one of the alcoves decorating the wall of the race course and relieved himself noisily behind an obscure philosopher.

Unfortunately the act reminded him of the body he had left behind another statue. Surely he couldn't be connected with it? But how long until he was able to be absolutely certain? Would he ever be assured he was safe?

He emerged, rearranging his garment. The nearby dome of the Great Church glowed in gathering darkness. Theodora's shade flying around indeed!

He realized he had stepped out into the midst of a group of young men, immediately identifiable by their partly shaved heads, braids of long hair worn in the Hunnish style, and rich, if barbaric, billowing garments with close-fitting sleeves.

Followers of the Blue chariot racing team.

"Why, it's Captain Felix." Their leader, a tall man with a scarred face, smiled in jovial fashion. He was standing much too close to Felix, blocking his path.

"Stand aside! I'm engaged in important imperial work!" Felix could hear his words were slurred.

"By the smell, you've been assigned to test the purity of wine," chimed in another of the group.

Felix pivoted, unsteady on his feet, to address the new speaker and before he could bark out a word, his arms were pinioned from behind, a hand clamped over his mouth, and he was dragged toward an archway leading into the Hippodrome.

There were a few people in the street who could not have helped seeing what was happening. They hurried on, faces averted. A knot of beggars settling down for the night inside the Hippodrome entranceway shouted encouragement to the Blues as they dragged Felix past.

Felix had no hope of escape. After all the wine he'd consumed he was barely able to stay on his feet, let alone put up a fight. The young men carted him as helpless as a baby through dark, deserted corridors.

What did they want?

Was it robbery? Then why address him by name?

Chilling gusts of fear began to clear wine mists from his head.

He bit the fingers covering his mouth. The hand jerked away reflexively but before Felix could yell for help one of his captors delivered a blow to the back of his skull.

A torch seemed to explode into sparks behind his eyes

The next thing he knew he was on his back staring up into the night. Above him, silhouetted against a dome of sky faintly illuminated by the city's innumerable lamps and torches, loomed a gigantic serpent, reared up as if to strike.

He cried out and tried to roll over and unsuccessfully push himself to his feet.

Coarse sand stuck to his palms.

Strong hands yanked him upright. A bolt of pain shot through his shoulder. His head throbbed and an ocean-like roar filled his ears. He blinked, bewildered. Row after row of seats glimmered in the gray light.

They were in the Hippodrome. His assailants had carted him out to the wall of the spina in the middle of the race track. The serpent was one of three huge, intertwined snakes which had once supported the sacred bowl at the Delphic Oracle before being carried off to Constantinople.

"Do you want to know your future, captain?" came a voice. "That prophesy is not very mysterious, is it?"

Felix saw what the man meant. From the serpent head jutting out over the track dangled a rope with a noose at the end.

Felix looked around, trying to control an overwhelming sensation of dizziness. "Who is in charge?" he demanded, trying to keep his voice steady. "Everyone knows Justinian supports the Blues, but if you believe the rumor that he exempts your faction from the law you are mistaken. When he finds out—" Someone shoved him from behind. He hit the ground face down, lifted his head, spitting sand, and took a boot to the ribs.

Idle class though the Blues were—for only the well-to-do could afford the extravagant clothing they preferred and the idleness in which they had earned their foul reputation—they hunted in packs like jackals, and once a group had their prey at a disadvantage, they dared any violence up to and including murder. They feared nothing, knowing Justinian was of the same racing persuasion.

The toe of a boot stung his shoulder. He averted his face, trying to protect himself as blow after blow descended. At some point he lost consciousness and returned to the world sputtering after a bucket of water was emptied over his head.

He started to turn to see his tormentors. A powerful hand forced his head down, grinding his face in the sand. Then it yanked his head up by the hair, pulling it back until he feared his neck would crack.

He could see the rope hanging, the hungry open maw of the noose waiting expectantly.

"What happened to the courier?" came a hoarse whisper.

"Courier?" Felix felt blood trickling from his forehead.

His interrogator pulled his head further back. "When you are hanging by your neck and gasping for the next breath which you will never draw, you'll wish you could talk. So you had better do so now. As you well know, I am asking about the man sent to your house who has not been seen since. More importantly, for men are many and riches few, what have you done with the relic?"

"Relic?"

"I see you are intent on trying to out-echo Echo," The whisperer's tone became more impatient. "The relic I am talking about is the relic you have been expecting. Since I have no objection to plain speech, I mean the holy mother's shroud."

The voice was dry and raspy. The voice of a man much older than the young thugs who had attacked Felix. And despite being muted it hinted at a sonorous quality, almost familiar. Felix tried to turn again and again was prevented from doing so by the hand on the back of his head. He decided to throw the knucklebones at a venture. "I admit I saw the courier but I don't know where he is now. As for the shroud, he may have had it once but he didn't when he came to me."

"Why would he arrive empty-handed?"

"That's exactly why I've been trying to find the scoundrel, to question him."

"Don't try to be clever, captain. We know he had it and we know he came to your house. I've had you followed all day, hoping you might lead us to the relic, but time grows short. Wherever you've hidden the shroud you'd best retrieve it quickly because it will be called for a day hence. We will find you, wherever you are, and you'd better have it in your possession when we do. I intend to take charge of the matter personally. Let's hope you recover quickly enough not to need further reminders of what you are required to do!"

With that, at a word to the group of men clustered nearby, the boots resumed their work until the dark heavens swooped down upon Felix again.

Chapter Twenty-one

Dedi pressed back against the shadowed wall of the Hippo-drome as a gang of Blues erupted from an archway, cursing and laughing.

"So much for that!" one grunted.

"A rope necklace solves a lot of problems," laughed another.

Dedi had halted abruptly just beyond the light from the torch beside the entrance. His attention shifted instantly from his own quarry to fear that he might spotted by the Blues and become a quarry himself.

Not that he would escape them for long.

Fortunately one of the beggars who clustered around the archway at night extended a grubby palm. Either he was blind or his humors were deranged, Dedi thought. Nobody begged from a Blue.

A Blue kicked the beggar's legs out from under him. The pack moved in and the man was reduced to a bloody heap in scarcely less time than it took them to cross the street singing a ribald song after they'd finished.

Suddenly there was a figure bending over the moaning beggar. It had appeared from nowhere, as if precipitated out of the thick, rank night air by the evil Dedi just witnessed. The figure straightened up and with a thrill of horror Dedi recognized the face of the hellish being for which he had been keeping a watch, the thing that had taken the form of Antonina's servant Tychon.

When the thing set off at a rapid pace parallel to the Hippodrome, it had two shadows. One its own, the other Dedi.

Its destination proved to be Baths of Zeuxippos. Why not? A creature mimicking a human would mimic human habits, Dedi reasoned as he stayed close on its heels. The creature paid the small fee to enter the baths and disappeared into the echoing portico.

Dedi, delayed at the entrance, finally located his quarry again near a fountain in the vast atrium. It was talking to two men seated on a curved bench. Dedi pretended to study the inscription on the base of a nearby statue of Demosthenes. From what he could overhear, the men were discussing palace scandals and whether the Green team had a chance of beating the Blues in the next round of chariot races.

"If the Blue charioteers are as savage on the track as their partisans are on the streets, the Greens don't stand a chance," the thing passing as Tychon said, and went on to describe what the Blues had done to the beggar. "He had a few coins on him. Enough to pay my way in here and buy me a drink."

The bronze orator looked on, tight-lipped, as if expressing disapproval of the artless conversation.

At last the demon set off again. Turning down one corridor after another, he came to a cold pool, deserted at this time of night.

Dedi lurked beside its entrance. Venturing a peek around the corner of the doorway he saw the thing begin to strip off its clothing. He held his breath. Perhaps it hadn't bothered to retain a semblance of humanity beneath its garments, nor would it bother to do so with no one, so it seemed, around.

Dedi braced himself for some vision of horror, hooves, a scaly tail.

There was only a pair of buttocks, paler than twin moons.

The cunning creature padded off to the pool. Dedi saw the thing dangle its legs into the water, which did not sizzle and boil at the touch of the infernal flesh as Dedi half expected.

Moving quickly Dedi crept into the changing room, pushed aside the tunic left crumpled on a bench, grabbed the woven belt underneath, and slipped silently away.

Unseen.

He hoped.

DAY FOUR

Chapter Twenty-two

John stood in the prow of the *Leviathan* staring into the fog. He could not make out the shore or even the waves rolling the deck under his sodden boots. Toward the stern crew members moved in and out of the mist, dissolving and materializing like phantoms, accompanied by the murmur of the unseen waves, the groaning of timbers, the creak of wet ropes, and occasionally a muffled, disembodied voice.

It was almost as if the sea had actually succeeded in catching him during the storm and dragging him into a dismal underworld. As he slid down the deck during the storm he was certain he was going to die. Perhaps he was dead and had not realized it yet.

The Lord Chamberlain—the man he had been—had died when the *Leviathan* sailed from Constantinople.

He tried to put the morbid thought away. An entire day and night had passed since the storm. The wind had gradually diminished, the heavy black shroud of clouds giving way to gray rags. A feeble sunset had glistened across the wet deck before another night of fitful sleep in the oppressive, rocking accommodations below.

Yet he could still feel himself sliding down the tilting deck.

The day had passed slowly, yet he could not recall exactly how he had spent it. He and Cornelia had not talked much. They found themselves adrift between a lost past painful to speak of and a future too uncertain to discuss comfortably.

Scanning the length of the ship he could make out a dull orange sun, the illuminated window of the captain's cabin. John wondered whether Captain Theon was inside drinking again with the mysterious passenger who lodged there.

To hear the sailors gossiping with each other, the captain had started drinking before they were out of sight of Constantinople. The two submerged rocks along the coast were clearly shown on the charts. A sober man could never have miscalculated the ship's position so badly.

The *Leviathan* had grazed one of the rocks, damaging a section of hull and the rudder. Anchors had been thrown out to keep the ship from being driven into the rock broadside until the seas calmed enough to attempt repairs.

These details John had learned by listening. The crew did not gossip with passengers.

The fog swirled slowly beside him and a voice spoke. "Let us hope an angel of the Lord stands beside us, as it did beside Paul when he was shipwrecked."

John recognized the pilgrim Egina accompanied by the shadow of her silent companion.

"This will be my final voyage," Egina said. "What a story I will have to tell my sisters! It is fortunate we have a number of anchors at the stern, as Paul's ship did, otherwise we would have found ourselves dashed upon the rocks."

"I am certain your prayers were of assistance," John said, diplomatically, recalling her incessant supplications during the night.

"I can tell you are a man of faith. When you reach my age you will understand that God assists those who can anchor themselves." She made the Christian sign and drifted away into the fog.

John walked carefully back along the slick deck and down into the hold where Cornelia was trying to nap, having been unable to sleep during the night. She sat up as John entered their tiny compartment. "It seems the fates are against your departing from Constantinople quickly," she said. "Peter tells me we are barely a day's ride from the walls."

"Provided one's horse is a strong swimmer or Pegasus." He sat down on the mat beside her, glad to be able to stop bracing himself against the ship's pitching.

"How bad is the damage? Can the ship stand being shaken around like this?"

"The crew seem more angry than worried. They have drawn cables around the hull, just in case, to hold us together."

Cornelia put her arms around him. "You frightened me. When I called and you didn't answer…"

"I couldn't hear anything above the wind and the waves. I thought the ship was going to capsize. But let's not talk about that again."

With her pressed against him, John could make out a remnant of the scent she often wore. He supposed it probably would not be available in Greece.

"I hope they can make repairs soon. You know Justinian's whims. I don't like being so close to his reach." Her grip on John tightened.

"The emperor's reach extends to the limits of the empire," John reminded her, then added, "I can't help wondering how Felix is faring."

Cornelia shook his arm in irritation. "That's all behind you now, John. Felix is no fool, he'll manage. If you want to wonder about someone what about that aristocratic looking man who rarely emerges from the captain's cabin? I wager he has something to hide."

"You may be right. He's got the look of the court about him. Peter overheard him speaking to Captain Theon. He didn't catch the man's name."

"You haven't set Peter to spying, have you?"

"No. He finally persuaded Theon to let him use the brazier in his cabin, on condition he would make some honey cakes and cook a meal or two for the captain and his companion, this fellow you just mentioned."

"I hope the ship's cook isn't upset. And that there's honey on board!"

"I suspect the cook's happy to do as little as he can get away with, given he's just a member of the crew who was assigned culinary duty. But I wasn't supposed to tell you. Peter wanted you to be surprised when he cooked our meal."

Cornelia chuckled. "I will pretend to be surprised. But what about this nameless aristocrat who is going to be enjoying Peter's honey cakes? Why is he on board?"

"That I can't say. Perhaps he's been sent to inspect some seldom visited family estates or he wishes to visit old temples."

"And recite poems to himself while he strolls through the ruins?" Cornelia scoffed.

"The muse might appreciate it if nobody else did. No, he's definitely more than he seems. Alert, watchful, carries a blade that's meant for use, not decoration."

Cornelia paled. "Is he…could he be an assassin?"

"You mean do I think Justinian sent him to dispose of me? If the emperor wanted me dead, he could have had me executed rather than sending me into exile."

"He might not simply want you dead, John. It might serve his purpose to see you dead by a particular means in a particular place."

John pulled her closer to him. "I'm glad we're going to Greece, Cornelia. You've been living at the palace for too long."

Chapter Twenty-three

Vast black wings beat around Felix, beating with the sound of a thunderous heart. Was he waking or slipping into unconsciousness? In his memory he saw a raven perched on a dry fountain.

"One raven stands for sorrow," John explained. "It is a fortune-telling rhyme I heard from the farmers when I fought in Bretania. Two black-feathered birds signify joy, three a letter, four for a boy."

But John was no longer in the city.

Five for silver, six for gold, seven for a secret...

The rhyme chased itself through the pulsing darkness in Felix's head. One for sorrow, two for joy...

Repeating itself maddeningly, it blotted out all coherent thought. Around and around it spun, like the sand beneath Felix's back.

Five for silver, six for gold, seven for a secret never to be told...

The wings beat in the darkness and Felix felt the wind of oblivion against his face.

Eternity. Eight was for eternity, nine for the devil.

And ten, what did ten black birds mean?

What did those dark specks soaring into the limitless blue dome of sky predict?

Did he see ten or nine ravens?

Felix realized he was awake, although groggy, and still alive, lying on his back, staring straight upwards. He remembered where he was. On the track at the Hippodrome.

He could feel his heart pounding. With each beat pain flared in his sides, reminding him of the beating he'd taken.

A shadow passed across his face, retreated, returned.

He dared to move his throbbing head slightly, and was relieved he could do so. Until he saw again the rope hanging from the sculpture of the giant serpents. The rope with the noose he had seen hours before.

Now it was taut with the weight of a dangling corpse.

A man whose face was nothing but a bloody piece of meat.

The corpse swung forward once more, until its shadow again reached Felix's face, then it swung back as the enormous raven clinging to the gore spattered shoulder finally yanked the remaining eyeball free of its socket.

The carrion eater turned its glassy eyes toward Felix, then with a convulsive flap of its dark wings took to the air, leaving the hanged man to spin slowly, unseeing.

John's voice rang out clearly in the deserted Hippodrome. "Ten for dying."

Felix blinked away the last fog of oblivion.

Fully awake, he realized John could not be present. John was on the sea.

Yet the clarity of the words had been such they continued to reverberate in Felix's head. Ten for dying?

No, Felix thought, as he managed to roll over and began to push himself to his knees.

No. Not yet.

◇◇◇

Anastasia carefully washed Felix's bruised and bloody face, grimacing as if it were she who was in pain.

"If you think this is bad you should have seen the other fellow," Felix told her. A poor jest, since it immediately brought back the image of the hanged man's shredded face.

Nevertheless, Anastasia chuckled. It sounded forced. "Fighting again! You would do well in Italy!"

Her long elegant fingers worked the silk cloth with the delicacy and precision he had come to expect from them. He felt a sharp stab of guilt at having drunk so much, betraying his promise to her.

There was also the fact that had he not been drinking he would never have been caught unawares. And even had he been ambushed, as a trained fighter he would have left more than one of those callow ruffians dead before the gang overpowered him.

Felix groaned. "I wish I was on the battlefield. Then I'd know who my enemies were."

They sat, hips pressed together, on a bench in the shade of a fig tree in Felix's garden. "Tell me again what happened. I waited all night for you. I was frightened."

Felix related the events of the day before, leaving out the tavern visits. "It was dawn when I woke up next to the spina and there right in front of me was a man hanging from the noose I thought was waiting for me. For an instant I feared I had left my body and was looking at my own corpse."

Anastasia shuddered. "Don't say such things, Felix." She squeezed her cloth out in the copper bowl of water at her feet. "Did you recognize the dead man?"

"No." He refrained from explaining why. "Perhaps it was somebody else who had been asked about the missing relic and gave unsatisfactory answers. Possibly he was killed to frighten me."

"That would be hard to do, you big bear!"

Felix gave her a bleak smile. It made his split lips sting. "They succeeded sufficiently in that I'd gladly hand that miserable rag over if I had it."

"Which is what they're counting on. If you don't produce it on time, that will prove to their satisfaction that you don't have it."

"Or else they will think that's what I hope they think. I'd be better off finding the damned relic than trying to guess what those thugs might be thinking. And even if I can even lay hands on it, what about after that?"

"What do you mean?"

"Consider. Justinian orders me to look into the theft, although it's already under investigation by the urban watch. Why should the captain of the excubitors become involved?

Perhaps the emperor's counting on me failing or appearing to entangle myself with the perpetrators so…"

"So he has an excuse to eliminate you," Anastasia completed his thought. "You don't have to be afraid to speak the truth to me. You are a close friend of the former Lord Chamberlain. The emperor may want to be rid of you as well. These are delicate times. With Theodora gone, half the court is jostling for power."

Did Anastasia assume Felix was in that half of the court, he wondered? Yet wasn't he ambitious, if the truth were told? Wasn't he hoping General Germanus would replace Belisarius? "If you want me to speak plainly, there's also the matter of the murdered courier. Who will believe I didn't kill him to get possession of the relic and then pretend he never had it?"

"Not the Blues who ambushed you. Bend your head down. You're still bleeding."

Obeying her command, he continued. "There are other possibilities. Whoever stole the relic from the courier and murdered him would be happy to pin both the murder and that theft on me. If they can't, they certainly won't wait around for me to find them and retrieve the shroud. Likewise, whoever originally stole it won't care to be tracked down either. In fact, they might actually believe I have it, or know where it is." He winced as Anastasia began to clean the deep cut on his forehead.

"That would be whoever is ordering Blues to terrify you into returning the relic? Anyone who orders Blues about is a brave man indeed."

"Brave perhaps, but not as clever as he thinks."

Anastasia straightened up from her task. The silk in her hand was stained crimson.

"He didn't allow me to see him. Grabbed my hair and yanked my head back, staying behind me. And he tried to disguise his voice," Felix went on. "But I recognized him all the same. It was Porphyrius."

"The charioteer?"

"That's right. You don't sound shocked?"

"Everyone knows he's fabulously wealthy, beyond what even the most famous charioteer of all ought to be. He seems to be involved in everything going on in the city. Why not this matter?"

"Yes. Racing for both the Blues and the Greens ingratiates you with everyone, and who doesn't want to bask in the reflected glory of a famous charioteer?"

"And if to do so means throwing a business opportunity his way, legal or otherwise, what of it?"

"You are too astute for a woman, my dove. Sometimes you remind me of our late empress. I've spoken to Porphyrius a number of times and won a fair bit wagering on his races, but I never thought I'd meet him again lying on my face with a noose dangling nearby!"

Anastasia bit her lip and nervously kneaded the bloody cloth. "So the emperor might want you dead, and whoever stole the shroud surely wants you dead, as does whoever robbed the original thief or thieves?"

"No doubt someone else wants me dead too. I'm losing count."

"But not hope," she said firmly. It was not a question.

"No."

Anastasia leaned back against the tree trunk beside the bench. "Why a fig tree?"

"For the shade, I imagine. I didn't plant it."

"Why do you suppose Jesus cursed the fig tree?"

"What?"

"Naughty bear." She grabbed the chain around his neck and yanked it out from his garment, revealing a cross hanging from it. "When I gave you this, you promised you would read and study."

"Well, I...I haven't got to that part yet."

"Did you ever suppose that Jesus cursed the fig tree because it is the sacred tree of the pagan god Mithra?"

"No," Felix offered, truthfully. It made him uncomfortable when she started to talk about her religion. Was she serious about it, or merely serious about the political ramifications of not being a Christian at a Christian court? "What does this have to do with what we were discussing?"

She threw her cloth into the bowl and brushed stray hairs off her forehead, leaving a red streak. "It could be very important, Felix. Men have been known to save their skins, as well as their souls, by finding faith at the right time." Her eyes shone feverishly and with the blood blazoned on her skin she looked as ferocious as a Pict.

"Yes, I understand." Felix clumsily tucked the chain back into hiding.

"I don't like the idea of Porphyrius being involved," Anastasia said. "Why not write to the former Lord Chamberlain? He visited the Church of the Holy Apostles with you. Perhaps he has some advice. He's had plenty of time to think the matter over aboard ship."

"He'd be in Greece before—"

"Use the imperial post. A relay of riders would be able to overtake a merchant ship that's trading locally. You know how they meander from port to port."

Felix shook his head vehemently. "No, I can't. I won't involve John. He's on his way to a new life. What if the emperor were to find out he had tried to help me?"

"There are more hiding places in Constantinople than there are stars in the sky, even if the relic is still in the city. Where will you start?"

"I'm not certain. If I can learn exactly who was trying to sell it and who wants to buy it, that might give me a path to follow." He started to get up. Dizziness hit him. There was a roaring in his ears. He sat down heavily.

"You need rest," Anastasia told him. "I'm acquainted with a woman who can make up a potion to help revive you. She also has protective amulets."

Felix tried to push himself up but realized he was too weak. He had managed to stagger back from the Hippodrome but his panic had passed and the effects of the beating were beginning to make themselves felt. "I'm not superstitious enough to want an amulet," he said, thinking of the Jingler, "but something to sooth the aches and pains would be useful. Hypatia, John's servant, made such potions, I recall. Who are you thinking of?"

"Antonina, Belisarius' wife."

"You know Antonina? How?"

"Does it matter?"

Felix shook his head violently and when it throbbed he wished he hadn't. "No, I don't think so. I wouldn't want to… impose on her."

Anastasia looked at him curiously.

"People will gossip," Felix stammered.

"Gossip? About what?"

"They don't need anything to gossip about to gossip, do they?"

She stared at him then laughed. "Why, you nasty bear! You know Antonina too, don't you? Where did you…meet her?"

"Don't be foolish! I never, um, met her. Not the way you mean. Everyone knows General Belisarius—"

"A tryst! Where, I wonder? When? I shall have to ask her."

"No, please, I mean, she wouldn't remember anyway. I was a young idiot. Who are you to be questioning Antonina about such delicate matters anyway?"

Anastasia pulled her features into a parody of hurt feelings. Then leaned forward. Her breath scorched his neck. "I am devastated."

"It meant nothing then and less now," Felix mumbled.

"Prove it to me."

She nibbled at his neck, then bit harder.

"You shouldn't do that!"

"Mmmm. Why not? No one will notice another little wound."

Chapter Twenty-four

It was past midday when Felix left his house. He kept self-consciously fingering his neck, as if anyone would notice the delicate, purpling bite mark amidst all his bruises, cuts, and abrasions.

He had slept the morning away like a dead man. Anastasia had awakened him, having fetched various preparations which she duly administered. If nothing else the vile taste of the potions and the hideous burning of the salves got him on his feet. She had neglected to bring an amulet. Perhaps, on second thought, she had decided the cross she'd given him was protection enough.

She had insisted he wasn't well enough to go out. Unfortunately there were people Felix did not want to talk to but needed to consult. And soon. He decided to have the conversation he least wanted to have first.

He had received written orders from Justinian to investigate the theft of the relic, the sort of task the urban watch would normally carry out. Was the emperor really deeply interested in the relic? If confronted, perhaps he would decide he didn't need Felix investigating after all.

A succession of the largely ornamental silentiaries stationed in the innermost recesses of the imperial residence respectfully permitted the captain of the excubitors to pass through doorway after doorway until he reached the hall leading to Justinian's private study. In theory, these guards were to serve as a counterweight to the excubitors. The reality was different. The silentiary who appeared to escort Felix into the emperor's presence made it plain how easily the excubitors would prevail if they decided to mutiny.

The silentiary presented a ridiculous figure in robes studded with cut-glass gems and a helmet topped by a dyed ostrich plume. He carried a spear so long it probably couldn't have been put to use without knocking frescoes off the corridor walls.

What did not strike Felix as ridiculous was the man's identity. It was his old colleague Bato, the fellow who had accosted him while he was trying to dispose of the courier's body.

"Felix! What a coincidence! I haven't seen you for months and now we run into each other twice in two days. I hope your lady friend was pleased with what you delivered?"

Felix forced a smile. He didn't think Bato suspected anything, but how could he be certain? He'd been staring right into the cart at the blanket-wrapped body.

"I see the silentiaries are treating you well, Bato. And so now you're rubbing elbows with the emperor." Bato and Felix had both served as excubitors years before but Bato had left to join the silentiaries, who were less likely than the excubitors to engage in fighting, a decision Felix had never understood.

"Don't change the subject," Bato said. "Was your client satisfied? Has she ordered more of your goods?"

"Would I tell you if she had?"

"If we were drinking together like we used to you would."

They stopped before a wooden door into which were carved crosses and angels. It looked as if it had been looted from a monastery.

"The emperor is entertaining a cleric at the moment. The visitor should be leaving soon."

"Justinian is still knee-deep in theology, then?"

"Up to his neck, to judge by the piles of parchment on his desk. Theodora's death hasn't been easy for him to accept."

It was well known that when he was troubled the emperor tended to retreat into theology.

"Have you overheard any talk about this stolen shroud?"

"What? Am I a spy for the excubitors?" Bato smiled. "If you're looking for imperial secrets it'll cost you a drink. Maybe two."

"As soon as I've got this job I'm working on finished we'll get together."

"We can talk about the old days. Well, listen to me! I never thought I'd be old enough to want to do that."

A draft had found its way into the center of the palace, catching at the yellow ostrich plume, making it sway back and forth.

"Are you happy in the silentiaries, Bato?"

"It's an easy living if not very exciting. But wait! You've already tried to worm imperial secrets out of me. Are you trying to get me to rejoin the excubitors? You're not thinking of emulating Justin and seizing the throne for yourself?"

"Hardly." Felix laughed. That was Bato, always jesting.

He was, wasn't he?

"I hear you've thrown your lot in with General Germanus."

"Now who's asking for secrets?"

Before Felix could decide whether Bato was merely up to his usual bantering or whether he had a more serious intent, the carved wooden door opened. Felix was surprised to see the priest Basilius emerge. Basilius looked equally surprised to see Felix, but he went past without acknowledging him.

Bato directed Felix into the study and closed to door behind him. Outside the sun shone, but in this windowless room deep within the imperial residence the night never ended. Felix imagined that it was here that Justinian had buried himself almost continually since Theodora's death, sleeping fitfully on a simple cot, poring over the religious texts piled on the wooden shelves and desk behind which he now slumped. The light from a single lamp showed how the flesh had fallen from the emperor's normally round, bland face, revealing the grim skull beneath.

Felix began to bow.

"Never mind the formalities, captain. You've arrived at a convenient time. I interrupted my studies to speak with Basilius about the stolen shroud. Do you have any news about it? How is your investigation going?"

Felix's spirits fell. He had been hoping to find Justinian was not concerning himself overly much with the theft. Apparently the opposite was the case.

He began by outlining his efforts to question people in the vicinity of the Church of the Holy Apostles.

The emperor appeared bored and tired. "From those cuts on your face, it looks as if some of the people you approached did not take kindly to your questions."

"Indeed. It was nothing serious." He didn't dare say anything about the assault by the Blues. How could he explain the motivation behind it without putting himself under suspicion?

"That is all you have to report?"

Did Justinian know about the attack? Was he wondering if Felix would tell him about it? Felix studied the emotionless features—which many called the mask of a demon—but as usual they betrayed nothing.

"Caesar, may I ask why you have involved me in this matter? The urban watch know the city better than I do and they are accustomed to investigate crimes. I should be working with my excubitors to insure the palace is secure, in case your enemies mistake your mourning for a sign of weakness."

"Do you suspect there are plots being hatched?"

Was that it? Did Justinian want to keep him away from the palace, away from his excubitors? Was he afraid their captain might have his eye on the throne?

"I know of no plots, but whenever the empire suffers a blow, there are those who seek to take advantage."

"As by stealing one of the city's most sacred relics? This is the very time we need the Virgin's protection the most."

"And naturally the theft upsets the populace."

"There is that also."

"If the theft was in aid of a plot all the more reason I need to be at my post."

"All the more reason our protection must be found and returned, Captain." The emperor's tone was sharp, a sudden contrast to his previous lassitude.

Felix uneasily shifted his feet, resisting his habitual nervous tug at his beard.

As a Mithran he had never given much credence to the Christian god and his relics. It was wise to treat them with respect, of course, whether those of the Olympian gods, or local deities, or the handiwork of sorcerers, just in case. There were supernatural powers, both good and evil, abroad in the world.

Justinian was rifling through parchments and half unrolled scrolls on his desk. "Though the saints are everywhere at once, they still linger most strongly in the vicinity of their relics. I was reading a treatise only days ago, but I can't seem to put my hand on it. It all has to do with lines of force. Since a saint's relics were once a part of his person or in contact with him, there remains an attraction between saint and relic, the attraction that holds spirit and matter together in the earthly sphere. Ever since the shroud was taken I have felt an absence, as if an invisible cloak of protection has been lifted from the city. Basilius tells me the Church of the Holy Apostles feels empty to him now."

"The reliquary in which the shroud rested was most certainly empty, Caesar. But if you will excuse me—I am an ignorant soldier. Why could not the shroud protect itself?"

"Ah, I see a military man may also be a philosopher. That is a good question, captain, and the answer is clear. We are being tested by God. Of course the shroud could have reduced the thieves to dust or brought lightning down on them. Even now the Lord could drop it right onto this desk. But that is not the way He works. It is up to us to please Him and not the other way around. Yes, it is even true the emperor must please God. To do that I must see the shroud returned and I am depending on you to assist in its recovery. Don't disappoint me."

Felix's stomach churned as he left the Great Palace. He was suddenly aware of the innumerable crosses pointing to heaven from the rooftops, of the magnificent churches he passed on many streets. The mithraeum where Felix worshipped was hidden underground. Symbols of Mithra were nowhere to be seen in public nor, if one was wise, in private also. The Jesus that Christians talked about—that Anastasia and the emperor worshipped—was not Felix's sort of man, not with all his prattle about love and peace. Yet somehow he and his followers had achieved what the sword had not, the subjugation of the Roman Empire.

And no doubt He wanted His mother's shroud returned. What son wouldn't?

Felix tugged at his beard in consternation. He had visited Justinian hoping to find the emperor was not really concerned about the matter of the relic and that Felix could let his investigation slide without angering him. Now he wasn't only risking the wrath of the emperor but the emperor's omnipotent god as well.

Chapter Twenty-five

As Felix walked into the Hippodrome he hoped this interview would be more successful than the last one.

He didn't bother to see if anyone had taken down the hanged man. Surely the corpse would have been noticed and removed hours before. Instead he took a ramp behind the starting gates and descended into the maze of stables and storage rooms under the racetrack. The sound of his boots hitting the concrete echoed back into the corridor. He smelled horses, hay, and dust despite a strong draught blowing from the direction of the great arena.

He was almost certain Porphyrius was the man who had threatened him. The aging charioteer wanted the relic for one reason or another, so why not start with him?

Felix did not find him in the stables. Try the track, he was told. He returned the way he had come, hurting with every step as if he were filled with shards of broken glass.

The great charioteer was sitting in the stands overlooking the track, the sole spectator in an arena designed for tens of thousands. He was instructing a younger man driving a chariot, shouting a mixture of praise and lurid oaths.

As Felix clattered up the marble benches Porphyrius leapt to his feet and bellowed "You'll never win a race like that. Stick as close to the inside of the track as you can instead of wandering all over it like a child in the market! It's a sure way to end up crippled or worse!"

The young charioteer grinned, flourished his whip, and came racing by, leaving his teacher coughing, choking, and cursing in a cloud of dust.

Porphyrius had been a wonder in his day, admired and feted. Statues had been raised to him and he had made a fortune, wresting it from the sweat and fear of racing, somehow avoiding serious injury. Considering the number of years he had raced and given he had raced for both Blues and Greens at one time or another, it was a miracle he had survived not only racing but had also escaped a blade in the back from a supporter of one of the competing factions, intended to even the odds in the next contest.

"Ah, the captain of the excubitors," Porphyrius remarked as Felix approached. "A little early for the racing, are you not?"

"It's not racing I'm here for." Felix sat down next to him. The sun had made the marble hot.

"So then…?"

Felix glanced at the man at his side. He was squat and powerfully built with a broad face and a laborer's arms. Despite the gray in his hair, he looked like the sort of man you wanted on your side in a fight, the sort you didn't want to oppose. And his booming voice was unmistakable. Felix was certain now that Porphyrius had been present on the spina the night before.

Felix looked back toward the center of the track. No sign of the hanging remained. Having confirmed to his satisfaction the identity of one of his assailants, Felix was unsure what to do next. "There was a man found hanging on the spina this morning," he finally said.

Porphyrius looked away from Felix toward the far side of the track where his student's chariot moved slowly, engaged in some exercise. "Is that so? The urban watch must have got out of bed earlier than usual this morning." There was a sneer in his voice.

"A murder on the racetrack could hardly have escaped your attention."

"I did hear some such tale when I arrived about an hour ago to put our latest recruit through his paces."

"Is the dead man's identity known?"

"Not to me. I didn't even see the man."

"No? I'm surprised. Granted, from where I was lying on the track I didn't have a good view. And the boots in my face didn't help."

"I don't know what you're talking about, captain."

Without being aware of it, Felix rubbed nervously at the sore spot on his neck. "If you suspect the poor fellow was involved in robbing the courier you should have allowed him to live. He might have had a better idea what happened to the relic than I do."

"Relic?"

"The shroud of the Virgin stolen from the Church of the Holy Apostles."

"I don't know anything about it beyond the fact it was stolen," came the curt reply. "What good are relics anyhow, apart from enticing the ignorant geese to visit the city, the better to be plucked at the races?" Porphyrius broke off to shout another mouthful of abuse at the young charioteer now passing below them.

It seemed to Felix that inexperienced charioteers were trained less kindly than their horses. "I'm surprised to hear you have no interest in relics. Charioteers are a superstitious lot, aren't they? What about curse tablets? They've been found buried under the track and I remember members of both teams were more than upset. Why, there were fist fights in the stables over whose supporters were responsible."

Porphyrius shrugged his massive shoulders. "Indeed, fist fights are the least of it. But if I were attempting to ensure my team won I would do it in a more practical way. Tampering with the other faction's chariot, say. Not that it's easy to get at them, given we all keep them well guarded. But what of it?"

"It would be highly valuable for many reasons, such a relic," Felix plunged on. He was developing a headache and jagged glass inside him kept shifting in agonizing fashion. He couldn't seem to get his thoughts to march in proper order. "What was your role, Porphyrius? Were you involved in stealing it for someone for a considerable sum? Is that why you want it back? This is official business. I am investigating the incident on behalf of Justinian."

"Should I be impressed? Justinian is one of my greatest admirers. Why would you think I knew anything about this relic?"

"You were here in the Hippodrome with several Blues last night and we had a conversation about it. A rather one-sided conversation."

"The sun has affected your humors, captain. You really don't look well at all. I was nowhere near this place. I was visiting a lady friend, as a matter of fact."

"What you forget is your voice is very distinctive. You were just shouting at that young charioteer and sounded very like the man who shouted in my ears not so long ago, questioning me about that missing relic and what I had done with it."

"Perhaps it isn't the sun affecting you. Have you gone back to drinking again? Spending your nights in the taverns? I see from your condition you've been brawling. The physicians say a blow to the head can cause all manner of strange results. Why, after one crash a few years back the Blue charioteer insisted he saw strange billowing curtains of color in the sky over the Great Church."

Felix glared at him. At least his companion now knew he had been identified as in some way involved in the theft. Although whether that made Felix safer or put him in even greater jeopardy was hard to say.

The young charioteer drew to a halt in front of where they were seated and Porphyrius motioned him he could leave, then stood up. "If you are so concerned about this matter, shouldn't you be seeking it, rather than talking to me? After all, time flies."

Felix rose painfully. "If I knew the identity of the man you had hanged last night it might be helpful. Despite what you may imagine I was not associated with him, though he probably had accomplices, if he was in fact involved in the theft. And they might know where it's gone. Think about it."

"I will. You may be hearing from me later." Porphyrius grinned in an unpleasant fashion. "By the way, I would see to it that puncture on your neck was well cleaned. More men have died from human bites than dog bites."

Chapter Twenty-six

Another precious hour had passed before Felix turned down the street leading to the Jingler's abode. He knew that his quarry, a slave to habit, would shortly emerge to make one of his regular trips to the Baths of Zeuxippos. Felix hoped he would prove more helpful than the beggars—and sometime informants—he had confronted after leaving Porphyrius. He had become increasingly angry and frustrated over their ignorance, or feigned ignorance. How was it possible not one of them had noticed a boisterous gang of Blues up to no good, or a fleeing demon?

Not that there was much chance that anyone on the streets had noticed anything useful. But then Felix was given to wagering hopefully against the odds. Otherwise, he reflected ruefully, he wouldn't be in the fix he was in.

The Jingler had been as close-mouthed as Porphyrius during their first discussion but that had been before Felix had come into temporary possession of a dead courier and besides, this interview—by design—would take place outside the safety of the Jingler's lair.

Felix was looking for an unobtrusive spot to wait when he spotted another ragged professional acquaintance.

The man must have seen Felix at the same time because he turned on his heel and hobbled in the opposite direction.

Felix caught up with him in a few strides and clamped a hand on the man's bony shoulder. "Wait, Euphratas. I need to speak to you."

Euphratas shuffled around to face Felix, reluctance plain in his white-bearded, wizened features.

"I'm surprised to find you still in Constantinople," Felix told him. "I thought you would have collected sufficient funds to complete your pilgrimage by now."

"Alas, the price of carriage travel is exorbitant. These old bones would never survive the accommodations aboard a merchant ship."

"The streets of Constantinople are much less taxing, I take it. How long have you been begging for your fare? Six years? Seven?"

"The price of travel is shocking. If you could spare a coin to help a poor pilgrim return home…"

Felix ignored the familiar request. "As a pilgrim, during your extended visit here you must have visited the Virgin's shroud."

"Certainly…that is…uh…certainly not…or rather…did you say the Virgin's church? These old ears—"

"Hear perfectly, as you've bragged to me. Everyone overlooks an old man. They speak freely in your presence as if age made one deaf or simple-minded, or so you claimed whenever you had information to sell me."

Euphratas exhaled a humid blast of wine fumes that made it plain where his most recently begged travel funds had gone. "Time has passed since we spoke. It brushes by and we find it has robbed us stealthily as a pickpocket in a forum, until—"

Exasperated, Felix interrupted by jamming a finger into the man's chest, harder than he intended. Euphrates staggered back a step. "Speaking of thefts, what have you heard about the theft of the shroud?"

The old beggar's bloodshot eyes widened in their nest of wrinkles. "Theft?"

"Don't play the fool. Were you anywhere near the Hippodrome last night?"

"No, sir. Nowhere near. I was down at the docks looking to see if anything had been dropped. Found a coin or two." Euphratas paused and scratched his beard, dislodging a scrap of grilled fish. "You're thinking about those Blues attacking a beggar at the track last night, aren't you? Glad to see someone taking an interest. The urban watch are useless. The only thing they're expert at is telling people trying to sleep in a corner to go elsewhere."

While an attack on a beggar was not the type of information he sought, nevertheless from force of habit Felix asked "You witnessed this attack?"

"No. I was at the docks, as I just said. Heard about it though. He was only sheltering in an entrance, minding his own business."

Felix studied the man. Was he lying? Had he, in fact, witnessed such an attack. Or had he actually seen Felix being dragged off? Even if he had, it wasn't likely he'd care to identify Felix's assailants, given the Blues ruled the streets on which Euphratas lived.

He pointed out the doorway to the Jingler's tenement. "Do you frequent this area? Have you seen anyone going in and out of there? Anyone unusual? At odd hours?"

"I hardly ever come this way, sir, and never at odd hours. It's not an area to be caught in during the night."

True enough, Felix had to admit. He put a coin into the man's hand. "This should get you part way home, or as far as the next tavern anyway. When we get older we can become forgetful, so if you remember anything else about last night you can expect a larger reward. You can go now."

Old though he looked, Euphratas scampered away as nimbly as a child and Felix sought out a vacant entranceway, not to sleep in but in which to lie in wait for the Jingler.

His vigil was brief. The door to the Jingler's tenement opened a crack, then after a long pause it opened wider and the Jingler stepped hesitantly into the sunlit street looking this way and that, as twitchy as a hare emerging from tall grass. Felix squinted against the flashes where sunlight caught amulets of metal and cut glass sewn to the man's garments and dangling from gold and silver chains.

If only everyone were like him, Felix thought, adhering to a strict routine and so easy to find when needed.

The Jingler went through what appeared to be a complicated ritual that involved touching amulets, muttering to himself, and a peculiar pattern of footsteps. Felix remained out of sight until the Jingler finally started down the street and neared his hiding place, then stepped out in the man's path.

"Julian!"

The Jingler stopped dead and turned the color of a drowned man. He trembled like a spindly, windblown tree, his amulets setting up a tintabulation. "What...what...is it? I...I don't have time right now."

"I do, and what I want to know is—look out, there's something behind you!"

The Jingler swung around in terror, causing the amulets to chime more loudly. "What? Is it a devil? Kill it!" he cried tremulously.

"Yes, yes, look, it's going into your house!" Felix drew his sword and waved it around.

His companion shrieked again and leapt at Felix, grabbing his arm. "Quick, get it before it can hide!"

Felix pushed the Jingler away, slicing his palm on a sharp-edged charm in the process. "Too late. It's gone."

The Jingler burst into tears. "I'll have to move! Oh, they're cunning, you know, very cunning. But I am more cunning still! They still haven't managed to grab me and carry me off!"

Felix sheathed his sword. "Yes. Don't worry. It ran off when you screamed. It didn't get inside. I wonder if it could be the same one that stole the holy shroud?"

The Jingler was furiously rubbing at the hand with which he had touched Felix's arm, apparently trying to rub off something visible only to himself. He looked at Felix, utterly bewildered. "But what would it be doing here? Are you sure it didn't get in?"

Felix glanced around before answering. The only living thing within sight was a young child curled up on a worn step, fast asleep despite the commotion, or more likely pretending to be asleep. He spoke in a near whisper. "Even if it's not the same one, it might be another, after...well, certain items of which we better not speak."

The Jingler gasped. "You mean holy items may attract devils! Yes, it's true!"

Felix nodded. "In fact, I was coming to tell you I think whoever gives you instructions ought to know about the danger. At the very least we ought to get paid more for handling them. Don't you agree?"

"The man who gives me instructions?" The other looked puzzled.

"Yes, that man."

"Oh, him? Yes, yes, I think you're right. I'll certainly tell him."

Felix doubted it. He had deliberately thrown the Jingler into confusion and fear with his pretense of seeing a demon. His puzzled look at the mention of his supposed superior, followed by his awkward recovery confirmed Felix's guess was right and the Jingler actually knew more than he was telling. That and the fact that the Jingler had inadvertently admitted he knew very well what was in the packages he handled—holy items—despite his earlier denials.

"Who was supposed to receive the shroud of the Virgin, Julian?"

"You can't imagine I had anything to do with that theft?"

"Can't I? I might not have had read much philosophy or poetry but you'd be surprised what I can imagine. I only wish I could imagine the dead courier in my courtyard away. Who was the courier? You gave him packages to deliver."

"And you received the packages. I didn't know more about him than you do."

"Your...superior must know."

"Yes. I suspect he does. He communicates with me anonymously."

"So unfortunately you can't give me his name." Felix noticed that Julian's jingling had ceased indicating the man had, unfortunately, got his wits about him again. Or as near as he could ever get to having his wits about him.

"I'd like to get to the bottom of this as much as you would."

"Why? Has Porphyrius threatened to hang you too if you don't produce the missing relic?"

The Jingler began to rattle loudly again. "Hardly."

"Then why are you shaking?"

"Just the idea…"

"Is he your superior?" The idea had suddenly struck Felix.

"How would I even know?"

"Perhaps he supplies manpower. His Blues work to enforce his wishes."

"In the same way you supply excubitors for transport? As for my superior…I can't say who else he employs."

Felix was at a loss how to question the man. The possibilities were endless. Felix wasn't John. How could he know what line of questioning to follow? It would help if he wasn't so woozy and his legs didn't feel weak. He wondered, had it been prudent to question the Jingler about Porphyrius?

"I don't know what I was thinking." The Jingler was examining the hand which had touched Felix, turning it this way and that in the sunlight.

"Never mind, you didn't hurt me," Felix growled, totally perplexed. "Except for that sharp amulet." He showed the Jingler a bloody palm.

The Jingler shuddered with a faint ringing.

There was no point in continuing the questioning. Felix's head was spinning. He'd make his humors as unbalanced as Julian's.

Chapter Twenty-seven

Perhaps Felix had lost his wits. As he neared his house, the sinking sun lengthening the shadows of columns and statues and passersby, pulling them taut, made him think of hangmen's ropes.

"Anastasia," he called, striding across the atrium. There was no answer. Had she returned to Antonina for more medical advice? What did she have to do with Antonina, anyway?

He sat down in his study and pulled off his boots. Not that he could give his feet a long rest. Much as he would have liked to linger while Anastasia applied hot poultices to his aching limbs he didn't have time.

"Nikomachos! Wine!"

Had he convinced Porphyrius or the Jingler that he did not possess the relic? Or had they in turn convinced whoever was in charge of the smugglers, if indeed it was a party unknown to Felix? Perhaps after all one of his informants would remember he had seen something useful, or Porphyrius or the Jingler would decide their best course would be to discuss matters further.

His servant did not appear promptly. It was not unusual. Felix got up and inspecting the jugs sitting here and there found one still partly filled and poured himself a cup. He decided to visit the nearest excubitor barracks. Despite his misgivings he would bring a contingent to the house and if Porphyrius did send men to carry out his threats Felix would have them arrested, pursuant to the investigation Justinian had ordered. As he'd explained to Anastasia, the consequences to his reputation when people began to talk to protect their own skins would be devastating, but what else could he do? Better his reputation than his neck.

Assuming his neck was spared.

His hand went to his neck, finding only the sore spot where Anastasia had nibbled.

He looked at the wine cup. Suddenly he was dizzy. Were the wine and potions he'd taken warring or was it the lingering effects of kicks to his head? He pushed the cup away and shouted for his servant again and at last heard a footstep at the doorway.

Turning he growled his displeasure. "About time. You do at least have two legs, if you'd choose to use them!"

"True enough, captain." The speaker was a short, bent, almost dwarfish man, as bald as a vulture. His plain looks were emphasized by their contrast to the sumptuously embroidered silk garments he wore.

"Narses!" Felix stared at his visitor. From the atrium came the clatter of boots and raised voices. Armed men appeared in the doorway beside Justinian's trusted official. By rank Narses served as imperial treasurer but in practice, as had been the case with John, he carried out whatever duties the emperor ordered.

"I bring you greetings from the emperor," Narses went on in a reedy voice.

Despite the wine, Felix's mouth had gone dry. "He wishes a report of my investigation so far?" he managed to say, trying to feign a hope he did not really feel. "I regret I have not yet discovered much of assistance, and—"

Narses made an impatient gesture. "You will be able to report personally to Justinian on your way to the dungeons, although not as captain of the excubitors. You are relieved of your command. Guards!"

Two men stepped forward and yanked Felix to his feet.

"On what grounds?" Felix demanded with a scowl.

"You question imperial orders?" Narses snapped.

"There is always the possibility of misunderstanding." Felix contemplated the distance between himself and the door and wondered if surprise might give him a small chance of escape.

Was it worth the wager? The palace dungeons were escaped as frequently as the grave.

His captors evidently sensed his thoughts or noticed the direction in which his gaze had flickered. He felt strong fingers dig more tightly into his bruised arms.

Two more guards entered the study. There were others nearby. Felix could hear voices and the slap of boots on tiles. They were probably searching the house. Luckily, this time, there was nothing to find.

Narses smirked up at him. "Hardly a misunderstanding, Felix. You see, the courier you murdered was not a complete fool. He left a note saying where he was going and when he didn't return his wife sent a servant to inform me. It's well known I do like to keep a keen watch on court matters."

More like watching for the next fly to blunder into a web of intrigue so you can benefit in some way, Felix thought. Narses was so close he could smell the cloying perfumes with which the eunuch official drenched his heavy robes. The years had not wrinkled his face like that of a natural man but rather seemed to have worn it as smooth as the face of an ancient sculpture.

"If you believe every schemer who tries to bring down his enemies with lies you must be very busy, Narses. I have no idea what you're talking about."

"No? It was another big, bearded fellow who deposited a naked corpse behind a statue of Aphrodite?"

"What are you talking about? What statue is this?"

"We have a witness. The streets are full of witnesses. No crime goes unglimpsed."

"You mean beggars will gladly agree to see anything you want them to see to avoid a beating."

Narses chuckled. His vulturine head bobbed up and down as if he were feeding on a carcass. "The wife of the victim, and I am sure I do not need to name him for you, identified his body. You had stripped the man but the corpses one finds on the street are rarely well fed, healthy, and clean, so the connection was made immediately."

"What connection? What makes you think he was here? The Blues have been allowed to roam the city like hungry dogs. No doubt they robbed the fellow and disposed of his body."

An visibly excited guard came trotting into the study and handed Narses a short jeweled cloak. "Found it in a servant's room, excellency."

"Ah!" Narse's thin, colorless lips curved into an imitation of a smile. "Yes. His wife said he was wearing a cloak exactly like this one." He held it out for Felix's inspection. "Familiar? Isn't this what your visitor had on when you killed him?"

Felix stared dumbly at the cloak. He remembered the dead courier, crumpled against the courtyard wall. An aristocrat obviously, judging by the richly embroidered robes. But a jeweled cloak? "No. It's a lie. He wasn't wearing—I mean —"

"Ah, you did see him then. So you admit your guilt?"

Felix said nothing. He could make no sense of it.

Narses signaled the guards and they yanked Felix in the direction of the door.

"Wait! You're not going to drag me off with bare feet, are you? If I have to die, let me die like a soldier with my boots on."

Chapter Twenty-eight

Felix fumbled with his boots. He hadn't had such a difficult time getting them on since he'd learned to dress himself as a child, but then he wasn't in a hurry to begin his long march to the dungeons. He had sent enough miscreants there to have wondered what it must be like to make that last walk through the city, seeing the sky for the final time, hearing a burst of laughter from a tavern, catching the rich odors of fruits and spices and the tang of the sea, before descending into the dim, dank, stinking underworld beneath the palace, never to emerge.

"Be quick about it!" Narse's voice was the bark of a small, bad-tempered dog.

Felix rose. And saw Anastasia appear in the doorway behind the guards. She carried a metal bucket gingerly, almost at arm's length.

Noticing Felix gaping over their shoulders, Narses and his men began to turn.

Anastasia swung the bucket.

Felix understood what was happening an instant before his visitors.

They roared with pain and shock as a torrent of glowing coals from the kitchen brazier pelted them.

Felix dodged to the side and was out the door and racing down the hall while they cursed and slapped at their hair and the smoldering spots on their clothes.

He realized he was abandoning Anastasia. But what could he do? He had taken off his sword when he arrived home. He was unarmed. Clearly she had wanted him to escape.

The guard left at the back gate must have left his post when he heard the commotion. Running across the courtyard he looked startled to see Felix barrel out of the house. He barked out a warning and raised his sword, and looked even more startled when Felix rushed forward and bulled into him, knocking him to the ground.

Then Felix was out the gate. He ran down the alley behind his house until he reached the street. On the far side lay the passage which had been too narrow to admit a donkey cart bearing a corpse. For a man fleeing on foot it offered a dim, inviting refuge. Once into the noisome maw, Felix risked pausing to peer down the street. Guards had emerged from the house and were shouting at a couple of passersby who were going through the usual ritual of shaking their heads and averring they had seen nothing. Nothing at all. Less than nothing if you insist on pressing the point.

Unfortunately, a cadaverous ragged man lounging against a nearby wall eating a piece of bread was apparently less learned in city ways or else hoping for a reward.

The man nodded and pointed a skeletal finger, akin to the finger of Death, directly at the alley's mouth.

Felix whirled around and fled. He splashed through puddles of green-scummed water and leapt over piles of refuse whose foul smell suggested much worse then rotting vegetables. Coming to a cross alley, he glanced up and down before veering left and increasing his pace.

The pounding of his footsteps drowned out any noise of pursuit but he was certain the guards could not be far behind.

He wondered what would happen to Anastasia.

Had she been able to escape in the confusion or was she even now being dragged to the palace to face…?

He didn't want to think about it.

Emerging in a street of shops, he sprinted across and down another narrow passage. The door of a tenement stood open, showing twilight at the end of a filthy hall. Ducking into the building, he ran through it and came out in a square, little more than a rectangular space of packed dirt somehow overlooked by centuries of builders.

Pausing to catch his breath, he listened for his pursuers.

And heard running footsteps echoing in the hallway he had just left.

He spun on his heel, dashed across the square, went around a corner, leapt down a flight of slippery stairs.

He zig-zagged through back streets and shadowy alleys until, at last, his panic faded and he realized night had filled all the narrow ways in a sheltering darkness as deep as the depths of the sea and he was alone, except for rats rustling through the middens piled against brick walls.

With a shock he saw that Fate had led him to the very place he feared. He was several pools of shadow and one torch-illuminated space away from the gate to the Great Palace.

But, he thought, that would be the last place anyone would search for him.

Had Narses put the excubitors at the gate on alert? Why would he?

Was it worth another wager?

"Mithra help me," Felix muttered. Then for good measure he briefly touched the cross hanging from the chain around his neck. He'd gambled himself into this predicament and the only stake he had left was his life, for which no reasonable man would give a copper coin for at the moment.

He walked through the shadows and the patch of light.

Narses and the emperor might have known that he was a condemned man, but to the guards who lowered their lances respectfully he was, for a while yet, still captain of the excubitors.

Unless they had been ordered to let him into the palace.

Could it be a trap?

There were no signs of one as he forced himself to saunter slowly across the palace grounds, more worried about Anastasia than himself. Eluding capture had given him renewed hope. He could leave the city, could follow John to Greece for that matter. Admittedly the long imperial arm could still reach out for him but it would be a shrewd move to retreat, go to ground, and see what happened.

For Anastasia flight would be next to impossible.

Why had she chosen to sacrifice herself for him? Certainly he had enjoyed being with her. Well, he had been obsessed with her. And she, apparently, with him. But did she think that meant… well, what did it mean?

His feet led him unthinkingly to the cobbled square where John's house sat across from the excubitor barracks. Felix couldn't risk showing himself to his men. Even if they didn't realize he was a fugitive, what could he do? What would he say? "Good evening, men. Justinian has accused me of murder so let's go and depose him. All hail, Emperor Felix!"

John's house appeared to be unguarded. With its owner gone, naturally no lights showed in the windows, which began on its second story.

Felix remembered the key John had given him.

The key sitting in the study of his house, he realized when he reached the ponderous nail studded door.

He pushed anyway and to his amazement the door groaned open.

It was obvious why whoever had been there last had neglected to secure the door. There was nothing in the unlocked house worth stealing. John had told Felix to take whatever he wanted before the emperor did. He was too late. The emperor, presumably, had taken everything. The place had been stripped bare. The atrium was a stygian cave. The faint, ambient illumination of the city night filtering down through the rectangular opening in the ceiling glimmered on the water in the impluvium.

Felix climbed the wooden stairs. Their creaking echoed through the empty shell of the house, the cries of ghostly voices. How often he had trodden those stairs before! Perhaps the emperor's men—for surely it was Justinian who had ordered everything be taken away—had left a bed. If not John's then Peter's in the servant's room on the third floor.

Felix was feeling the results of his exertions. If necessary, he would lie on the boards and try to get some rest, plan his next move.

Passing the kitchen where John had eaten his meals at a scarred wooden table not fit for the lowest inn, he could see the lights of Constantinople through the many-paned window. It was as if the great flaming mosaic of the starry sky had come loose and settled down over the earth.

He paused at the study where he had so often shared a jug of wine with his friend.

On impulse he went in. Dim light entered from the window overlooking the cobbled square which, Felix was relieved to see, remained deserted.

No furniture had been left but on one wall the mosaic with its rustic scene glinted. Felix hoped that John and his family were going to a countryside in reality as peaceful as that depicted in the pieces of cut glass. The scene had not changed…except…

Felix stepped toward the wall and knelt down.

There was shown in the lower part of the scene a young girl. John had called her Zoe and had been in the habit of confiding secrets to her that he would not share with many who were flesh and blood.

Or rather, Zoe had been there, all the years Felix had been visiting the house. Now there was only a jagged space, where tesserae and plaster had been torn away, leaving the bare wall behind.

He reached out and touched the gap.

Could John have taken Zoe with him?

He couldn't imagine his friend doing such a thing.

A furtive gleam caught his attention. He picked up a tiny piece of glass from the floor. It was pure, glossy black. Part of Zoe's somber, all-knowing eyes?

He was pondering the mystery when he heard footsteps downstairs.

Chapter Twenty-nine

"That's an ugly burn. You're going to have a scar." Antonina smeared white unguent along the side of Anastasia's hand, then wrapped a scrap of cloth around the affected area. "Perhaps it's time to end this little romantic adventure of yours."

Anastasia drew her lips into a pout. "Just when it's getting exciting?"

"It's also getting too awkward, don't you think? It's one thing to want the men to burn for us, but to use hot coals…"

The two women were sitting beneath the gaze of the painted empress in Antonina's reception room. Anastasia couldn't help feeling that Theodora—long time champion of General Belisarius—was frowning at her in a reproving fashion. "You don't approve of Felix because he's allied with Germanus."

"I do wish you had made a better choice, but let's not speak of that again. There's no point allowing our men's rivalries to come between us." Antonia replaced the lid on the ceramic unguent jar, sat it down on the side table, and picked up the jewel box there. The box was of polished wood, inlaid with ivory crosses. She opened it to reveal a collection of amulets.

"I pray for Felix every day," Anastasia said. "But he refuses to let go of that pagan deity of his. Do you think the Lord answers prayers for pagans?"

"The Lord works almost as mysteriously as the emperor. Still, you're probably right, an amulet can't hurt. Although, from what you told me, it may already be too late." She rummaged through the collection, which ranged from smooth pebbles one might pick up on the sea shore to medallions made of precious metals.

"I prayed for him in the Great Church," Anastasia went on. "I think prayers work better there. When I pray in my room I feel as if I'm talking to myself. In the church I feel a presence, in the light and the shadows up in the dome."

"How about this one?" Antonina handed over a carnelian suspended from a silver chain. "It's been engraved with magick symbols. How you intend to give it to him however…?"

"He'll find his way back to me."

"Indeed. I can tell you are still under the captain's barbaric spell. A brawling ruffian is quite a change from courtiers who fight with poisoned tongues. You're like our dear Theodora, except she kept her bears caged and you prefer them in your bed."

"And what about you? You like keeping wild things around. Didn't you say that many of your servants had been recruited from the factions because you liked their spirit?"

"That's not to say I sleep with all my servants."

"Oh? You have always advised me that the best way to stay young is to remain open to new experiences. Since we're talking in confidence, what happened to that young man you brought back with you from Italy? You are keeping him well hidden. He never showed his face at the court."

"Karpos? I couldn't tell you where he is right now. I don't keep my men on a chain, regardless of what people say."

"I thought maybe you didn't trust me. I might try to steal him."

"Really Anastasia! I would never suspect you of such a thing. It's servants who steal things. In fact lately I've noticed petty thefts—a bracelet missing, a jar of cosmetics."

"Perhaps the thief is that demon your servants were afraid of?"

"More likely it is Tychon. A tough fellow. One of my wild things as you put it. In his case the faction was the Blues. I suspect he's been helping himself to my wine on the sly. I have devised a little trap for the thief, whoever it turns out to be."

"When you catch the culprit, let me know who it was. Maybe it is Karpos!" Anastasia stood up. "I'd better get back to Felix's house now."

"If you must. Do you really expect him to elude the emperor?"

"If he doesn't then I shall have something to say about it!"

"I'm sure you will. Be careful. These are not normal times. This game might not turn out as you wish."

"Oh, Antonina! You're just cross because you know Belisarius will be retired and underfoot before long and Felix will commanding troops in Italy!"

◇◇◇

Felix took a step toward the door's barred window before the chain around his ankle brought him up short. Feeble light from a torch somewhere in the corridor made its way through the bars and trembled around the bare and otherwise windowless cell. Leprous plaster fallen from the walls revealed the bricks beneath. White flakes littered the concrete floor.

This diseased hole in the earth was the last place he was likely to see.

Narses had allowed him to escape, hoping he would lead the guards to the stolen relic. It should have been obvious. How could Felix have been so stupid as to imagine he was really outrunning trained military men half his age?

He'd put up a good fight, however, when they'd cornered him in John's study. At least one of those callow bastards was going to have a permanently flattened nose to remind him of Felix.

Felix kicked and yanked at the chain, which was firmly attached to the wall.

Mithra!" It was a curse rather than a prayer. He didn't feel like praying, either to his own god or Anastasia's Christian one. They could both go to Hell as far as he was concerned, along with Narses and Justinian.

What evidence did Narses really have against Felix? Not that it mattered. He had trapped Felix by bringing that jeweled cloak to the house and having his guard pretend to find it. If Felix swore the courier hadn't been wearing the cloak he'd be admitting he had, indeed, found the courier in his courtyard and disposed of the body.

How the stinking eunuch had enjoyed ordering Felix to lie on the floor of the emperor's reception hall. When Justinian ordered Felix to stand he was pleased to see a huge, red blister on Narse's naked scalp, the result of one of the hot coals Anastasia had flung.

"I am deeply troubled, captain," Justinian had said, his bland features looking as untroubled as one of the marble busts decorating the hall. "Is there no one left whom I can trust? No one except Narses? The theft of the Virgin's shroud is not the only matter for which you have to answer. In addition, you were observed talking to the disgraced Lord Chamberlain not long before he left the city. Narses has told me he suspects a plot. I tend to agree."

He would. Justinian's predecessor as emperor, his uncle Justin, had been captain of the excubitors, although in Justin's case he had outmaneuvered a scheming Lord Chamberlain to seize the throne.

There was no reason for Narses to fabricate such a plot on Felix's behalf. Theft of the relic was more than enough to cost him his head. No doubt the treacherous eunuch wanted an excuse to pluck John out of the safety of exile.

Felix wished he could warn John.

But the best he could hope for was to resist confessing to Narse's inventions under the ministrations of the imperial torturers.

And that was a doubtful proposition. He had seen what was left of those from whom the torturers had torn the desired confessions—mindless, bleeding husks. By the time their mouths had babbled the required words any semblance of reasoning or humanity had long since fled.

This was what Felix anticipated in the near future. Not only death but agony beyond imagining and the knowledge that in the end he would surely betray his friend.

He shuddered. The malodorous air was clammy, but the chill he felt had nothing to do with the moisture. He stared through the bars into the corridor. The flickering torchlight gave no clue as to the time. What difference did time make here? For those who entered the emperor's dungeons time had ended.

But surely, in the world above, it must be near dawn.

Felix heard voices. Approaching steps.

The light from the corridor dimmed, blocked by a figure in front of the cell door. A huge man.

A key rattled in a lock and the door swung forward, its hinges giving off the high, thin shriek of a terrified woman.

DAY FIVE

Chapter Thirty

At sunrise a placid sea cradled the *Leviathan*, which still lay at rest, helpless as a baby. Already the sound of hammering echoed through the dim hold. The crew had worked through the previous day without managing to finish repairs. John suspected that the damage to the hull must have been more severe than anyone wanted to admit. Obviously Captain Theon did not trust the vessel enough to pull up the anchors and escape the rock upon which they had run partly aground.

Or so John understood. He might have grasped it wrongly, given when approached Theon gave nothing but short grunts of annoyance. After all, who was John to be wasting the captain's time? Just another passenger, additional cargo. The crew seemed to have been ordered to say nothing about their predicament so John was forced to piece the situation together from inadequate snatches of overheard conversation. It was frustrating for a man to whom Justinian had confided the secrets of the empire.

He was also left to worry that a weak spot might suddenly, catastrophically, give way, allowing the sea to burst into the hold and drag the *Leviathan* down.

John sat below, trying to distract himself by watching Hypatia, seated on the mat that served for a bed, make protective charms.

"In case the weather turns foul again," she explained.

Peter assisted her, dutifully tearing strips off an empty grain sack. Hypatia tied intricate knots in each strip before fastening the ends to form a loop. She held one of them out to John. "You might want to wear it around your wrist, master."

John slid the loop over his hand to be polite. It didn't ease his anxiety. At times he wished he could believe in magick. "Why does this bring good luck?"

"Knots keep things secure, don't they? And these are very special knots. They hold onto good fortune."

"I should think a cross would be sufficient," Peter sniffed.

"Perhaps," Hypatia replied, "But in Egypt we think differently. And what about what you call your lucky coin? The one you found in Derbe when you were on campaign?"

"Oh, but that's different!"

"Is it?"

Peter looked baffled and fell silent.

John heard Cornelia's laugh. She came in from her walk on deck, dropped down beside John, and poked him in the ribs with her elbow. "I think Hypatia has won that argument, at least for now! All the same I'll be happy when we reach dry land again."

John nodded. Thinking of the greedy sea slapping on the wooden boards at his back made him uneasy. He distracted himself by turning his mind toward the matter of the stolen relic. Hypatia had advanced a possible explanation for the visions those in the church had seen. Would it be of assistance to Felix?

"I wonder if Felix has located the stolen shroud yet?"

Cornelia looked at John sharply. "You shouldn't dwell on that business. Felix can take care of himself. Besides, there's nothing you can do about it."

"I could send a letter."

"A letter from the exiled Lord Chamberlain? You might as well send him a bottle of poison."

"Yes, you're probably right." He looked away from her scowl and watched Hypatia's fingers move almost too quickly and nimbly for him to follow. She might indeed have been tying up Fate. The knots she was forming looked more complicated than those needed to hold anything physical.

She handed a knotted loop to Cornelia, who put it on.

Peter tore off a new strip to add to the pile beside him. He got to his feet. "That should be enough for now. I need to start preparing our meal. Captain Theon is well provisioned, but I can never find the proper utensils."

As Peter left, John noted that despite his protest, the servant was wearing his own bracelet.

"If Felix hasn't found the shroud, he must have at least unearthed new facts about the theft," John mused. "The question is whether they are sufficient to lead him to the solution of the mystery. If I were there just long enough to hear the results of his investigations, I feel I could help."

Cornelia gripped his arm and dug her fingers in. "John! What are you thinking?"

"A letter might be intercepted. But if I were to ride back to the city, in disguise, for just long enough—"

"No! Don't even think about it!"

Hypatia averted her eyes, embarrassed. Who was Cornelia to give orders to the Lord Chamberlain?

"You can't leave us, John," Cornelia continued, her voice urgent. "You wouldn't return. You know that. The emperor would find out and…"

"Yes, you're right, Cornelia." John excused himself and went up on deck. He walked with small, uncertain steps, like a sick man, ever aware of the slight rolling of the anchored ship. Wasn't anyone else troubled by the incessant motion? Would he ever feel solid ground beneath his feet again?

From somewhere below came a burst of hammering.

Then there was an inarticulate cry, followed by shouts, running footsteps.

Crew members were converging near the rail beside the captain's cabin, looking down into the water. Someone pointed.

He made his way to the crowd as fast as he dared.

The pilgrim Egina was there. She turned an anguished face toward him. "Sir! It's your servant. He's fallen overboard."

Chapter Thirty-one

The enormously fat jailer loomed in the doorway to Felix's cell. Behind him, two guards held short lances at the ready.

"You are wanted now." The jailer's thick lips formed an unpleasant smile as he lumbered in and bent with a grunt to unlock the shackle around Felix's ankle.

Felix went out into the corridor without protest. There would have been no point in resisting.

Once outside the cell Felix saw that the jailer's tunic was filthy with stains, as if worn by a butcher. Perhaps the man was a torturer rather than a jailer?

Felix was led past a series of thick plank doors, banded with iron, each with a tiny barred window. From behind one door came low moans of pain, from behind another there issued an even more chilling sound, a snatch of mindless, bubbling laughter.

Here and there the walls and floor were slimy with a rusty excrescence which could have been either mineral or mold. Moving numbly, Felix slipped once and stumbled against a cell door. The jailer—Felix preferred to think of him as a jailer— turned ponderously to grab his arm to steady him. The fat man's fingers were incongruously long, pale and delicate, the fingers of a woman's hand.

The air began to have the stench of an abattoir.

They passed through an open doorway into a room brightly lit by oil lamps.

Their light danced across shining metal instruments hanging from the walls and piled on shelves, a display of a variety of cutting edges and razor-sharp points to put an armory, or a surgeon's office, to shame. Amongst these were countless weirdly articulated devices whose purpose Felix did not care to guess at.

The jailer came to a halt and looked around, the gleam in his eyes matching those of the metal instrumentalities surrounding them. He turned his head toward Felix. The tip of his tongue emerged maggot-like from between his bloated lips, then withdrew as the wistful look of a departing lover passed over his porcine face.

"Ah, what a waste," he sighed, before grasping Felix by the arm and dragging him forward, through another doorway, and into a whitewashed room with benches along the walls.

The man seated there looked up as Felix entered. He had the profile of a classical Greek sculpture. Though not as old as Felix, his thick curly hair was tinged with gray.

Felix recognized him.

John's good friend, Anatolius, the lawyer.

Anatolius was a lawyer now but Felix still thought of him as the foppish poet he had been when younger. The two men were well acquainted, largely because they had tolerated each other for John's sake. Now they studied each other uneasily across a wobbly round table at the back of a tavern next to the Baths of Zeuxippos.

With barely a word of explanation, Anatolius had rushed Felix away. Both knew Justinian might change his mind and decide to have Felix arrested again as quickly and inexplicably as he had agreed to his release.

Felix never imagined he could be so happy to see the a cloudy sky or to simply walk out of the palace gate. The sour tavern air smelled sweet. His wine cup shook as he drank deeply, wiped his mouth with the back of his hand, and shuddered.

"I keep expecting to be arrested again," he muttered. "How was it you knew?"

"A senator, who insists of remaining anonymous, contacted me, on behalf of a person whose name he was not at liberty to reveal."

"I…I have to thank you, Anatolius. I was convinced I was a dead man. I don't know how you managed to persuade the emperor to let me go. You must be a better lawyer than a poet. That is…I mean…"

"I will take that as a compliment from you, Felix. As it happened, Justinian didn't need much convincing. I suspect he had already made his mind up to release you. He may have some ulterior motive. I can't say. It was definitely on his orders you were arrested." Anatolius leaned forward on his elbows and said in a near whisper. "What in the name of Mithra have you got yourself involved with now, Felix?"

"I wish I knew. I told you about the dead courier and the missing relic. But I had nothing to do with them."

Anatolius glared. "Pretend I am John. Would you lie to him?"

Felix buried his face in his cup and took another long drink. "I'm not lying!"

"Weren't you expecting that courier? Justinian seems to think so."

"I…I…meant I had nothing to do with the courier being dead. No idea who he is."

"What about the fact that his cloak was found at your house. In the servants' quarters, I was told."

"You don't believe it was really found there, do you? Narses must have brought it with him, supplying his own evidence."

"Then you don't think the courier's wife actually identified the cloak as belonging to him?"

"I don't know that he really had a wife, whoever he was. She's probably a fabrication."

"That may well be. I wasn't told any more than you know. Unfortunately the corpse that at one point was on your property and was later found behind a statue of Aphrodite elsewhere in the city is not a fabrication. You do admit you found the body?"

Felix paused, confused. "Did I? Oh, yes, I suppose I have."

"Palace rumor says you've taken to drink and gambling again. You're up to your helmet in debt."

"People at the palace will say anything."

"Anything is exactly what goes on at the palace."

Felix tugged at his beard. "All right. Yes. It's all true. Or was. I've sworn to cut down my drinking and I haven't placed a wager in weeks."

"Because you can't afford to or no one trusts you enough to take your wagers? At least you admit your problems. That's a start. Now I want to know the details, how you see them."

Assisted by much prompting, Felix obliged.

By the time he was finished Anatolius looked as if he was attending Felix's funeral rather than talking to him across a table at a tavern. "Let us review what we know. Perhaps it will suggest a road to follow."

Felix mumbled his wish that John were in the city to assist.

"Indeed, but he isn't so we must do the best we can all by our poor selves, a simple lawyer and the captain of the excubitors."

"Former captain."

"I stand corrected. Justinian has not rescinded your demotion." Anatolius tilted his chair back until it rested against the wall. "Now, as I understand it, embroiled in certain arrangements we will not mention, you discovered one of your colleagues in this enterprise dead on your premises. There was an official visit but you managed to conceal the evidence, and then removed the body but were seen in the act of disposing of it. Meantime, the deceased's wife notified the authorities, or so we have been told. This led to the second official visit and subsequent arrest. Along with the guards finding that damning cloak."

"That sums it up very well. I swear, the man was not wearing that cloak when I first saw him."

"What was he wearing?"

Felix tried to remember. He closed his eyes and tried to blot out the suddenly distracting noises of the tavern.

"Certainly you can't have forgotten finding a corpse in your courtyard. It must have been very startling. Or wasn't it?"

"Yes, yes. I was shocked. That's just it. The only thing that made an impression on me was that there was a dead man lying against the wall. It must have driven everything else straight out of my mind."

"But you said you remembered he wasn't wearing the cloak so—"

"That's right. Now I recall. His robes were embroidered rather ostentatiously, even for a courtier. That's what caught my attention."

"You can't remember any more details? Could the fancy clothes have included a jeweled cloak?"

Felix shook his head. "No. I'm certain."

"Do you suppose one of your servants stole the cloak and hid it?"

"What? Found the body and took the cloak, without alerting me?"

"How many month's wages could a cloak like that be sold for?"

"I see what you mean. I hadn't considered that, what with fleeing for my life and expecting to be tortured to death momentarily."

"Quite understandable. You should look into this when you get home. But let's continue. Meantime, Porphyrius—as renowned and respected as he is wealthy—has you beaten—or so you claim—and threatens that unless you produce the relic recently stolen from the Church of the Holy Apostles there will be dire consequences."

"And hangs a man to show he does not make idle threats," Felix added.

"I should like to know why this particular man was chosen. But you said he was, unfortunately, not recognizable. Then there's the man with jingling clothes from whom you took instructions. Who, like Porphyrius, may or may not be the leader of this enterprise we do not specify. So many things are unknown, and so little of what we know makes sense." Anatolius paused to take a sip of wine. "The natives of Hell, I think we can discount. I am willing to believe you haven't been dealing with demons, aside from those who emerge from wine jugs."

Felix started to retort but bit his lip. Anatolius had saved his skin, and he might well require the lawyer's assistance to keep it.

"If you promise to supply me with a list of your creditors we'll say no more about that," Anatolius told him. "You might not think any of them have a hand in any of this, aside from driving you to become involved in dubious matters for financial reasons, but I'm not so sure." He pulled out his coin pouch preparatory to paying for their drinks, and gave it a shake. It reminded Felix of the Jingler. "Money is the mother of lawyers."

"There'll be no problem with me paying you, Anatolius."

"I wasn't thinking about that. I was thinking that no matter what problem clients come to me with, it usually all started with money. I wouldn't charge a friend. Look, from what you've told me we have roads leading to the Hippodrome, the palace, and possibly to an unknown person who could be anywhere directing matters. Not to mention the church authorities naturally wish to have their treasure restored and Justinian ordered you to assist in finding it. There is some irony in that. The kind of irony that puts one behind iron bars."

Felix licked his lips, dry despite all the wine he'd consumed. "So what do you advise?"

"Given all you've told me, speaking as a lawyer, I have to tell you that the only reasonable course of action is to flee the city immediately."

Felix stared at him, speechless.

Anatolius went on. "But as your friend, if you prefer to stay, unwise as that may be, I am prepared to make some inquiries and see if I can help. Perhaps I can find out who the dead man was."

Felix nodded his assent. Anatolius put coins on the table. He paused. "Felix, apart from legal matters…you can't become a slave to Bacchus again. You're not as young as you were. You're ruining your health. You look terrible. Look at all the bruises and cuts and the red patches on your hands and cheeks. When I first saw you I feared the torturers had already begun their work. Your payment to me will be a promise to imbibe less. Imagine it is John admonishing you. You know he would if he were here."

"I told you I've sworn off overindulgence. But a drink now and then keeps one calm."

"Find a better way to stay calm." Anatolius got up to leave. "And come to think of it, maybe you should visit Isis. You spent plenty of time at her establishment in the past."

"We both did, Anatolius. But she's not running a brothel anymore. Why would I visit her refuge for former prostitutes?"

"To let Isis give you some advice on how to mend your ways, my friend. I am serious. If Isis could change her ways to such a great extent, surely you could change a few things about your behavior."

Felix stayed at the table for a while after Anatolius had gone. He had no intention of visiting Isis. It would be embarrassing for both of them, he imagined. Besides, he wasn't a prostitute in need of reforming. He was a man who enjoyed his wine.

His thoughts were interrupted by shouts, laughter, and curses. A number of Blues crowded through the doorway.

Though Felix remained rooted to his chair his heart was racing. He had totally forgotten. It had not even occurred to him while he rambled on to Anatolius.

During the night, while he awaited his fate in the cell, the deadline Porphyrius had set for the return of the Virgin's shroud had passed.

Chapter Thirty-two

The javelin hissed past Felix's shoulder and buried itself in the forehead of the figure sagging against Athena.

General Germanus, who had flung the weapon, strode across the flagstones to the statue of the goddess and admired his aim before yanking the projectile from the crudely painted face. Then he turned angrily toward Felix.

"Are you trying to kill yourself? You almost walked into my throw. Did you suppose I could call my javelin back once I'd let go of it? What are you doing here?"

"My apologies. I needed to see you urgently."

Germanus stalked across the garden to the edge of the colonnade where another javelin lay, along with a bow and arrows. He was engaged in target practice with the dummy propped up against the statue of Athena. His enemy consisted of a faded garment stuffed with straw, now protruding from numerous wounds, and topped by a similarly stuffed sack on which were daubed simplistic representations of eyes, mouth, and nose.

"Haven't I made it plain, captain, that when I need you I will summon you?"

"I wouldn't have disturbed you if it wasn't necessary, general. I find myself in certain difficulties."

"This is of importance to me?"

Surely, thought Felix, Germanus must have heard about him being relieved of his command. Should he say anything about it? The javelin whistled past Felix again and thunked into the dummy. The shaft quivered, jutting from one painted eye.

"Could we possibly sit somewhere?"

Germanus walked past him to the target and jerked the javelin free. "Well," he snapped, "are you just going to stand there like a stuffed tunic? I might mistake you for my target." He placed the point of his javelin on Felix's chest. "How did you get those cuts and bruises? Have you been brawling, or have you found a very spirited mistress?"

He grinned, showing his big, square teeth to the guards, who laughed in appreciation of his jest.

Felix felt his face grow hot.

"General, my only concern is to be ready to assist you when required. You told me you needed information that might be harmful to Belisarius. But presently, I fear I am being impeded due to certain…uh…certain circumstances, and I…"

Germanus laughed. "Do you think I require your assistance in convincing the emperor to remove Belisarius from his command? The word I have is the great coward is sailing up and down the coast, too frightened to land. He hasn't taken his armies out of sight of the sea in years. He won't fight without an escape ship at his back."

Felix nodded. One didn't disagree with Germanus. Yet the assistance of the captain of the excubitors was not to be lightly dismissed. Many powerful aristocrats and office holders would oppose Belisarius' removal. Who could guess what lengths they would go to? Then too, once in charge of the Italian campaign, Germanus would need commanders personally loyal to him, with more reason to want him to succeed than to wish for the return of Belisarius.

But there was no point in Felix telling Germanus what he already knew. What he didn't seem to know—or more likely knew but didn't care about—was that Felix had lost his position. He must suppose that Felix still had the loyalty of his men. And now had a grudge to nurse, in addition to being desperate, and so might prove even more useful.

If so he would assist Felix.

He had to. Who else could?

"General, all I require is for you to have a word with the emperor or with Porphyrius, and the difficulty is solved."

"Porphyrius? What's he got to do with me?" Germanus turned his back and strode away toward the colonnade and the weapons piled there. Felix went after him. He caught up when the general stooped to exchange his javelin for the bow.

"Porphyrius has threatened to kill me." He knew it was dangerous to make accusations about a wealthy and powerful man, but what choice did he have? John might have been in a strong enough position to assist Felix but he was far away.

Germanus' expression did not change. He selected an arrow, placed it in the bow, and pulled back, testing, apparently more interested in the tautness of the string than Felix's predicament. "You come to me to accuse a prominent and respected citizen of threatening your life? Why would Porphyrius do such a thing?"

Felix stared past Germanus toward the target. The dummy's hideous painted face, straw bursting from its forehead and one dead black eye, might have been the half-formed visage of a devil. "It's all a misunderstanding. He thinks I have the Virgin's shroud."

Germanus lowered his bow. "You're mixed up in the theft?"

"Of course not."

"But Porphyrius thinks you are?"

"Yes. Why, I don't know."

"So it is a minor matter. A few words will smooth it over?"

The tightness in Felix's chest relaxed. "Yes. Exactly. I hesitated to tell you the whole story but I know you are a fair man."

"And the little matter of you being thrown into the dungeons under suspicion of murder? That, I take it, is too insignificant to mention."

The breath went out of Felix.

"Do you think I'm stupid, ex-captain? Do you imagine a man who drinks and gambles and mixes himself up in crimes, a man suspected by the emperor of murder, can be of any use to me?"

"But it's not true. It's a misunderstanding. A word from you and my position will be restored."

Germanus showed his teeth in a snarling smile. "I thought it was you who was supposed to assist me. Get out of my sight, ex-captain. Leave the city immediately and never approach me again."

Chapter Thirty-three

Everyone knows that demons breath darkness, which is why they need to keep to the shadows during the day, and why if one ventures into a demon's lair it is best to do so during the daytime.

This common knowledge was the reason Dedi didn't wait for night before invading Antonina's mansion. He felt safer relieving its guard of his key and strolling through the back gate in the middle of the afternoon.

The guard was slumped on his stool making wheezing, grunting noises, dead to the world thanks to the potion the Egyptian magician had easily dropped into the inattentive fellow's wine jug, the same potion he'd used to drug the doorkeeper of the mausoleum. Magicians were well practiced at sleight of hand.

As soon as Dedi was inside he slipped through the shrubbery around the exposed, sun-drenched courtyard. From outside, the trees visible above the high walls had made it obvious most of the grounds behind the mansion consisted of gardens. He peered out at the courtyard. Short as he was, there was no need for him to crouch to keep his head below the carefully trimmed greenery. A servant emerged to empty a bucket of water.

Dedi loped away, keeping to the shelter of ornamental bushes, flower beds, arbors, and clusters of tall, frond-like grasses. Scattered vegetation cast light shade here and there, but insufficient for a demon to breath properly. He was not surprised to see Antonina's garden featured a large collection of satyrs in all shapes and sizes, in granite, marble, bronze, copper, and porphyry, every material imaginable except flesh and fur. Or so he hoped.

What resembled a miniature Greek temple jutted from the back of the house. The roses blooming nearby did not quite conceal the smells of herbs, incense, and smoke emanating from the peculiar structure. There were other odors, strange and pungent, evidence of substances that Dedi knew should never be coaxed into existence. This no doubt was Antonina's workshop, where she brewed the nostrums she gave to her wealthy friends—and also practiced her magick.

Dedi's fish-like mouth puckered in disapproval. Why did the rich insist on dabbling at what others needed to do to earn a living?

Not far away, he located the servants' entrance to the main house.

This was the place he needed to access, the servants' quarters, where the demon disguised as Tychon lurked.

He pulled a small clay pot from his robe, unstopped it, and shook some of its contents, a fine gray dust, in the doorway. Then he knelt and traced an intricate pattern in the dust with his forefinger while reciting an incantation.

Dedi had concocted the magickal substance by burning Tychon's woven belt, stolen at the baths, and combining the ashes with several ingredients. The ingredients, it was true, could be purchased at any number of shops along the Mese, but one needed to know the precise amounts and combinations and the guttural words of the incantation had never before been heard in Constantinople.

At least by human ears.

When he was finished Dedi stood and scuffed at the pattern, obliterating merely its physical presence, then moved silently into the house. There was no sign of anyone, so he continued to cast spells in each doorway he came to until his pot was empty.

Laughter shrilled from around a corner of the corridor.

Dedi tucked the pot back into his garment and skittered off, unheard and unseen.

Now he only needed to wait. As soon as Tychon passed through one of the doorways, the spell would encircle him as surely as the belt had encircled his waist and the demon would be in thrall to the diminutive Egyptian.

Dedi found a well-concealed spot beneath a huge clump of rose bushes, lay down on the soft earth, and dozed.

Chapter Thirty-four

Felix lay flat on his back, gazing upward.

His bed was a ship caught in a maelstrom. The fluffy clouds on the ceiling whirled madly, the pretty painted birds circled like vultures. His stomach heaved but there was nothing left to eject. He gagged and choked.

Anastasia, perched on the edge of the bed, mopped his burning forehead with a damp cloth. She picked up a green glass bottle from the table beside her. "Here's one of the potions Antonina supplied."

She slid her free hand behind Felix's head, pushing it up as she lowered the bottle toward his mouth.

He flailed his arm weakly. "No. It's her poisons did this to me. I won't take any more of them."

"Silly bear! It's those kicks to your head. You shouldn't have been running all over the city so soon afterwards. Now take this."

He opened his mouth to protest again and she poured the contents of the bottle between his lips. He spluttered. Some dribbled out over his beard. She dabbed it up with her forefinger, then thrust the finger into his mouth. "Let's not waste any."

She released his head and he settled back, defeated. "What do you know about getting kicked in the head anyway?"

"You gave me a pretty good kick in the head the other night when we were—"

"True, but I wasn't wearing boots at the time."

Anastasia placed the bottle back with several companions. "You need to stay in bed for a day or two."

"Impossible. I have to find that relic. No one has come after it yet?"

"No."

"You should leave, Anastasia. If you're here when they finally show up, you'll be in as much danger as I am."

"Which is to say, no danger at all. Why would Porphyrius kill you if he really thinks you have the relic hidden? Then he'd never be able to get his hands on it, would he?"

"Tell that to the fellow they hanged."

"They didn't hang you, did they?"

Felix closed his eyes to blot out the careening ceiling. He had to get back to work. Unfortunately to do so meant he would have to stand up first, and to stand up, sad to say, he had to manage to sit up. It was all so complicated. "I can't just lie here and wait for a knock at the door."

"You're not capable of anything else right now. That potion will have you on your feet soon enough. Rest."

"I wish I could. Now I've made an enemy of Germanus too."

"Nonsense. He needs the captain of the excubitors on his side. He just enjoys bullying people."

"How is it you know General Germanus?"

Anastasia shoved a pillow under Felix's shoulders. "Try to sit up."

To his surprise he managed to lever himself up slightly and risked opening his eyes a slit. The room looked a bit more stable. "Ah. Good."

Anastasia handed him a silver chain from which was suspended an engraved carnelian. "Hang this around your neck. The symbols on the stone are magickal."

Felix slipped the chain over his head, alongside his cross. He tapped at the chain bearing the latter. "Will that charm get along with—"

"Antonina knows what she's doing. Ask all the men she's bewitched."

"They don't necessarily know they're bewitched, though, do they?"

"Oh, my. Are you thinking about that time—"

"Isn't that what you were referring to? But let's forget it." He couldn't help recalling his own long ago encounter with Belisarius' wanton wife, which Anastasia seemed to have guessed. The last thing he needed in his state was an argument.

Anastasia giggled suddenly.

He looked at her as sharply. "What's so funny? You're not picturing me and—"

"You do feel guilty, don't you? This talk about potions reminded me. Antonina said her servants had been stealing wine. So she added a little something that would cause the thief to reveal himself, and teach him never to do it again." She covered her mouth to stifle further giggles.

"I wouldn't care to work in that house! But how do you come to know Antonina so well? She was great friends with Theodora. Is that it? Is Antonina acquainted with all of Theodora's attendants?"

Anastasia stopped giggling and looked at him in a way he'd never seen before. Totally perplexed. "You great oaf! You really don't know, do you? And I thought you simply wanted it left unsaid."

Felix stared at her in bewilderment. The room was no longer spinning but he felt even more disoriented. "Don't know what? Didn't want anything said about what?"

She bent over and playfully kissed the tip of his nose. "I'm not a lady-in-waiting or any kind of attendant. I'm Theodora's sister."

Chapter Thirty-five

"Why are you looking so shocked, Felix? You know that Theodora had sisters."

"Anastasia is such a common name. Anyone could make the same mistake. I've seen Comita at the palace from time to time but—"

"I avoid the court and in particular public ceremonies, They are both so terribly boring." Anastasia dropped onto the bed next to Felix. The bed's motion sent a shot of pain through his side. "I'm still the same woman."

Felix tried to avoid wincing. "Why didn't you tell me?"

"I thought you knew and did not want it mentioned. As I said."

Her tone didn't sound convincing. Felix was about to say as much when she grabbed his beard, pulled his face toward her, and gave him a lengthy kiss.

"There. Do my kisses taste different?"

"No," he admitted.

But now he was afraid the honey concealed a bitter poison.

"You're worried it isn't safe to be involved with Theodora's sister, even if the empress is dead. That's it, isn't it?"

As always she seemed to read his thoughts. Felix ran his tongue nervously over his lips and said nothing.

"Remember, you aren't a common soldier. You're the commander of the excubitors, the imperial guard."

"Was the commander, you mean."

Anastasia waved her hand dismissively. "The trouble with you is you don't have the courage of your ambitions. You're too loyal."

"Justinian prizes loyalty."

"And where has it got you?"

Felix grunted. "Right now I'm not concerned about getting anywhere. Just remaining out of the dungeons is enough."

"As soon as you're rested and healed, you'll be longing for the battlefields of Italy again."

"A few hours ago I was sure I'd be dead by now, or if not, wishing I were." A chill went down his back as he thought again of passing through the room full of torture instruments.

"If you don't stop getting your humors deranged you'll kill yourself without any help from Justinian or Porphyrius. You don't look well at all. Just look at the backs of your hands.'

"Yes, I know, Anatolius pointed out the same thing. What am I supposed to do? I'm in grave danger, and so are you. We must proceed with great caution."

"Me? In danger? Hardly! Did it not occur to you that in your current predicament you are extremely fortunate to have the empress' sister for a lover? Do you think I can't protect you? Who do you suppose spoke with Justinian after he'd ordered you hauled off to the dungeons? Who told the senator to engage Anatolius?"

Felix looked away from her. "I see. The empress' sister is even allowed to throw hot coals at guards if it amuses her. And to think, I feared—"

Anastasia placed a finger on his lips. "Hush. I'm sorry if you were afraid for me."

"You've been playing with me, Anastasia!" The words burst from Felix. "All I am to you is a…captive bear. Like the one Theodora kept in her menagerie."

"That's cruel, Felix."

"And how can I be sure you don't know who the courier was? How can I be sure it wasn't you who—"

"Don't even think such a thing! And if I knew anything, wouldn't I tell you? Maybe I can find out who the dead man was." Anastasia put her arms around him. Reflexively he tried to draw away.

"Please, Felix. Don't turn against me. If I could erase my birth to please you, I would. But what does it matter? Isn't it obvious that I'm your slave? Is there anything a servant girl could give you that I haven't?"

"It's not…it's just that…well…" He let his voice trail off. How could he tell her he felt humiliated, having been saved by a woman. Grateful, certainly. Relieved. But nevertheless humiliated. "I need to speak to Nikomachos," he said instead.

"About what?"

"That cloak Narses claimed was found in the servants' quarters. I want Nikomachos to question the staff. I'm sure Narses supplied the cloak himself, but Anatolius is of the opinion one of the servants might have stolen it."

"Without bothering to tell you there was a dead body in the courtyard?"

"Thieves who rob corpses are not noted for their honesty."

"You might ask him to conduct his own search. In case the guards overlooked something else that might have been stolen. That might give away the courier's identity. If you trust Nikomachos…more than you seem to trust me."

"Nikomachos has been with me for years. He's perfectly trustworthy. Servants tend to be light fingered, but with only one arm he's twice as honest as most."

"Perhaps you would have more faith in me if I had only one arm," Anastasia sniffed. "I'll go and get him. He should have looked in here to see if his master required his services. I'm not that frightening, am I?" Without waiting for a reply Anastasia left Felix alone with his thoughts.

They made for very poor company.

He felt dazed. Theodora's sister! Thank Mithra, or the Lord, or whatever deity wouldn't take offense, that the empress was dead. Even so…

Anastasia was gone much longer than Felix would have

expected. Did she have to search the house to find a servant who was supposed to be nearby, ready to attend to Felix's every wish?

Finally she returned, looking grim.

"Nikomachos isn't here. I looked everywhere, asked the whole staff. No one has seen him all day!"

"He might have gone to see if he could do anything for me."

Anastasia's lips tightened. "That's not the first explanation that would have sprung to my mind. However, we will know soon enough if your servant has run off, for whatever reason. In the meantime I've had an idea."

She came over the bed and held out a torn bit of cloth the size of her palm.

Felix looked at it without comprehension. "What is that?"

"Part of the Virgin's shroud." She shook it insistently in his face.

He took the scrap from her, holding it gingerly between his thumb and forefinger as if it might come alive and bite him. His heart raced. "What do you mean? Is there more you haven't told me? It looks like, well, just a bit of rag."

Anastasia put a hand to her mouth to muffle a laugh.

Felix's simply gaped at the cloth, holding it at arms-length. "I don't understand, Anastasia."

"I tore it off a cleaning cloth. It's part of that relic everyone is seeking."

"What? My servant's been cleaning with the Virgin's shroud?"

Anastasia snatched the rag back. "Of course not, foolish bear! But from now on, we pretend it's been torn off the relic."

"Lie about it?"

"Of course. I know you are more comfortable with brute force but a lie is more effective than a sword here in the capital."

He eyed the rag dubiously. "And how am I supposed to use this weapon?"

"To start negotiations with Porphyrius. I'm certain once he sees it he'll be willing to come to an accommodation with you. Especially when you explain that you will continue to bring him pieces until he agrees to terms. Or until the shroud ceases to exist."

◇◇◇

Porphyrius' laughter boomed around the stables behind his mansion. "You expect me to believe this piece of rag is from the Virgin's shroud?"

"If you want the shroud returned you have no other choice." Felix kept his voice calm. It was a struggle, particularly since the great charioteer had designed the frontage of his private stables to resemble the starting gates in the Hippodrome. The beating and threats Felix had suffered in the latter were still fresh in his memory and on his flesh.

Besides, he had never been a good liar.

Porphyrius returned the scrap of cloth to Felix and rubbed his fingers briskly on his leather breeches. "But I don't want the shroud returned. I have nothing to do with the unfortunate theft. I have explained that to you already."

"Then why did you agree to speak with me?"

There was no reply. Porphyrius stamped across the hard-packed dirt, stopping at a gate to look into the stall beyond.

Felix followed, determined to extract some admission. Anastasia had brought him around to her way of thinking. It was safer to allow Porphyrius to think he had the relic. If he convinced the charioteer that he, in fact, had no idea where it was, Porphyrius might very well have him killed for knowing too much about his affairs. But Porphyrius wouldn't dare kill the only person who might lead him to the relic, would he?

Felix leaned on the gate beside Porphyrius. From within the stables came the odor of hay and horses but the stall was empty. The charioteer had been staring at nothing. Pondering the offer, perhaps?

"We're both familiar with the races," Felix said. "We both know something about gambling. If you choose to believe what I showed you wasn't torn off the shroud, you're free to do so. But we both know that's a losing bet, either way. If you're right, and I don't know where the relic is, I can't retrieve it for you. On the other hand, if I am telling the truth—and I am—then

I will destroy the relic in stages, as I described to you, unless we come to terms."

"Perhaps you should tell all this to whoever it was threatened you the other night."

"Tell a gang of anonymous Blues? Where do I find them? I'm sure you can identify them more readily than I can."

Porphyrius' face remained impassive but muscles tightened in the massive forearms leaning on the gate. "You're hardly in a position to harass me about this, are you, Felix? I could offer you a job cleaning my stables if you're looking for work."

Felix shrugged. "We both know Justinian is prone to sudden whims."

Porphyrius pushed himself away from the stall and nodded toward the guard stationed in a corner of the enclosure. The man, who had been watching the conversation, shifted his lance and strode over. "My servant will see you out."

Felix looked down at the scrap in his hand then closed his fist around it. "When you want to talk about obtaining the rest of this, let me know."

He left, deep in thought. Had he made the desired impression on the charioteer? If he had succeeded in buying himself time, what happened if time ran out again before he found the relic?

Chapter Thirty-six

Germanus and his guards tramped noisily into the immense atrium of the building the populace referred to as the Palace of Narses. The clatter of boots on marble reverberated around the Greek statuary and multi-colored pillars, rising toward the distant vaulted ceiling from which depended golden lamps on silver chains, as numerous as the stars over the Marmara.

Narses came forward to meet Germanus. The eunuch's own guards remained at a discreet distance, posted all around the atrium. Shrunken, bent, and bald, Narses appeared an insignificant figure before the tall, muscular general. So too did a vulture look insignificant perched on the corpse of a lion.

"Do you really need to march in here like an invading army?" Narses' reedy voice sounded petulant. His beady gaze swept along the tracks created when the men had entered. "You could have knocked the dirt off your boots, couldn't you?"

"Dirt has never bothered you, Narses."

"What business do you imagine you have with me?" Narses asked.

"The captain of the excubitors tells me he has been threatened by Porphyrius."

"If the former captain says that a former charioteer is threatening him, why do you come to me? And why would you care what transpires between those two anyway?"

"I made inquiries. Whether or not Porphyrius is out for the captain's blood, you certainly are."

"You speak plainly, Germanus. Should I not be on guard against those in high positions who plot against the emperor? And again, why should you be interested in this complaint? Ah, but wait, Felix is a friend of yours, isn't he? Or should I say follower? Or ally?"

Germanus resisted rubbing his watering eyes. All around the atrium smoky tendrils from burning incense coiled up from silver urns. The air was as thick as that in the inner sanctum of an oracle. Perhaps the creature he confronted required this exotic atmosphere to survive. "If the captain of the emperor's excubitors claims that a private person is threatening him, shouldn't that be looked into?"

"Felix never reported the matter to the urban watch. Nor to me, although why anyone would report such threats to me…"

"Because you are close to Justinian and anything that endangers the emperor's officials endangers the emperor. This assault—"

"It is an assault now?"

"Perhaps you're working with Porphyrius," Germanus said.

Narses' vulturine eyes glistened. "Why would I? I'm not interested in racing."

"I'm not surprised. It's much too straightforward a contest for those like you. Perhaps you want Felix out of way for your own reasons, just because he was a friend of John's. Or perhaps because he is, as you put it, a friend of mine."

"I assume you mean because he was a friend of yours. It would not do your reputation any good if you were known to a close associate with a traitorous criminal."

Germanus scanned the vast, smoky space. He could see Narses' guards looking in his direction, no doubt meeting the gazes of his own bodyguard, exchanging silent challenges, sizing each other up. Which was why he had come here. To engage Narses, to put him on notice if he intended to work against him, in whatever way, for whatever reason, Germanus would push back hard.

Germanus said, "You mean you hope to make Felix look like a traitorous criminal to blacken my reputation enough that Justinian won't dare appoint me to replace Belisarius."

"So you admit it! Your ambition is to replace the heroic Belisarius!" Narses voice had grown shrill.

Germanus smiled. "Yes, I admit what everyone in the city knows and what most desire, considering the shambles Belisarius has made in Italy."

"Granted, he has been a disappointment. But do you suppose you are the only candidate to replace him?"

"Who else could?"

"I could."

Germanus stared down at the dwarf-like figure in disbelief. "You? You're old enough to be my great grandfather, if you were actually a man!"

After the brief meeting had ended with nothing apparent accomplished and Germanus had returned to his home, he kept thinking in amazement about the twisted little eunuch's ambition. He had pictured him as a vulture perched on a dead lion. Now he saw a vulture perched on the carcass of a once mighty general.

Chapter Thirty-seven

A pale figure floated silently through the dark halls at the rear of Antonina's mansion. Now it paused beside a closed door, listening, now it peered stealthily around a corner, now it eased a door open a crack to see the dim shape of the cook's assistant sleeping on her cot within.

Antonina's servant Tychon, going about his nightly rounds, was certain he had heard a noise, something more than a rat in the walls or a cat prowling the gardens.

He bent down where two corridors intersected. The dim light from the guttering oil lamp in a wall niche slanted across the floor, picking out what looked like scuff marks. Tychon ran a finger across them, detecting a hint of dust.

Hadn't the hallways been cleaned during the afternoon?

He got to his feet and stood, a pallid apparition. In the nearby rooms the rest of the staff slept. He heard the cook's muffled cough, the sonorous snoring of the pretty little cleaning girl.

Nothing unusual.

Perhaps he had been imagining things. Even after years of working for Antonina she still frightened him, witch that she was. He much preferred the house when she was away on expeditions with Belisarius. At least Karpos was gone. Wouldn't Antonina have liked to know how her young man had been prowling the servants' quarters looking for a girl more his age?

It had created some problems for Tychon, but now that was all resolved, and Tychon knew how to keep his mouth shut.

He went out into the garden. Is this where the mysterious sound had emanated? Had it been the rustle of bushes heard through open windows? There was no breeze to stir the vegetation. Shrubs, trees, and flower beds were clumps of deeper darkness in the night. Over the enclosure's high walls the night sky shone with the faint, gray luminescence from the city. The smell of roses filled the humid air, stronger at night than in the daytime.

There was nothing to see or hear. A few steps away the miniature marble pillars of Antonina's workshop glimmered. Enough laboring, Tychon told himself, as he strode into the workshop.

Sufficient light came through the doorway for him to pick his way through the familiar room. Although outwardly it had been designed to look like a Greek temple, inside it resembled a kitchen with a long brazier and heavy wooden tables. Bottles lining shelves gave off faint glitters, captive stars. The acrid stench of the last mixture Antonina had been brewing almost overpowered the dry scents of herbs tied in bundles hanging from the ceiling and a vague, incongruous odor of incense.

Tychon knew the workshop well. Without needing to search for them, he could put his hand immediately on belladonna, equally prized for enhancing women's eyes and disposing of enemies, or the walnut infusion favored by ladies of the court for treating blemishes of the skin. There were small pots of soothing emollients tinted and perfumed with rose petals, jars of comfrey leaves, a number of the forked roots Antonina called Circe's plant, a jug of the elder bark purgative much disliked by the household servants, and a hundred other ingredients for nostrums and potions. He also knew where his mistress kept the excellent aged Italian wine she drank when the brazier filled the workshop with infernal heat.

He retrieved a cup he kept hidden behind empty amphorae in the bottom of a cupboard and filled it from the enormous lidded earthen jug sitting beneath a tall, narrow window at the end of the room. He would never have dared drink from any unfamiliar container from the workshop, no matter how well cleaned. Seated on a stool he could just see through the window into a black tangle of rosebushes.

He took a sip of wine. It was the sort meant for the lips of emperors. Not servants. Which was what appealed to Tychon more than the taste. To his palate it hinted at mold. The effects the wine had, on him at least, were no different than those of the near vinegar one could buy for a couple of copper coins at the lowest tavern. Did the aristocrats who imbibed such rare ambrosia as Antonina kept in stock experience some heightened form of inebriation in keeping with the cost? Tychon doubted it.

He sat drinking contentedly. He deserved this bit of extra compensation, didn't he? The difficult job he had been entrusted with had gone as planned. As far as he was concerned, it was over. He had been understandably on edge since that night, startled more than once by half-glimpsed shadows and stealthy noises such as he had been hearing earlier. Just deranged humors and imagination.

Again he dipped his cup into the jug, took a gulp, and contemplatively smacked his lips. This was different than usual. Did he detect a hint of bitterness? Perhaps it had been a bad year, a less than stellar vintage. Had Antonina brought a new batch back from Italy with her? It had been a bad year for generals, why not for grapes also?

Suddenly he was very tired. It was all catching up to him. More wine would help.

The tangled rose bushes beyond the wind moved, as if in a breeze.

Had the wind risen? There might be another storm on the way.

The bushes writhed like a nest of entwined snakes.

Was something hiding there?

Tychon put his cup back behind the amphorae, turned, and banged hard into the edge of the nearest table. Strange. He knew the workshop like the back of his hand. Actually the back of his hand was trembling. He ran toward the door, stumbling, feeling as if he were inexplicably going down hill.

He burst out into a nightmare landscape of looming grotesques. Shadows were swaying, crawling through the dark pool of night caught between the house and the garden walls. No, they were only trees and shrubs. For all their apparent movement they remained anchored to their spots. Except…

One shadow darted away from the side wall of the workshop. Tychon gave chase.

A street urchin who had managed to creep in, judging by its size.

Yet the proportions seemed all wrong. And the loping gait was unlike that of a child.

An ape, Tychon thought. It's an ape!

Sure enough, as the creature came to the garden's perimeter it clambered up into a yew and then vanished over the top of the wall.

Some part of Tychon's mind begged him to pause and consider the likelihood of Antonina's garden being invaded by an ape. But it pleaded to no avail with the irrationality that had taken hold. He was to the gate and out into the street before the guard could react. He raced along parallel to the wall. His mouth was filled with the weirdly bitter taste of the wine.

There was the ape, blocking his path. staring straight at him.

No, a short creature with a hideous face, a mouth moving like that of a landed fish.

"Demon! By the Goddess of the Frogs, I command you!" The monstrosity waved its arms.

Demon. Yes, that's what it was! "No," Tychon cried. "I meant no harm!"

The horror came hopping at him, reaching out with clawed hands. Now Tychon saw that every shadow in the street had come to life, waving phantom arms, slithering through the gutters. Was this the way an angry god dealt with malefactors?

He screamed and ran.

Reason, locked deep inside his panicked mind, pounded helplessly, unheard, at the door of its dungeon as he fled through the streets, alleyways, and squares pursued by a shape that was part Fury and part avenging angel.

He burst into an open promenade overlooking the water. The last thing Tychon saw were city lights reflected in the water far below the sea wall.

DAY SIX

Chapter Thirty-eight

Peter lay stretched out on his sleeping mat, eyes closed, hands clasped peacefully on his chest. As if he sensed John looking at him, he opened his eyes. "Master? What is it?"

"I didn't mean to wake you, Peter. I wished to question you again, in case you recalled anything more."

Peter propped himself up on his elbows. "I tried, master, but my memory isn't what it used to be."

On the mat next to his, Hypatia stirred and sat up. She looked at John crossly, but addressed Peter. "Your recollection has nothing to do with age, Peter. Why would you remember every single thing you saw and did right before? You weren't expecting to be thrown into the sea!"

Peter looked in distress from John to Hypatia and back. "I'm sorry—"

"Never mind, Peter. Hypatia is right. Go back to sleep. It's barely dawn and you need to rest."

"Really, master. I'm all right. I can swim, you know. And thank the Lord, I also had the protection of Hypatia's charm." He lifted his arm to display the knotted bracelet around his wrist. "It was just the shock of it. When you're standing there minding your own business and someone grabs the back of your—"

"Yes, I understand." John did not want to contemplate what it would be like to be grabbed from behind, hoisted over the rail, and dropped into the bottomless waters. Which is what had happened to Peter, as he had already told John.

He had also told John several times that, no, he had not managed to see the culprit. All he had time to notice was the water rushing up at him.

No, he couldn't say who had been on deck when he emerged from the captain's cabin. A few crew members no doubt. He had no reason to take note. He'd just wanted to get a breath of air while the pot on the brazier came to a boil.

No, he hadn't heard his attacker approach.

The captain's cabin had been empty when he arrived so he fanned the brazier's embers to life and began cooking stew. He had had to search for a knife suitable for slicing onions. Cooking utensils were jumbled on the shelves with hammers and files and the like. Jars of olives were mixed up with jars of ointment. Much of what Peter needed was hidden under a stack of packages, pouches, and navigational charts. The disarray was shocking.

John was amazed Peter seemed more upset by the disorder in his adopted kitchen than he was about his near encounter with Poseidon.

He went on deck to search for the captain and found the plump, red-faced man at the stern where the huge, iron crosses of the anchors had been winched on board.

"Are the repairs completed?"

"Patched up well enough to reach the shore. Needs a new rudder, among other things. Hope you're not in a big hurry." There was a sneer in his voice.

John wondered if he had been apprised of who the tall Greek and his party were and the reason for their journey.

"I'm not concerned about that. Did you find anything out about who tried to murder my servant?"

"Been a little busy as you might have noticed."

"Too busy to question your crew about attempted murder?"

The captain screwed up his features and scratched a pink, bristly chin as if pondering the question. "Questioned my men. None of them seen anything. Merchant ship's no place for an old relic like that one. Standing around, always in the way. Someone brushed past him, busy, concentrating on his job, and the old man loses his balance and over he goes. Or perhaps he had one of them falling spells as them that's his advanced age often has and just imagines he was pushed. He wouldn't be much of a loss, if you ask me."

"You like his honey cakes well enough. You and your traveling companion."

"I'd miss those cakes, certainly. As for the passenger you're talking about, you won't get nothing out of me. It's no one's business who takes ship on the *Leviathan*. All I want to know about my passengers is they put the proper number of coins into my hand. I don't know who they are. And even if I do know, I don't know. And now, if you don't want us to drift back onto them rocks…" He turned and waddled off, barking instructions at the crew.

Before long the sails billowed and the *Leviathan* began to move with much groaning of timbers, like an old man trying to get out of a chair.

John had spent hours after Peter's rescue interrogating the crew without the slightest result. Even when he expressed his gratitude and offered them coins as a reward, they remained suspicious and close-mouthed. Not surprisingly. On board the only person they needed to fear was the captain and it seemed clear to John he had ordered them to remain silent.

He talked to the other passengers.

The farmers, as John supposed they were, spent most of their time below deck, sitting in the shadows, sullenly throwing knucklebones. Both apparently lost with every throw, to judge from their sour expressions. It strengthened John's impression they had traveled to Constantinople to petition the emperor on a matter involving land or taxes, and had not been satisfied with the answer.

"We might've heard a yell, then feet stamping around overhead," one of the farmers admitted. "But after staying two weeks in that inn behind the Hippodrome we were so used to hearing fights in the alley under our window we thought nothing of the noise."

Cornelia, Peter, and Hypatia had been intent on making charms. None of them could say whether the farmers had, truly, both been occupying their usual dark spot at the time. The pilgrim and her companion claimed they had been on deck and had heard and seen nothing.

"You were nearer than I was to where Peter went overboard," John had noted.

"But we were on the opposite side of the cabin, contemplating the sunrise. As it says in the Scriptures, the sun emerges to run its course with joy."

"That would be the eastern side of the ship, where Peter went overboard."

"Don't you remember, Egina?" the companion put in. "The sun was well up by then and we had moved around to the other side to see if it was clear enough for us to glimpse the shore."

"Oh, that's right. She is correct, sir. I had forgotten that. All this excitement has been too much for me."

As for the nameless passenger, he haughtily informed John that although it was none of his business, he had been making a round of the ship but had seen nothing. "Consider with whom you are dealing. The boys who crew this ship are nothing but the lowest of ruffians. One saw that old scarecrow leaning out over the rail and thought it would be a good joke to introduce him to the fishes. Boys like that don't think past their impulses."

The speaker was nothing but a boy himself, John noted, though he certainly did not give evidence of being prone to impulses. At least not the impulse to talk out of turn.

"I don't like that young man, whoever he is," John told Cornelia when he found her standing in the prow, contemplating the sparkling wavelets rippling past the moving hull. "Not that he would have any reason to drown Peter. This journey must be very hard on Peter, although he will never complain. The sun beats down so strongly, exhausted, coming out of that dim cabin into the sun, he might have become dizzy—"

"You know that's not the case."

John shrugged. "No one on this ship has any reason to hurt Peter."

Cornelia looked in the direction of the as yet invisible coast. "Did you consider whoever did it wanted to hurt you?"

"Hurt me? Are you imagining an assassin again? Surely he would target me, not Peter?"

"But only after you have watched your family pay, murdered one by one, for whatever your crimes are supposed to be."

"But…who could be that full of hatred? Except one person we both know is lying dead in a mausoleum at the Church of the Holy Apostles."

Chapter Thirty-nine

"A team of laborers unloading a grain ship say they heard Tychon yelling about demons. His screams carried all the way down to the docks. When they looked up they saw him come flying over the sea wall. Not that he flew far. It took a while for someone to get up on the roof of the warehouse, but judging from the shape Tychon was in he must have died the instant he hit it. Antonina is extremely upset."

Anastasia let her silk tunic drop onto the tiles beside the bath and stepped down into the water to sit beside Felix, Aphrodite, descending into the sea. Looking at her made Felix ache in a way that almost drove the ache of his injuries out of his mind. Almost.

"Why should Antonina be upset? You told me she'd drugged the wine to teach the thief a lesson. So she not only did that, she also executed him." Felix leaned back against the rim of the basin and watched tendrils of steam climb up toward the round patch of sky visible through the aperture overhead. He had ordered the water be made much hotter than usual. Anastasia's skin had already turned rosy.

"She didn't want anyone to die! The potion is supposed to cause visions. She meant to give the culprit an unpleasant experience. She suspected Tychon. An unruly sort. Ran with one of the racing factions at one time, she claims. Capable servants are difficult to replace." Anastasia shifted, pressing her hip against his.

"Perhaps Antonina wouldn't have been so upset if the culprit had turned out to be one her less capable servants?"

"That's unfair, Felix."

"Didn't it occur to her that the victim might have visions, might even see fiends? From what you've told me, most of the household already imagined they were besieged by them."

"Perhaps they are."

Felix shook his head. "As I already told you, that was probably the leper who was lurking around here. I mistook him for a demon, but only for an instant."

"Turn around and let me see to that back. What a nasty purple mess it is!" She splashed some water onto the wounds. "Does that hurt?"

Felix grunted and Anastasia replied with little sounds of sympathy. "It's my belief the evil spirits came out to do mischief as soon as my sister died," she continued. "When the world's not right, when everything is turned upside down, they see their chance."

She gently kneaded his sore muscles and Felix began to relax. Could she be right? The workers at the church swore they had seen demons fleeing with the relic. Perhaps the supernatural was, in fact, involved. What about the frogs in the mausoleum? There was something unnatural about that. And the doorkeeper said he'd seen an ape or something resembling one. Still, Mithrans knew there were forces of darkness at work in the world. "It's not that I don't believe demons exist. Demons of some sort, somewhere, some time. But right here? Right now? I don't expect to see any."

"Why not? Devils are everywhere. Look at how many Jesus cast out. He drove two thousand from one poor soul into a whole herd of swine."

"At that rate there wouldn't be enough swine in the world to dispose of the demons inside the Great Palace alone!"

"Oh, Felix, I'm serious." Anastasia slapped the back of his head, lightly, but hard enough to make him wince, given the lump there.

"So am I. There's evil in the world, but it works though human beings. There's no need for demons to get involved. Well, most of the time anyhow."

Yet what if such beings really were involved in a matter with which he was inextricably entwined? Better not to think about it. Then again, every new possibility that occurred to him was just as puzzling as the previous ones. "What about your friend Antonina? Tychon was her servant. If he was seeing demons, could it have something to do with the stolen shroud? Might Antonina have an interest in relics?"

She stopped stroking his back and slid away from him. "How can you say that? Why don't you accuse me of involvement too?"

He turned to face her. "I'm just trying to think of all the possibilities."

"And you think that's a possibility?" Her face was flushed and not just from the hot air which had beaded her face with perspiration.

"I'm just trying to follow the trail of—"

"Don't say any more." She stood, making the steamy mist swirl. Rivulets streamed down her sides, sparkling in the light from overhead. She was achingly beautiful. And angry. And the sister of the late empress. Felix had the sudden, humiliating feeling of being targeted by the wrath of a goddess.

"Can't you understand? How long do you think the ruse with a bit of cloth is going to stop Porphyrius? If there are people higher up than Porphyrius or the Jingler, they've hidden themselves well. I'm not even certain what the relationship between Porphyrius and the Jingler is, or if there is any. I'm totally in the dark!"

Anastasia pushed her damp hair back from her face. Her rigid features softened. "Poor bear! I hate to see you in such a state. I have a suggestion that might make you feel better."

"Yes?"

She pivoted and stamped up the steps out of the bath, showing him her perfect buttocks. "You'd better speak to the Jingler again."

Chapter Forty

Julian the Jingler counted to seven, touched the magickal bracelets on both stick-thin wrists, murmured a guttural phrase in an unknown language that he had found through assiduous study of an obscure work by Apollonius of Tyana, and emerged from the bath.

This was the most dangerous time of all.

Few devils cared for water, fiery creatures that they were. But for the few steps it took him to reach the changing room and dress himself, Julian was protected only by the scanty number of amulets and charms it was possible to wear on neck chains and bracelets.

One or two bathers, new to the baths, gaped at the slight figure, white as a phantom, creeping across the tiles. The regulars had long since ceased to pay attention. There were many strange sights in Constantinople.

Julian did not hurry. He forced himself to remain calm. Devils had keen noses for fear, like street dogs.

As soon as he reached the bench where he had laid out his robes in the usual pattern he put on his sandals, left one first naturally. Why would he put on his right sandal first when devils had never swooped down to carry him off so long as he favored his left foot? If something worked, it was best to keep using it.

He methodically donned his clothing, so heavy with charms it made a comforting jangling like spiritual chain mail. Once he had armored himself again, he sighed with relief. Now he had only to return to his rooms by his invariable route—a route that had proved secure again and again.

He left by the front entrance, walked to the open square of the Augustaion, and passed warily through the crowds.

People drew away as he approached.

He was glad of it.

How did the inhabitants of this evil city, reigned over by a devilish emperor, survive living so blindly and haphazardly?

Or did they? How could anyone tell? Was the woman seated in the shadow of Justinian's column, selling live birds from a wicker basket, nothing but an automaton animated by the devils which had evicted her soul to wander the underworld? For all Julian knew he might be the sole human being in Constantinople and only his amulets prevented the devils from seeing that he was not one of them.

A shadow passed over him.

He stopped abruptly with a fearful jingling.

It was only a raven. It landed on the discarded scrap of fish which had lured it into the crowds, stared malevolently at Julian, then flapped away, prey clutched in its claws.

A close escape perhaps?

Heart pounding, Julian passed along the side of the Great Church. He was no less troubled than Felix by recent events involving the missing relic, but it was necessary for him to concentrate on reaching home safely. Once he was back behind his locked door, surrounded by protective magick of every variety, then he would think about the problem.

He had never known the devils to be so active. He could feel their presence as he made his way through the streets. From the mouth of an alley came the almost imperceptible chilly draught as a gateway to the underworld opened and shut somewhere.

There was no apparent reason for the zig-zag route he followed. Julian himself could not have said why it was necessary for him to go down this alleyway or cross that square. It might be that the geography of the place inhabited by the devils did not match that of this world. If it were possible to see into that other world, it would be obvious why he needed to proceed exactly as he did to avoid unwanted encounters.

Finally he reached the street where he lived. He found it hard to breath, hard to restrain himself from breaking into a run which would alert the devils swarming in the city.

It didn't matter how many times he completed his daily journeys successfully, the nearer he got to safety the more anxious he became.

Then he was mounting the stairs. He heard no pursuit from behind.

The hallway leading to his apartment was clear.

He tested his door. Still locked.

There remained only to open it, go in, and—

As the door swung open an enormous hand grabbed the back of his neck and flung him inside.

Chapter Forty-one

Anatolius contemplated the one-armed man seated on the other side of the desk. "You would be Felix's servant."

"Nikomachos, sir."

"I remember seeing you at his house in the past."

"Most people remember me, sir. Perhaps it is my blue eyes."

Anatolius tapped his reed pen on the skull grinning up from the mosaic decorating the desk top. "Have you brought me a message from your master?"

"I regret I have been forced by circumstances to take a temporary absence from my employment."

"By circumstances you mean stealing a valuable cloak from a dead man and possibly murdering him as well?"

"I assure you I did not kill the courier, sir. You are correct, however, that I have been forced to abandon my duties for fear of being accused of murder."

"Why are you here, Nikomachos? You realize that I should summon the urban watch immediately."

The absconding servant did not appear to be perturbed by the possibility. "I know you are a friend of the captain's. I had to leave in a hurry and did not realize the full extent of the serious trouble he was in. Since then word has spread all over the city. I thought I might be able to help."

"It's plain enough you wouldn't dare approach the City Prefect. How do you suppose you can help Captain Felix by coming to me?"

"I know that he did not kill the courier."

Anatolius slid a sheet of parchment over the skull and dipped his pen into the ink pot sitting at one corner of the desk. "How is this?"

Nikomachos settled back in his chair and reached over with his one hand to clasp the stump of his missing arm, coming as near as possible—disconcertingly so as far as Anatolius was concerned—to crossing his arms. "The morning the corpse was found in the courtyard I rose at my usual hour, Which is to say while it was still dark and long before the rest of the household. As I was going about attending to my duties at the back of the house I heard voices. It isn't uncommon to hear people passing by in the alley but something in the tone caught my attention, so I stepped outside. At that instant a figure dropped down from over the wall. A robber, I thought. But before I had a chance to raise the alarm, I noticed that the form by the wall didn't move.

"I got a lamp and crept forward. The figure just lay there. He didn't react. I could tell right away he must be an aristocrat because the lamp light sparkled off jewels sewn to his short cloak."

Anatolius' pen scratched at the parchment. "So naturally the first action that occurred to you was to steal the dead man's cloak and hide it in your room, where it was soon found by the urban watch."

"I thought the intruder was so intoxicated as to be unconscious, sir."

"Surely you realized he was dead?"

"After a closer examination, yes. But I'm not here to defend my actions. I don't try to defend them. We must take care of ourselves. A dead man does not miss his cloak. Life is cruel and sometimes we must act cruelly." He shrugged and tapped his stump. "But you see my point? The captain would hardly have killed the man and then dumped him in his own courtyard."

"True, provided anyone would be prepared to believe your story."

"I have found that a war wound tends to corroborate one's testimony, sir. But in fact, I offer my story in case it might encourage you to unearth other witnesses."

"Did you recognize the dead man?"

"I recognized him as a man who came to the house on occasion, delivering packages. I did not know who he was and I never heard him addressed by name."

"And you happened to observe these meetings?"

"At my job, one needs to be alert. But I am also discreet."

Anatolius made a few more scribbles, pondering on what he had been told. He suspected Nikomachos was interested in saving his employer to save his employment. His actions hadn't been reasonable. Then again most of the distressed clients Anatolius met in this office were there because they had acted without reasoning things through carefully. "Did you by any chance relieve the courier of a package as well as a cloak?"

"I did not, sir. I took a few coins, I admit. And a small dagger. He was not carrying a package."

"Are you certain?"

"I searched the young man well enough to know he did not have a package on him. The dagger was well hidden beneath his garment."

Felix's haughty servant departed without revealing anything else of value. He was hiding at a friend's but wouldn't say where.

Anatolius picked the parchment up and studied it. So Nikomachos had confirmed Felix wasn't the murderer and the courier had only arrived in the courtyard after he was dead and the package had been taken from him, if indeed he had been carrying it in the first place. If, that is, one were to believe Nikomachos.

Was that useful?

Would anyone of importance believe a thieving servant?

If nothing else, it reminded Anatolius of his promise to Felix to investigate the matter.

He laid the parchment down. There was nothing on it but a detailed sketch of a grinning skull. Yes, he was definitely getting better at drawing that skull, although he still hadn't got the toothy grin right.

◇◇◇

The grin of the dead man who was stretched out on the concrete floor of an underground room at the City Prefect's offices wasn't right either.

The face had been torn away, leaving a partially fleshed skull framed by dark hair. The ravens hadn't got far with the neck, which still exhibited an indentation akin to a necklace, the gift of the hangman in the Hippodrome.

Anatolius straightened up, keeping his sleeve pressed over his nose and mouth as Flaccus, the attendant, yanked sackcloth back into place, covering the horror. Flies immediately descended and started searching for an entry.

A dozen or so shrouded heaps were scattered over the floor of the chamber. The humid air was alive with flies, several of which crawled across Flaccus' bald, sweating scalp. He appeared to be oblivious to them.

"No one's identified him?" Anatolius asked.

Flaccus' extraordinarily wide, toothless mouth, curled into a gum-revealing grin almost as hideous as that of the faceless corpse. "You just seen him. What do you think?"

Anatolius had had reason to speak with the short, corpulent attendant before. This was where the urban watch brought unidentified bodies—a crop Constantinople produced in abundance—on the small chance that someone might claim them.

"What kind of man was he? Are there any indications?"

Flaccus' puckered his lips in thought. "He weren't carrying nothing. His tunic was coarse, unbleached cloth, but fairly new. Calloused hands, but only slightly. A man who worked but not one who done hard labor. A house servant, I'd say. His owner will come inquiring about a missing slave eventually but we'll have to bury him sooner than that for obvious reasons." He sniffed, not without a certain air of enjoyment, the way one might sniff at a fine, ripe cheese.

"If you find out anything more let me know. I'm really more interested in the fellow found naked in the embrace of Aphrodite."

"He's gone home, he has."

"And who was he?"

"Ah now, there's a deep, dark mystery for you. The Prefect himself come down with the widow. Ordered me out before she identified him."

"All the more reason for you to have ascertained his identity, Flaccus. Where there's secrecy there's usually gold to be had. People overhear conversations, they happen to see official reports, word gets around."

"Word might get around, but we're duty bound not to let it get out, if I may say so respectfully. As I'm sure you understand, working for the Prefect's office I am a representative of the law, sir, just as you are."

Anatolius watched a fly make its stately procession across the glistening dome of the representative of the law. "I realize there's murder involved and that it might involve a sensitive matter, Flaccus, but I'm not interested in any of that. My only interest is the widow."

Flaccus leered at him but said nothing.

"I'm not thinking of romance! I'm a lawyer. Widows usually need legal assistance. There will be an estate to handle, various formalities to attend to, that sort of thing. As a matter of professional courtesy, naturally you'll be entitled to a fee."

The grotesque grin stretched across Flaccus' face from pink ear to pink ear. "I understand now, sir. It hurts to think of unscrupulous legal cheats lying in wait for a poor young widow. I'd be doing a good turn sending her an honest man such as yourself."

Chapter Forty-two

"So the traitorous Lord Chamberlain is still plotting against me with the captain?" Justinian dropped the parchment onto his desk.

"Former Lord Chamberlain and former captain, Caesar," said Narses.

Justinian sat at his document littered desk in his study deep inside the imperial residence. He had barely emerged from this sanctuary for days.

"Are you sure it is authentic, Narses?"

The eunuch's bald head bobbed up and down, catching the fitful lamp light. The stark shadows gave him a devilish appearance. "I have had Felix's home under surveillance. We intercepted a private courier leaving."

Justinian pushed the parchment away from him with a forefinger. "Yet it appears to be written in a feminine hand."

"Dictated, naturally. And practically as soon as he returned home." There was no reason for Narses to say aloud that Justinian should have heeded his advice and kept Felix in the dungeons. The plain fact hung almost palpably between them in the airless room. It angered Narses that the whim of Theodora's sister outweighed his own good judgment. But what else would one expect?

"He asks John for assistance in his investigation of the theft of the Virgin's shroud."

"Do you believe that is all he wants assistance with? He also suggests John return to Constantinople in secret."

Justinian released a sigh akin to a death rattle. "I do not wish to distress Anastasia. I expected Felix's visit to the dungeons might dissuade her from this particular little adventure. If only Theodora could speak to her! Anastasia was always wilful and insists on going out in the city without attendants even though she knows how dangerous it is."

That was the least of her transgressions against good sense, Narses thought, while maintaining a respectful silence.

"Returning to the matter of the relic," Justinian went on. "We are in the grip of evil, Narses. Where will it lead? I must study the problem further and pray for guidance. You have my authority to take what steps you think best."

At least he was out of the dungeons, Felix thought as he approached the street where the Jingler had his lair. He ought to be grateful for that. Grateful that Anastasia had saved him.

Thinking about her assistance made him wince. He should have been able to save himself. He was on his guard now, determined not to be surprised again. He didn't trust Justinian's whims. The emperor's mood changed hour by hour. It worried him leaving Anastasia alone at his house even if she was the late empress' sister so she had promised to spend the afternoon safely at the palace.

Why did she remain by his side? A man she had known for a couple of weeks? Love? The sheer excitement? Theodora's sister wouldn't be harmed, in the end, would she? How much power did the younger sister of a deceased empress possess really? It might well benefit her to be married to a leading commander for Justinian's new supreme general, Germanus, supposing the emperor's cousin did replace Belisarius as everyone at the palace expected. A husband of high military position would enhance what standing she gained through wealth and family connections. If Germanus succeeded Justinian as emperor Felix might well take over Germanus' position. And who knows, Germanus might die…

Although only a short walk from the palace Felix was day dreaming about, the area where the Jingler lived might have been in a different world. A drifting miasma of smoke from the forges in the Copper Quarter dimmed the sun and the rickety tenements, blackened by years of soot, leaned tiredly against one another. Pedestrians trudged along as if employed in transporting the weight of the world. Even the feral dogs looked discouraged.

Felix told himself it was just his imagination.

He scratched idly at the back of his hand.

Those cursed red bumps. Was he falling ill? Well, a few spots on his hands and face were the least of his problems.

He went up the stairs to the Jingler's rooms. The stuffy air inside the building was hotter than outside. It smelled of boiled fish and onions and mildew. By the time he reached the top floor he was breathing hard and wishing he didn't need to inhale at all. His head had begun to throb. He touched the lump under his hair and winced.

Catching his breath and trying to put the pain out of his mind, he rapped at the Jingler's door. To his shock it swung open.

In the middle of the cluttered room, Julian was hanging by his neck from a rope. The lifeless body, twisting slowly, jingled a faint dirge.

Felix stared.

The pounding in his head was worse and there was a roaring in his ears.

He scanned the hallway. It was empty.

A fat fly buzzed out of the room straight at his face. He slapped it away.

There was no sound except for the awful jingling of Julian's useless charms and amulets. The poor man's eyes were bulging as if he was surprised all his magick had failed him.

The foul stench of old cooking was suddenly overpowering. Felix gagged and started down the stairs moving as quickly as possible without making a racket.

He guessed the Jingler hadn't been dead for long. His killers might be lying in wait.

He reached the street without incident, then thought of Anastasia. She was involved in this business almost as deeply as the Jingler had been. For all Felix knew whoever had killed the Jingler had gone straight to Felix's house. Murderers and those who gave them orders didn't necessarily care what one's position at court might be.

Felix broke into a run.

As he neared the archway that led to the entrance to his house he saw Anastasia walking along the colonnade.

He sprinted across the Mese and grabbed her arm, just as she was about to pass through the archway.

She spun around, breaking his grasp. Her eyes blazed with fury, her fists were clenched. Then she recognized her assailant and her snarl turned into a puzzled smile. "Felix! What do you think you're doing?"

He bent down. He saw that the dusting of ashes he had left under the archway—barely noticeable given the dirt and litter in the streets—had been disturbed, and not by only a single pair of feet.

"It looks like the whole Army of the East has been through here," he growled.

He led Anastasia around the corner, down a side street, and ventured a furtive glance down the alley leading past the back of his house. "There's a guard at the gate. Narses must be back."

"You didn't extend them a dinner invitation, I take it."

He laughed grimly. "What's more, the Jingler's dead. Hanged."

They moved away as quickly as possible without drawing attention.

"You're too closely involved with me," Felix said. "Whoever killed the Jingler might want you out of the way too. You have a safe place to stay. Go back to the palace and don't come out again. Better yet, leave the city. You've told me you prefer your country estates."

She took his face between her hands, pulled his head down, and kissed him. "Do you imagine I'd abandon you, foolish bear?" She pulled a ring off her finger and pressed it into his hand. "Go to the Hippodrome and ask for Maria, the widow of the bear-keeper."

Felix turned the ring over in his hand. It was a crude copper circle holding a bit of green cut glass. Hardly fit jewelry for an aristocrat.

"I've know Maria since childhood," Anastasia continued. "Theodora, Comita, and I grew up among circus performers. When you show her the ring, she'll know I sent you. She'll hide you."

"But for how long?"

"Long enough for me to speak to Justinian again."

"You don't really think you can keep persuading him I'm not guilty do you? Without proof?"

"There will be proof soon enough. The former Lord Chamberlain will surely return to assist you once he receives your letter."

"My letter?"

"The letter I urged you to write but you wouldn't. I've written it for you. Hurry up now. Get yourself to the Hippodrome. I have things to do."

She gave him a push, as if he were a balky child. He took several steps and when he turned to speak to her she was already walking briskly off in the opposite direction.

Chapter Forty-three

The primary objective in a battle was to outlive your opponent. At a given moment you might not be able to press the attack, might be forced into retreat, but as long as you stayed alive the fight could be renewed and won later. Which was why, Felix told himself, he had again taken orders from a woman.

That was the trouble with serving at the palace. You were always taking orders from women and perfumed courtiers and cowardly bureaucrats.

Moving like a sleepwalker, Felix shivered as he passed from the glaring sunlight into the shadowed concourse at the front of the Hippodrome. Not that the heat was much diminished inside, but rather he immediately saw in his imagination the hanged man by the spina, slowly twisting at the end of the rope, and then the man with the demolished face became the Jingler, his magickal charms chinking mournfully.

Then he saw Porphyrius the great charioteer looming above him, staring down, whip in hand.

This was not a mirage. It was the larger-than-life bronze statue that lorded it over the concourse.

His hand went to the chains around his neck. Were his own protective tokens as useless as the Jingler's had proved to be?

He opened his other hand to see the crude ring he carried, it being too small to fit his thick fingers. He was to entrust his safety to a bear-keeper's widow? A total stranger? A disreputable associate of circus performers?

"Look where you're going!" The man Felix had blundered into, a stable worker to judge by the stains on his tunic and his general air, gave him a shove.

The stable worker's companion made a disgusted noise. "He's not even looking where he's going. Must be demented!"

Yes, Felix thought, he was demented if he was thinking about consigning his life to this Maria. Already Narses might have grown tired of waiting and begun to detail men to scour the city. Knowing Felix's proclivity for racing, the Hippodrome would be the first place he'd search, wouldn't it?

Men ever fly for comfort to what they love.

What did he know about the woman who had sent him here anyway? Nothing, except she was Theodora's sister and she had lied to him about that by not revealing the relationship. Naturally he had taken her for an attendant to some great lady of the court. What else was she lying about? She was a friend of Antonina, the husband of Belisarius and thus the enemy of Felix's patron Germanus. His patron, provided that Felix would regain Germanus' good opinion after this crisis passed.

How did Felix know Antonina had not persuaded Anastasia to spy on him to discover what Germanus was planning? Was that the real explanation for her strange interest in the captain of the excubitors?

For all he knew Anastasia might be sending him into a trap.

Did he truly distrust her, or was his vanity inured at the prospect of her rescuing him once again?

But where could he go?

Germanus was angry with him. John was gone. Anatolius?

Anatolius had no real affection for Felix, did he? Besides, should a soldier throw himself on the mercy of a poet, even if the poet was masquerading as a lawyer?

But what had Anatolius advised him? To visit Isis, as he had in the old days although this time for a different purpose.

And why not? How long had Felix known Isis? Years. She would help.

While he was coming to a decision the armed men he had been fearing arrived.

Only his long ingrained military instincts saved him from detection. A murmur in the crowd, turning heads, caught his attention in time for him to dart through an archway leading to stairs just as the contingent tramped into the concourse, peering this way and that, swords at the ready.

They hadn't spotted him. He started down the stairs to the stables beneath the race track.

Five Blues climbed toward him.

Narses' men weren't the only ones Felix had to fear.

The husky, extravagantly attired young men didn't look familiar. There was no reason to think these particular faction members were being employed by Porphyrius. Holding his breath, Felix continued down. If it came to it he'd sooner be beaten to death inartfully by Blues than dragged to the palace by Narse's men to suffer at the skilled hands of Justinian's torturers.

The pack went by him without incident, although purposely refusing to give way, forcing him to plaster himself against the wall.

He continued on, as relieved as it was possible to be considering he had descended into the very lair of Porphyrius.

Felix took a zig-zag route through what amounted to a vast, underground horse farm, complete with stables, storerooms for equipment and feed, and offices for various levels of estate managers, before emerging at the far end of the Hippodrome. From there he worked his way through alleys and side streets to Isis' establishment not far from the Mese.

The courtyard in front of the building was open to the public. A few women, dressed in the chaste robes common to holy orders, were seeking relief from the heat in the shadow of the peristyle. Quite a contrast to the women Felix had seen here on visits in the past.

Although they were probably mostly the same women, Felix reflected, since Isis had simply changed the nature of her establishment. He knocked at the door and let his gaze wander over the women, looking for familiar faces, nothing else being uncovered under this new regime.

One, a stranger, appeared to be staring at him. A plump, painfully plain-faced woman dressed in what looked like her own shroud.

She smiled.

He gaped at the woman, removed a little weight, painted her face, and suddenly, shockingly, recognized the beautiful young prostitute with whom he had been enchanted before Isis' regrettable conversion.

"Well, what is it?" came a perturbed voice from the open doorway. Felix swiveled around to see a tall, stout woman holding what looked like a staff—the nearest Isis could find to a proper doorkeeper.

"I have business with madam—that is to say—your…uh… mistress."

Isis, it turned out, was not pleased to see him.

The plump former brothel owner, now clad like the other women Felix had seen in the plain white linen robes fit for the head of what she called her refuge, planted herself in front of her office door. He had hardly finished blurting out his story to her before she ordered him to leave, immediately.

"But Isis, I don't have anywhere to go. I've explained—"

"—far too much. Suspected of smuggling relics indeed. Only suspected? Would you have half the city after you, as you claim? I've changed my ways, Felix. You should have changed your own sinful ways long ago."

"I never thought I would hear the word 'sinful' from your lips, Isis. But what of this Christian charity I am told about?"

"Ah, Felix…you must realize I formed this refuge under the protection of Theodora and now she is gone, who can say what is store for us? I must think of my girls. If it were just me, it would be different."

"Yes, I understand. But—"

"I'm sorry, Felix. I will pray for you." She smiled sadly, as if she knew, despite her professed beliefs, how much good a prayer was likely to do.

He remembered the cross he was wearing and for an instant considered showing it to her and averring he had converted. Anastasia had advised him that faith could stand one in good stead, hadn't she? On the other hand should he risk offending either or both gods?

If he'd thought things through he would never have come here. He was still stuck in the past. He left. He had no desire to cause his old friend trouble, even if she was no longer his friend. But where could he go next? No one at the palace would welcome him. Would he have to rent a room?

Crossing the courtyard he stopped and glanced back at the women, lounging in the shade. He did not see the familiar yet unfamiliar face that had caught his eye. He walked over to the nearest of the women.

"Do you know where Lallis is? I'd like to speak to her."

The woman eyed him suspiciously. "Men are not allowed inside any further than the atrium."

"I don't need to speak to her inside. Out here would do. I'm an...an old acquaintance."

"I see." She looked him up and down and smiled coquettishly. Old habits die hard.

She left and soon returned with Lallis in tow. The woman—still a girl really—approached him almost shyly.

"I never thought I would see you again Felix. I hope you realize—"

"Don't worry, I am not here for any...um...well..."

"What is it then? Are you looking for spiritual comfort now?"

He stared at her without being able to tell whether she was joking. "No. I'm in trouble. I was hoping Isis would hide me but—"

"She is a stickler for the rules. But if you really need a place to stay I can help, for old times sake. We might renounce the pleasures of the flesh but we can never forget them."

She took hold of his wrist in a delicate hand. "Come with me. There's a back door where no one will see us go inside."

Chapter Forty-four

Dedi sat on a bench in the palace gardens next to a statue of Justinian and mournfully gnawed at a chicken leg stolen from the imperial kitchens while pondering what he might do next to revive Theodora. Dead, his former employer was of less use to him than the deceased chicken which was providing him a meal. For the time being he was managing to live like a rat in the walls but that couldn't go on forever.

He'd been thwarted in his initial attempt at the mausoleum, and a fine waste of frogs that had been! But what could you expect when demons were on the loose, interfering with rituals by raising the alarm? Clearly, his magick was powerful enough to achieve his aims. Look at how effectively he had controlled Tychon through the agency of the servant's stolen belt. A pity the result had availed him nothing. On the other hand, the obvious lesson was to obtain a memento of Theodora. Except that being dead she was no longer likely to invite him into her inner sanctum to entertain her.

Those had been the days! How Theodora had laughed when he presented the radish colored cat, a gray feline he explained as resembling a radish that had grown old and molded. And no matter how many times she had him tell the joke to her courtiers they laughed just as hard. Well, what choice did they have?"

His appetite suddenly gone, he tossed the remains of the chicken leg into the rose bush behind the bench. Two cats—neither radish colored, one as black as night and the other brown and white—appeared as from nowhere and commenced a vigorous discussion as to which would eat the remaining scraps.

It was at that instant he caught a glimpse through the rose bushes of Anastasia passing by.

Lady Bast sends a sign, he breathed, ignoring the marble Justinian's disapproving stare at such pagan blasphemy. For after all, was not Bast the protectoress of cats, women, and secrets? Surely his sacrifice of chicken to her sacred animals, unintentional though it may have been, would cause her to smile on his endeavor to use secret means to return the late empress to life?

Hadn't he been wondering how he might gain admittance to Theodora's private domain? Wouldn't something from her sister, a blood relative, serve to attract the interest of Theodora's wandering shade and be far easier to steal?

He jumped up and followed her, taking care to stay concealed behind shrubbery, hedges, and trees. Anastasia threaded her way across the palace grounds, passing under an arbor draped with grape vines, through a garden of Greek statuary set against a somber background of pine trees, past an artificial lake shaped as a map of the empire and inhabited by several swans that hissed as he crept by. Now and then she glanced back, as if suspicious she was being followed. Each time he crouched down, scarcely breathing, until she turned and resumed walking.

To his surprise, her destination was the Hormisdas Palace, where Theodora and Justinian had lived before he became emperor. More recently, Theodora had used the Hormisdas to shelter religious refugees adherent to the heretical sect toward which she was sympathetic. They were still in residence.

"By the gods of Egypt!" muttered Dedi, peering around the corner of a frescoed corridor at a raucous reception room buzzing with an assortment of ill-clad men attended by hordes of flies. The din was that of a public market, the smell a combination of refuse heap and public toilet. Apparently Theodora's protection extended from beyond the grave. At least until Justinian decided otherwise. He had always indulged his wife's whims but would he continue now that she was gone?

Dedi offered a prayer of thanksgiving for the crowds of humanity concealing him as he stalked after Anastasia. She had gone directly to the reception room, which still retained traces of its former frescoed glory despite the palace occupants' unfortunate habit of lighting fires on its floors, and from there up the wide, green marble stairs formerly guarded by excubitors and into a room with a gilt-decorated door a few steps to the right of the top of the staircase. After a short stay, she emerged and then trotted quickly downstairs, carrying a package.

Dedi kept her in sight as she exited via a polished oak door, passed through corridors, and out into a rapidly fading warm, gray twilight.

As twilight deepened into velvet darkness, Dedi kept close to Anastasia's heels.

She reached Antonina's house where she was bowed in through the front entrance. Dedi scrambled over the back wall of the grounds. Creeping along on all fours from sheltering bush to bush, ears strained for shouts of discovery, he finally rose to his knees and peeked through a window into a dimly lit room.

He was startled to see Anastasia and Antonina standing a hand's breadth away on the other side of the lattices. Had they spotted him?

They gave no indication they had. He heard Anastasia say, "I've brought something you might like to see."

What it was remained a mystery, because his gaze went past the two women and he gasped in mingled delight and fear.

His magick at the empress' tomb, though interrupted, had been powerful enough to work, after all.

Theodora was also in the room, staring out toward him.

DAY SEVEN

Chapter Forty-five

John was standing in front of the office of a shipping concern not far from the docks when he spotted the aristocratic stranger from the *Leviathan* prowling the opposite side of the square. The ship had finally reached a port where it could be properly repaired. He had wondered whether he and his family would be forbidden to go ashore. But apparently Captain Theon had not been instructed to insure that the former Lord Chamberlain was, in fact, delivered to his intended destination. Or else he considered there was no threat of John fleeing.

Then there was the further possibility that the mysterious passenger who was lodged in the captain's cabin had been dispatched to keep a watch on John.

John had seen the man loitering at a distance as soon as he and Cornelia and the servants had left the ship. Wherever John went, the stranger was there as well.

The square was surrounded by low buildings faced with stucco which might once have been painted blue. Beside the doorways competing shippers advertised their services in black and white mosaics depicting the type of sea and land transport available. Pedestrians and laden carts filled the square. Down a colonnaded side street could be seen inviting rows of shops.

Reluctantly, John had left Cornelia, Peter, and Hypatia scouring the marketplace. He supposed that whoever had attacked Peter on the *Leviathan* would not risk violence in public, and

Peter insisted on purchasing provisions—fruit, figs, olives—anything that didn't need cooking since Captain Theon had barred him from the makeshift kitchen in the cabin.

"He thinks I fell over the rail," Peter told John indignantly. "Says he's afraid I'll fall into the brazier and set the ship on fire!"

Hypatia, standing beside her husband, added, "Theon has no right to talk—a captain who sails his ship onto the rocks. He's only pretending to think Peter fell overboard. Peter's as spry as a young mountain goat."

John had seen Peter stumble on the stairs of the house in Constantinople. He was not so sure that the servant possessed the spryness of even a very old goat. He did, however, believe in Peter's unwavering honesty. If Peter said he'd been pushed overboard then he had.

It might actually have been John who was being attacked—or warned—through the attempted murder of one of his party. But about what? That he was not to think of returning to Constantinople? That no matter how far away John might be he would never be beyond the emperor's grasp?

He walked away from the shipping company, went along the alley hugging the building, and past the stables behind it. Beyond, a short street ran between three and four story brick tenements. John turned down the street, then ducked into the first doorway he came to.

He waited. Shortly thereafter a figure walked past his hiding place. The passenger from the *Leviathan*.

The young man paused just beyond where John had drawn back into the shadow, and appeared to study the street in front of him. Then he broke into a run.

When the young man turned the corner at the end of the street, John left his hiding place and returned the way he'd come.

There appeared to be nothing on the street to attract a one who didn't know the city. So, John deduced, the young aristocrat must indeed have been following him. With ill intent? To make sure he didn't abscond? Suspicious of what John might be doing—or persons he might be meeting?

John hurried back to the *Leviathan*. He had seen Captain Theon preparing to leave the ship to consult a carpenter about the rudder. With both Theon and his passenger ashore John would be able to investigate the cabin. He was convinced that Peter hadn't been banned from cooking there because of fear that he'd cause a fire.

The crew members left on board were all at the prow, throwing knucklebones and debating the best places ashore for drinking and women in anticipation of their watch ending. If they were keeping watch for anything, it was for Captain Theon's return. They paid no attention to John.

"Wait until we get to Crotone," said one of the men. "There's a temple to Priapus there!"

John did not wait to hear the ensuing argument about the veracity of the statement. He strolled along beside the rail keeping a prudent distance as he always did until he reached the stern. Peering around the edge of the cabin he waited until there was a rattling noise and the players' attention was fixed on the bones tumbling along the deck. Then he moved speedily to the cabin door.

Because the ship had been left in the care of a handful of trusted men, or from what seemed to be customary carelessness, the door was unlocked.

As soon as John stepped inside his boot landed on a stain on the plank floor. A reddish patch of half congealed liquid. Spilled wine to judge by the smell.

Beams of light lanced in through gaps in the closed shutters. The brazier sat against the back wall. Along one side lay rumpled bedding and dirty clothing. The walls were mostly concealed behind shelves cluttered with items ranging from small boxes and amphorae in wooden cradles to hammers and cooking utensils. On a wooden table stained navigational charts lay half-unrolled across dirty metal plates.

Apart from the absence of water it might have been the remains of a shipwreck on the bottom of the sea.

John stood still, listening carefully. He could hear the muted voices of the gamblers at the other end of the ship. No one came to the door. Apparently he had not been seen.

He went to work.

He searched the bedding and the chests, finding nothing but the personal items one might expect. Nor was there anything of interest on the table. He started to examine the shelves as silently as possible, shifting a box to get to the ceramic jars behind it and moving them aside to find nothing but a broken knife.

His shoulder banged a shelf. Something flashed down past him. He reached out reflexively and caught it before it smashed against the floor. It turned out to be an empty blue glass bottle.

He paused. Had he made any tell tale noise?

After a short while he resumed. He had broken out in a sweat. The hot, stifling air in the cabin lay against his skin with a pressure as palpable as that of water in a hot bath. Fat flies circled above the grease-encrusted brazier grill.

How long had he been searching?

At some point Captain Theon would be back, or the stranger would decide John had eluded him and return to the *Leviathan*.

He knelt down to examine the bottom shelves. He removed a sack. All it concealed was a large lidded pot.

This was what Peter had been doing before someone tried to push him overboard. Searching the shelves, in his case for cooking utensils. In John's case…

He pulled the pot forward and removed its lid.

Inside sat a small package, firmly secured and bearing a wax imperial seal.

He picked it up. It was light and felt soft.

Then there was a movement but before he could make sense of it or react a garrote was tightening around his neck.

For years he had lived at the Great Palace and dealt with intrigue more often than with weapons. But the reflexes from his fighting days as a young mercenary had never left him.

He reached back and ducked forward in the same motion and with a convulsive effort managed to pull his assailant half over his head.

A body crashed into a shelf sending down a torrent of wares.

John clambered to his feet. As he did so, the attacker leapt at him, driving him across the cabin.

John twisted away, trying to break his fall.

He saw the corner of the table coming up at him and then the world dissolved in a fiery flash.

Chapter Forty-six

Cornelia came into the atrium crying. She wore a plain, white robe like those worn by the girls at Isis' refuge. Felix noticed that, as was the case at the refuge, there were rows of close-set doors along the walls. Yet he knew this was John's house.

"My apologies," he said. "I realize I haven't visited recently. I suddenly remembered. How long has it been? Years?"

How could it have been years since he had seen his friend? Suddenly there was hollow feeling in his chest. How could he have forgotten him for so long?

Tears streamed down Cornelia's face as she approached. "It's too late," she said. "You waited too long. He's gone now."

"Gone?"

"It's your fault," she said.

"I don't understand."

"Read the letter." He realized she was holding a scroll out to him, although he had not noticed her holding it before.

He reached out and noticed then that the scroll was glistening red, dripping with blood.

Felix awoke with a start, lying on his back on the concrete floor of a cell. He stared up numbly, without comprehension as his dream dissipated in the shadows squirming across a low, whitewashed ceiling. It took him a little while to remember that the cell belonged to Isis' girl, Lallis. It was not locked or barred. Unlike the emperor's dungeons it was devoted to denial of the flesh rather than the flaying of it.

He had had no trouble denying his flesh since Lallis had ushered him in. She had not suggested they resume their former affair—or business relationship, if he were being honest. Perhaps she had actually changed her ways and not just her clothing.

And neither John nor Cornelia were in Constantinople any longer. They were both on a ship to Greece. And both were perfectly safe, weren't they?

Felix rolled onto his side.

Lallis was sitting on the bed, her legs drawn up under her chaste robe, staring at him as if he were some exotic creature. "I haven't had a man in here since Isis converted her establishment to a refuge."

"I should hope not."

She gazed down with big, brown, dog-like eyes. He had always thought her eyes expressive. Had it just been the way she'd outlined them in kohl?

"I thought I would like my new life. So much easier. But... I'm so bored."

"If you'd had the excitement I do, you'd wish you could be bored again." Though it seemed a wise thing to say, he wasn't so certain it was true. Anastasia seemed to revel in excitement. Was that why she was involved with Felix, because she was so bored?

Lallis' thin lips tightened into an unattractive pout. "It's all right for Mother Isis but she's practically dead. When she had some life in her, she had a lively time of it. How many prayers can a girl say? How many hymns can a girl sing?"

She bent suddenly and came at him with a kiss. He must have misjudged. She hadn't changed much at all. He moved his head and she got a mouthful of beard. He put his hands on her shoulders and held her away from him, uncomfortably aware of her warmth.

"Oh, Felix, don't you remember?"

"I recall what you charged."

She drew away. Her mouth trembled.

"I'm sorry," Felix said. "Yes, yes, it was more than that. Certainly. But we can't resume. It's impossible."

"Another woman!"

"No. Or, rather…well, it makes no difference. You have a good, secure life here. One that doesn't include lovers." He didn't feel capable of arguing.

Lallis looked at her lap and smoothed down the robe which had ridden up her legs. "I suppose you're right."

"And I know your life isn't all prayers and hymns, Lallis. Isis still has business interests. She owns shops. Surely you work outside this place frequently?"

"I know things aren't the same, Felix. But since you're here and no one knows, it wouldn't hurt, would it?"

"But it probably would hurt, Lallis. Some way or another it always ends up hurting. As it is, it'll be difficult enough if I'm found with you. If I cause you trouble…" He shook his head wearily. "I would never have imagined Isis would turn me away. She's a different woman."

"I know why she threw you out."

"Obviously, because she's a good Christian now."

"It's not that. It's because of that relic you were telling her about."

"You were eavesdropping?"

"I overheard. You told her you were being hunted by men smuggling relics. So needless to say she had to get rid of you as fast as possible."

"Why?"

"Because she's part of it! She's helping the smugglers."

Felix stared at the girl. "Not Isis! She wouldn't do that!"

"Selling relics is part of the way she supports the refuge. If you don't believe me, I'll show you. This is the day they're delivered, which is probably why she turned you away at once. She couldn't risk you staying even a single night in case of what you might see or hear, and later reveal if you were caught and questioned. The messenger arrives just before dawn."

She rose, opened the door a crack, and looked up and down the hallway. "It's all right," she whispered. "Isis doesn't require us to do early morning devotions, thank the Lord."

She motioned for him to follow. The hallway was empty, illuminated by a lamp on a wooden table at one end. Lallis crept silently in the opposite direction, into deepening darkness. Felix tip-toed nervously behind, past the closed doors lining the walls. Gone from beside them were the lewd mosaic plaques illustrating the pleasures available within. He thought of the rows of stalls beneath the Hippodrome. Each door here opened onto a bare, utilitarian box like Lallis' cell, equally suited to serving man or God.

At the end of the hall she stopped, put a finger to her lips, and waved him forward to peer around the corner.

He was looking down another long gloomy hallway. Felix recognized the door at the end as the back entrance which in the old days had been used by tradesmen and discreet high court officials. An orange light spilled feebly into the hallway then grew in intensity until Isis came into view, holding a clay lamp. She set the lamp in the niche beside the door, then slid back the bolt.

Felix felt a pang of guilt to be spying on his old friend.

But then, she'd coldly refused to help him, hadn't she?

And Lallis claimed...

But how could he believe that Isis was smuggling relics?

Isis pulled the door open. A figure stood in the darkness outside. No words were exchanged. The caller handed Isis a small sack. She opened the top and looked in. Apparently satisfied, she closed the sack. Coins flashed in the lamp light.

Then from down the hall came a shriek. "Lallis has a man with her!"

Felix heard doors opening and more loud comments from Isis' girls.

Isis heard the racket too and whirled around. The sack slipped from her grasp and hit the floor. Bones rattled out and skittered into the walls, as if invisible hands were playing knucklebones.

"Mithra! Just my luck!" cursed Felix, and ran after the caller.

Chapter Forty-seven

Fortuna had not abandoned Felix entirely. He careened past Isis who was startled into immobility. Bones crunched under his feet, then he flung himself out the door.

Isis' mysterious caller was still within sight. The man sauntered along, showing no sign of concern. Apparently he had not heard the commotion he had left in his wake.

Perhaps he was hard of hearing. Keeping his distance to remain undetected, Felix could tell he was a man of late middle age, sturdy. There was something familiar about him.

When the man passed through a pool of torch light in front of a closed shop, Felix recognized him—the lamp keeper he and John had interviewed at the Church of the Holy Apostles the morning after the theft of the Virgin's shroud. What was his name? Peteiros? He claimed to have seen demons making off with a sacred relic, yet hadn't he just delivered a bag of bones to Isis?

An ugly swarm of possibilities began to buzz around in Felix's head.

As the sun rose, light spilled into the streets. The squeaking and banging of metal grates being raised as shops opened for the day reverberated beneath cool shaded colonnades. Peteiros, if indeed Felix had identified him correctly, strolled along the Mese. Naturally, he would take his time, now he had nothing to hide. He carried only the coins Isis had handed over.

To be delivered to whom?

The answer seemed obvious.

But perhaps Peteiros wasn't going to the church. He might have taken the furtive job to make extra money. He could even be employed by Porphyrius. Peteiros would make an inconspicuous courier. Just as an aristocrat would not appear out of place arriving at the house of the excubitor captain, so a church worker would raise no eyebrows by going to the door of a refuge.

However, to Felix's dismay, at the spot where the Mese forked, Peteiros took the northern branch and started to climb the hill atop which sat the Church of the Holy Apostles.

All the way there Felix hoped Peteiros would turn from his route. He held his breath in expectation every time they approached a side street, but the carer of holy lamps kept straight along, dragging Felix's hopes lower and lower, until he finally entered the grounds of the church and vanished through its entrance.

Felix cursed silently. Already he was opposed by the emperor and a wealthy and famous charioteer. Now it seemed he had to worry about the priest of one of the city's largest churches. Who would it be next? The Patriarch?

How could he have been so stupid? Who had unrestricted access to the shroud except Basilius? He bore the responsibility for its security. All that nonsense about demons must have been concocted between the priest and Peteiros.

If he—or John—had given the matter thought Basilius could have been confronted immediately and Felix would never have run afoul of Justinian and Porphyrius. And Julian would still be alive.

Felix's spirits had been sagging the closer they got to the church, but as he went up the steps his despair turned to anger.

A deacon took one look at his grim face and directed him to Basilius. The priest was taking a morning walk through the grounds behind the church. He stopped in front of Theodora's mausoleum at Felix's approach and when he saw Felix's expression he blurted out, "Bad news? Is it the shroud? Please, Lord, let it be safe."

"You should be able to me whether the relic is safe or not. First explain the transaction at Isis' refuge this morning. Then tell me what you did with the missing relic. And no lies this time!"

"You have no right to speak—"

"A man with his life hanging by a thread has the right to demand information from anyone to save himself."

Basilius was making little gestures with his hands, pleading for Felix to be quieter. "You can't think I had anything to do with stealing the shroud?"

"I can, I have reason to think it, and I do."

"But you saw me after I consulted with the emperor about the theft."

"A good smokescreen. You knew the shroud was going to reside here for a while after Theodora's funeral. So you decided to take advantage of the chance. It was you who arranged to have it protected so inadequately. On purpose, I believe."

"That's not true."

"I know you've been selling relics to Isis. Do you expect me to believe it's a coincidence the most valuable relic in your church has been stolen?"

Basilius looked around nervously. There was no one nearby. "Isis? Who is Isis? Wait. Do you mean Theodora's model prostitute? The one who supposedly changed her house to a refuge?"

Felix's fists clenched. He forced himself not to grab the little cleric by the front of his robes and shake the truth out of him. "You know Isis well enough to have had your man Peteiros deliver a sack of relics, old bones to be precise. I observed the transaction myself and followed him back here."

Basilius seemed stunned. "This is true?"

"Why are you questioning me?" Felix thundered. "You're the one who's lying!"

The priest suddenly strode in the direction of the mausoleum. For an instant Felix thought he was running away, but instead he called out. "Timothy!"

The elderly doorkeeper came hobbling out, leaning on his stick and blinking. No doubt he had been sleeping, Felix thought. Or pretending to sleep. Was he involved too, with his frogs and amulets and implausible stories of apes and demons?

"Timothy, go and bring Peteiros. Tell him there's a man here making inquiries about his...um...activities. A man from the palace tell him, so he will know how to...uh...conduct himself."

The ancient fellow gave Felix a suspicious look and shuffled off. He took a very long time in returning with Peteiros. Time that Felix and the priest passed in an increasingly awkward silence. An unseen bird sang in a tree. If only the songs of those Felix interrogated were as simple and guileless at that bird's, he mused.

By the time Peteiros finally arrived Basilius had composed himself. He related in sharp tones what Felix had told him.

Peteiros was stricken. "Lord forgive me!" He wailed, dropping to the ground and groveling at the priest's feet in a display of debasement that Theodora would have admired.

Basilius took hold of the back of the man's tunic and yanked with surprising strength, urging him back to his feet.

Peteiros complied and stood swaying and moaning.

"It's true, then?" Basilius said. Felix would never have believed the little priest's tones could be so cold. "You've been pilfering holy relics and selling them to a...a...prostitute?"

"No! No, sir. Only a few small, useless things."

"It was quite a collection of bones you brought to Isis this morning," Felix put in.

"They were the foot bones of a donkey," was the reply.

Felix recalled one of the stories Anastasia had insisted he learn. "You mean the beast Jesus rode into Jerusalem?"

"Oh no, sir. It couldn't have been. There was still skin and fur attached until I-"

"You're talking about the donkey bones the old cart driver tried to pass off on us last week, aren't you?" Basilius said. "A dreadful case. The poor fellow was starving, without a beast to pull his cart. He must have prayed he wouldn't outlive his donkey." He turned to address Felix. "I gave him a few coins and sent him away, then I ordered the bones placed into our store room with all the other similar items. We receive an endless stream of blatantly fraudulent relics, for one reason or another. I had no idea—"

"Why should I believe you?"

"Because I'm telling you the truth."

Felix smiled wearily. "And you, Peteiros why shouldn't I hand you over to the authorities for stealing the Virgin's shroud? Because you're telling the truth too? You've admitted you were selling relics."

"Not relics, sir. Donkey bones."

Basilius broke in. "Why, Peteiros? How could you do such a thing?"

"But I was only tidying up a bit, wasn't I? And Mada and I, we hoped we might save enough to buy a bit of land for a farm."

"The relic with which I am concerned would be worth more than a farm," Felix pointed out.

Peteiros was almost in tears. "I'd never think of such a blasphemous thing, sir. My soul would burn. Those demons I saw would fall upon me and carry me off under the earth, into the eternal fires."

"Pray that you are not destined for the flames for your perfidy," Basilius told him. "How did you come to know such a woman as this Isis?"

Peteiros swallowed and licked his lips. "During the winter, when we needed to replace lamps and you wished me to find the least expensive…It was from one of the shops run by the refuge that I got the best bargains."

Felix saw Basilius' eyes widen slightly. He could imagine the priest thinking, in horror, "I have been walking in the light from a whore's lamps all this time!"

What Basilius said was, "You may go now, Peteiros. We shall speak about your future later."

Felix allowed the man to creep away. He didn't believe his story, nor did he believe Basilius was ignorant of his employee's activities. Hadn't he as much as instructed Timothy to warn Peteiros to conduct himself appropriately? Clearly the two had a story worked out between them in case of need. And Peteiros wasn't likely to deviate from it in front of his employer. Nor was Basilius likely to confess to any crimes, except perhaps to his god or Justinian's torturers, and Felix was trying to avoid the latter himself.

He wheeled and stalked off without a word.

Chapter Forty-eight

Isis flushed with anger. "I know nothing about the theft of this relic you're looking for. If I did know anything, I'd tell you. For a small donation for my girls' welfare, of course."

"Of course," Felix agreed. They were sitting on a cushioned couch in her office, her inner sanctum, not as elaborately furnished as in the past, but still retaining memories of luxury. He had grown fond of this room in the days when he had happier business to conduct. He was fond of Isis as well. He regretted having to pressure his old friend. Her color looked unhealthy. But what could he do? She was dealing in relics. She had managed to get herself tangled up in the whole mess. "You need to tell me about your recent visitor now. I may not be able to talk with you again."

Felix had returned to the refuge by back streets, uncomfortably aware that by now Narses would be probing every corner of the city for him, a vulture seeking the last, tender organ inside a stripped carcass. As he and Isis spoke, he half-listened for the imperious pounding on the door that would tell him he was discovered by a predatory beak.

She stared at him with a stony expression. "I don't touch true relics, Felix. My girls do sell mementoes. Yes, we realize that some may not be what they should be. We might even create a few in this house. The church owns many frauds. I am told there are four of Peter's fishing nets in one particular church, which seems a great many for a poor man, and so many leg bones attributed to Paul that he must have been a spider. Where is the harm if the buyer is convinced what he has purchased is what he believes it to be? His faith makes it holy. And is it not faith by which we are saved?"

"I'd say it is faith by which we are lost, when we put it in lies and liars, Isis. Peteiros claims he was the only one dealing in these relics, stealing them from under the priest's nose. Frankly I have no faith in that statement."

Isis glowered at him. "He told me he had sought me out on behalf of Basilius. Do you think I would have dealt with him otherwise? And he deals with me because he realizes I can exercise discretion, thanks to my previous calling."

"Yet Basilius denied any involvement. Are you certain Peteiros comes here under his orders?"

"Certainly. Have I ever lied to you?"

That was the question, wasn't it? How did Felix know if she, or anyone else for that matter, was lying to him?

"But could it be that Peteiros was lying to you about the priest being involved to convince you to cooperate? Have you ever dealt with Basilius in person?"

Isis looked cross. "No, but it isn't surprising. He wouldn't want to be seen with me."

"Can you swear to me you know nothing about the missing relic, Isis? All I care about is getting it back. If you can help me it would be best for you to do so. The emperor is sure to find out eventually who was involved, unless I can hand it over to him first."

"I understand, Felix, but I know nothing about this shroud." Isis' tone turned wistful. "If I actually had the such a valuable relic, do you suppose I would still be here? I know my business. I would have already sold it to the highest bidder, appointed a successor to run my refuge, and been on my way back to Egypt to live in luxury the rest of my life."

"Supposing the relic was not authentic, you mean? You just told me you don't deal in authentic relics. You don't think it is the actual shroud of the Virgin?"

"Fortunately I have no reason to give it any thought."

"I wish I could say the same, Isis. Your mentioning Egypt reminds me that there was that scarab left on Theodora's tomb the night of the robbery."

Isis made a gesture of contempt. "I am not the only person from Egypt living in the city. Besides that what about those who collect such interesting artifacts?"

"That's all very well, Isis, but—"

"Have some wine, Felix. You look overheated. You can think things out more clearly if you cool down."

Felix pushed up his sleeves and reached for the cup she offered. Isis leaned forward, then sat back and stared. The ruddy color drained from her face as quickly as the sunset blush fades from a marble statue.

"May the gods protect you, Felix! Those patches on your skin…I saw them in Egypt." She leapt off the couch and backed away. "You must leave immediately!"

He stood. "What is it?"

She cringed and backed further away. Her features trembled and twisted into an expression of horror and revulsion. "I'll have to engage a doctor to examine everyone in the house tomorrow. My girls! You've killed them! You've brought leprosy into my refuge!"

Chapter Forty-nine

Gordia, widow of Martinus, occupied what passed for a modest dwelling amongst the aristocrats of Constantinople, a domed, brick, two story house faced with polished granite, at the top of the hill north of the Great Palace. The dead courier's wife met Anatolius on a terrace from which could be seen the Golden Horn to the north and to the north east the Marmara where it met the Bosporos.

She had delayed their meeting but Anatolius had persisted. She was in her late twenties, one of the pretty, well-born women whose sole purpose seemed to be to decorate the home of a similarly well-born man. Anatolius knew from experience all of the carefully painted little statuettes were far more complicated than they seemed when one got to know them better, and also that it was not easy, and ultimately not desirable, to get to know them better.

"How can you help me?" Gordia asked. "Martinus is dead."

"But whoever killed him is at large. Surely you want him brought to justice?"

"It would not bring any comfort, if that's what you are implying."

Anatolius stared out over the sparkling waters where ships lay scattered like a child's abandoned toys. She had agreed to see him but had not offered a cup of wine, or even a seat. "You would not wish an innocent man executed for a murder he didn't commit, would you?"

"Martinus was executed for no reason at all."

He explained to her as vaguely as possible, without naming names, how her knowledge of her late husband's activities might provide vital clues which would prevent more innocent blood being spilled.

"But you see, I knew nothing about his activities."

"You knew he was visiting the captain of the excubitors from the note he left. Didn't that seem unusual to you?"

Gordia looked at him, the eyes in her blandly painted features wells of infinite weariness. "Martinus gambled. He was very deeply in debt. Everyone at court knows the captain is a gambler. I supposed it had something to do with that." Her cheekbones flushed with sudden anger. "No doubt you will tell me I should have expected it. That's what you get when your husband becomes involved with a bad element. That's what most of my friends have told me!"

"If we were all murdered for our weaknesses there would be no one left in the city."

"You do have a silver tongue, don't you? I apologize for not offering you any hospitality. I do not have a proper staff at present. Our head servant vanished a few days before…well…and I thought I had too much to deal with when that happened."

"Could there be a connection between this vanished servant and your husband's death? Did you report the servant missing?"

"Certainly not. I believe it was a case of Martinus not paying him his wages on time. It was always happening. Rather than paying the servants he'd bet on the races. It is not the sort of matter I would wish known." She paused. "I don't want you to think Martinus was a bad man. It's true he ran with the Blues when he was a boy and he came before the magistrates more than once because of it. He had put all that behind him and he would have put the gambling behind him too if he'd had the chance."

Anatolius was thinking rapidly.

Was Martinus' missing servant somehow also involved? Martinus had been in the same straits as Felix, who had admitted his financial problems led to his recruitment into the affair. Had that been the case with Martinus, who had once been a Blue and was now unable to refuse cooperating in the thefts for fear of consequences? Porphyrius had used Blues to administer the beating Felix had received. If Porphyrius was organizing thefts of relics, or even if he were merely involved, the situation began to look very like a web with the old charioteer squatting in the center. Or rather lurking unseen at one side, as spiders often do, ready to scuttle out when there was prey to claim.

"You're silent," Gordia snapped. "Have I helped you in any way or have you deepened my misery for no reason?"

"This is valuable information," Anatolius told her. He would need to get in touch with Felix and pass it on to him. "I will not inconvenience you further."

"Thank you. I understand you are a lawyer. There are things that need to be taken care of with regard to my late husband's estate. If you would be so good as to return next week…"

Chapter Fifty

Following Isis' pronouncement of doom Felix fled blindly out into the streets.

Leprosy! Already it had been neglected for…how long had it been since he'd noticed the spots on his face and hands?

He was sure he had washed himself sufficiently after his encounter with the leprous beggar in the alleyway but obviously he hadn't. Now the filthy disease was eating away at him. He was rotting like a corpse. That's what happened to lepers, wasn't it? He would end his days a pariah, alive but as good as dead.

What did he care if he was apprehended wandering about? Before it came to that he'd give himself up to Justinian. Better an axe or a noose end his suffering quickly. The imperial torturers wouldn't dare to work on a leper, would they?

He prayed to Mithra and several other gods he had learned about during his days in Constantinople, including—at the sight of a feral cat crossing his path—the Egyptian deity Bast.

"Please let this be a nightmare," he prayed. "Let me wake up!"

Every god answered his prayer. And every answer was the same. No.

Then he found himself in front of a church.

From the open doors came the sweet smell of incense.

He entered and walked through diffused shafts of light falling through the tall windows.

Tears ran down his cheeks and into his beard. The incense must be irritating them.

He pulled his cross out and pressed it to his lips, as he had seen Christians do, and fell to his knees and prayed to Anastasia's god.

His head cleared. The miasma of unreality which had surrounded him began to evaporate. He was aware of other worshipers kneeling and murmuring on either side of him and suddenly he flushed with humiliation.

What was he doing? A military man on his knees, blubbering?

He felt a hand on his shoulder.

He tensed, turned, expecting to see one of Narse's guards. Instead an elderly priest looked down at him.

"You are in distress, my son."

Felix nodded.

"What troubles you? I will add my prayers to your own."

Felix displayed the back of a spotted hand. "You shouldn't touch me. I am unclean."

The priest scowled and then smiled benignly. "Those are not the marks of a leper."

"But I was told—"

"I have ministered to enough poor souls in my lifetime to know a leper when I see one."

Felix stood up, still clutching his cross. It felt hot in his big fist.

"Do not look so astonished," the priest told him. "I have not healed you. Thank the Lord that you do not have leprosy."

Felix went out into the sunlight. How long had he been roaming the city out of his wits with horror? He was lucky Narse's men hadn't found him.

Yes, lucky. Thanks be to Fortuna.

Felix sat in the shadows in the back of a dingy and dimly lit tavern nursing a single cup of wine, deciding where to go next. He examined the spots on his hand. Was it true that he didn't have leprosy? It would be the first thing that had gone right in the past week.

He had conflicting diagnoses from a former prostitute and a priest. Who should he believe? Doubtless the priest had seen more prostitutes than Isis. In the stories Anastasia insisted he read, Jesus had forever been healing lepers.

Could Isis have been correct? Might the Christian god have healed Felix there in the church?

No, the blotches looked no different than they had when Isis had become hysterical over them.

It seemed out of character. But so was her conversion to Christianity. Well, she was getting old. Felix was getting old. He reached inside his tunic and pulled out the cross, intending to tear it off and toss it away. Then he remembered Anastasia had given it to him and refrained.

Things had been simpler when he was young. They had been better. He would gladly give up his high position to be Emperor Justin's bodyguard again.

Justin, now there was a man. He walked through the gates of Constantinople with dirt under his fingernails, a peasant farmer, and he died an emperor.

Over the years it had passed through Felix's mind that, if circumstances allowed, he might follow in Justin's path. But he was loyal to Justinian—weak and unwarlike as the current emperor was—and time went by so quickly. Anastasia had made him feel like a youth again. She had rekindled what he had thought were the dead embers of his ambitions.

Purposefully?

She had denied any desire to use Felix but why else would Theodora's sister have entangled herself with him?

What bothered him most was how she had kept her relationship to the late empress a secret. No matter her excuses, could he really trust her, knowing she had deceived him from the start?

He wished he could, but at the palace wishful thinking could get you killed.

In his dark corner Felix tensed as he saw a large youth sporting the hairstyle of a Blue enter the tavern. After a moment or two, when the youth gave no indication he was there for anything but a drink, Felix relaxed. He had to fear every Blue he saw, and every guard and member of the urban watch, not to mention whoever Narses and Porphyrius, and perhaps others besides, had hired to work incognito.

Maybe he had even to fear donkeys, if Anastasia was right and his donkey might betray him.

He remembered her coming into the bath, telling him about Antonina's servant, who saw demons and had thrown himself over the sea wall. He had wondered vaguely at the time if the man could have had some connection with the demons who had stolen the holy shroud. And if Antonina could have had some interest in relics.

Anastasia knew her. Might Anastasia also have some interest in relics?

But Anastasia could hardly be working with Antonina. Clearly Anastasia hoped that Germanus would supplant Antonina's Belisarius as Justinian's chief general. She was counting on Felix being given a command by Germanus.

And maybe counting on him being placed a step away from the throne.

Or so he imagined.

But then again, Anastasia, as Antonina's friend, might have agreed to spy on Felix in hopes of discovering what Germanus was planning.

More than one strand of this sticky web in which Felix found himself struggling led back to Antonina. He needed to talk to her. But how could he? Especially considering their past history, brief as that history had been.

He took another sip of his wine. The blemishes on the back of his hand which had so frightened him caught his attention.

Ah. There was his answer.

Chapter Fifty-one

"Did Anastasia send you to me, Felix?" Antonina smiled coldly. "And if so, why?"

"She didn't," Felix said, "but I know you are a friend of hers and she wanted to ask you for a cure for my, er, skin problem... but, after all, a man must make his own decisions about these things. So I said I would think about it, and I only just decided to, um, well...do you have anything suitable?"

Now that he was face-to-face with the woman, Felix had no idea how he was going to question her.

Antonina laughed. "Oh, Felix, you're trying to pretend you have forgotten our little tryst in the Hall of Nineteen Couches, aren't you?"

Felix looked at the floor and said nothing. His broad frame was perched on a delicate gilded chair, suited to the aristocratic ladies Antonina normally entertained.

She bent, gave his beard a playful tug and whispered in his ear. "Surely you haven't forgotten? I would be insulted if you had. But it will remain our little secret."

Her warm breath was as welcome to him as a fiery gust from the gates of Hell. "I haven't come here to resume our...uh...I'm just following Anastasia's advice. I take it she's a very good friend of yours."

"You're here to interrogate me about your lady love then? Not very gallant."

"No, certainly not. I wouldn't presume to pry. It's this hand, as I told you."

He held it up for her inspection.

"These little red patches? That's what worries you?"

He nodded and drew his hand away quickly. "I've been told it's serious."

Antonina straightened. "I have a remedy for any complaint of the skin." She went out of the room.

Felix tried to think. She was already suspicious. And why not? He had no real business showing up here. He was surprised, and unnerved that she had even recalled their encounter so many years, and so many liaisons, ago.

Antonina returned with an alabaster pot shaped as a miniature head of a woman whose hair was dressed in the classical Greek style.

Felix shuddered as she plucked off the head. The action reminded him too much of possibilities awaiting him. The contents of the pot proved to be a greasy ointment.

"The pot is valuable enough," Antonina remarked, "but the ointment more valuable still. It's made from the juice of Jove's beard mixed with rendered fat, so use it quickly before its virtues are dispersed. Many court ladies have employed it for skin eruptions, but I do believe you're the first military man." Giving him a crooked smile, she handed the pot to Felix.

He set it on his knees and clumsily smeared part of the contents on his lumpy patches. It made his skin tingle unpleasantly.

"I'll give you more to take with you but don't let Anastasia see it or she will be jealous," Antonina remarked. "I know about the difficulty in which you find yourself, Felix. Aside from your blemishes, that is. My advice is to leave the city immediately so you won't risk compromising Anastasia. And when I say immediately, I mean as soon as you have had a cup of wine."

"Leave the city? On foot? I don't think—"

"I shall give you a horse for Anastasia's sake. You can always go to Greece and take shelter with the former Lord Chamberlain.

Stay here until evening. Darkness will cover your shall we say strategic retreat?"

Cowardly retreat, Felix thought. Did he have a choice? And why should she care if he stayed or fled, unless she were involved in the affair in some way?

It again occurred to him that Anastasia might be working with the enemies of Germanus, spying on Felix, a key ally of Germanus. Did he dare trust Anastasia any longer? How he could he possibly sort it out, while pursued by both the emperor and Porphyrius? Maybe he should take Antonina's offer, escape while he still could.

He immediately chided himself. He had too much pride to run away and it was unworthy of him to mistrust Anastasia. What reason had she ever given him to doubt her?

A few streets away Anastasia rode behind the closed curtains of one of the less gaudy imperial carriages, unaware she was accompanied by Dedi, who, clinging to the back of the conveyance, prayed he would neither fall off nor be discovered.

Passersby glanced with curiosity as the carriage clattered past, wondering what elevated personage might be concealed and for what reason an aristocrat or high official was out and about in the city. And if there was a strange, little man hanging onto the back of the carriage, what business was it of theirs? The wealthy and powerful were often given to peculiar whims. On the other hand, if the twisted little creature was unknown to the passenger and up to no good…well, what business was it of theirs?

Dedi's perch was less than salubrious. He was coated with dust churned up by the hooves of the horses' and the carriage wheels. It gave his shriveled face a mummy-like appearance. He suppressed a cough, felt grit in his mouth, and spit mud.

Nevertheless, further from the palace he would have a better chance of escaping with whatever he managed to pilfer from her.

He needed a token from her to control her sister.

Although he had managed to recall Theodora she had chosen to fly to Antonina rather than subject herself to Dedi's will. He had no way of knowing why. As soon as he glimpsed the empress through the window Dedi had ducked away to avoid detection. Antonina was well-versed in magick herself and might have detected his presence. No doubt she intended to employ Theodora's reanimated shade for her own purposes.

The carriage hit a rut and the jolt nearly threw Dedi into the street. He tightened his grip. Darkness had fallen. He could see they were approaching the Church of the Holy Apostles because of the light pouring from its windows. The carriage came to a halt behind the building.

How odd. Why would Anastasia be carrying a package to the church?

Sticking his head around the side of the carriage he recognized the priest, Basilius, standing in the grounds, apparently waiting. When Anastasia alighted from the carriage he came over to greet her.

"You have brought me something, as you promised?" Dedi heard Basilius ask.

The carriage had drawn up in front of Theodora's mausoleum. Dedi dropped quietly to the ground and crept underneath the carriage, out of sight of the driver but nearer to where Anastasia stood with Basilius.

Anastasia presented the package to the priest. "A small offering for the church. A chalice specially blessed by certain clergy in whom Theodora took a particular interest."

Basilius looked at the package suspiciously. "You don't mean those heretics of hers?"

"Surely you would not decline a tribute to the late empress?"

"No. Certainly not." He took the package gingerly as if it were filthy.

Dedi was studying Anastasia carefully. His mouth widened in a gleeful grin. Tonight was one of particular good fortune, for Anastasia was wearing a necklace of garnets and silver he knew had once belonged to Theodora, and indeed had been a favorite of hers.

He sprang from beneath the carriage, grabbed the necklace, snapped its chain, and was gone into the night before either Anastasia or Basilius could do more than gasp in surprise and horror.

Chapter Fifty-two

Felix lay on a red-upholstered couch pinned down by the dark-eyed glare of a life-sized portrait of the late empress. He hadn't meant to fall asleep while waiting for evening. In fact, he had intended to use Antonina's invitation to linger to devise some method of questioning her further. But exhaustion had over-taken him. Unless…his gaze fell on his empty wine cup. Unless Antonina had given him something to help him sleep.

He felt his chest tighten and his heart beat faster. Though he had looked away he could sense the painted empress staring at him. Theodora's image brought back the same wary reactions that her physical presence had caused. The aura of menace that had accompanied her alive seemed to emanate from the colored plaster. In reality the aura only existed in Felix's mind and in the minds of many at the palace and in the city. Thus the empress lived on in the fear she had struck into those who had known her. Felix knew that very well, and yet…

He jumped at the touch of a hand on his shoulder.

"You are awake." Antonina perched on the edge of the couch. "I gave you a little potion to help you relax. You've slept a long time. It will be dawn soon."

How could he have been so stupid as to drink anything Antonina had offered him? Then again, he had used the potions and ointments Anastasia had obtained from her friend. Maybe Antonina had only wanted to help him. He didn't remember. That frightened him.

He sat up. The garden visible through the window was brightly lit. But no, that was also a painting.

"Why did you come here, Felix?"

He looked down at his hands, glistening in places with ointment. "I explained…"

"You don't think I believe you dared to come here because you had some eruptions on your skin, do you?"

"Some eruptions? Is that what you call leprosy?"

Antonina laughed unpleasantly. "Leprosy? Do you think I'm a fool?"

"I was told it was leprosy."

"By who? A fool?"

"No." Felix had never thought of Isis as a fool. He had concluded she had been mistaken because she was upset, or as a result of age. Or had she intended to get rid of Felix quickly by frightening him?

"You did hope to interrogate me, didn't you?" Antonina said.

"What would I want to interrogate you about?"

"Really, Felix. Can't you do better than that?" She looked fixedly at him. Her blue eyes resembled shining cutting tools, torture instruments ready to slice him wide open and lay bare every vein and sinew of any secret he might have inside his body.

"I did wonder about your servant, Tychon. Anastasia told me the poor fellow threw himself over the sea wall. My own head servant has just vanished, you see."

Her next remark caught him by surprise. "How much do you know about the theft of the Virgin's shroud, Felix?"

He tried not to look startled. Did she realize that was what had brought him here? And did that imply she had a connection to the matter? "What do you mean? Why do you want to know?"

Antonina smiled. "Don't look so shocked. Anastasia told me about your investigation. Naturally I am interested. Her sister's tomb, my dear friend's tomb, was desecrated." She nodded in the direction of the painted Theodora. Felix had an irrational fear that the dead empress would respond. However, she remained silent and motionless. Her implacable gaze did not waver.

"It was only an amulet and a few frogs," Felix said. "A lot of frogs, I admit."

"And there were demons involved?"

"If Anastasia told you all about it, why ask me?"

"She didn't say whether you knew anything further about the demons, where they might have come from."

"From the underworld, I imagine. Well, that's why I asked about Tychon. Anastasia told me that according to witnesses he cried out that he was being chased by demons. Why did he think that? Were they the demons—or so-called demons—who stole the shroud? Was Tychon perhaps—"

"Where did the demons go after running out of the church?"

"I wish I knew. I'm not even certain the workers I spoke to at the church were telling the truth about seeing demons. I'm not sure if anyone has told me the truth."

"Including me?"

"Why do you think I'd suspect you of lying? About what? I merely came here for assistance with these spots—what I thought was a serious condition."

Felix's heart beat faster and he began to feel hot. He'd hoped to grill Antonina but now he was the one on the grill.

"What about the dead man in your courtyard?" Antonina pressed on. "Who was he? Didn't you recognize him?"

"No. Or do you suppose I was lying to Anastasia about that?"

"You must have seen the man at the palace, Felix. He was an aristocrat, I understand."

"What does it matter to you who he was? Or what I know?"

She reached out and playfully tugged his beard. "I am a curious person, Felix. You know that. I don't like secrets, unless I share in them."

"Any secrets I might have to share, Anastasia has already shared with you, or so it appears."

Antonina sighed. "I would be less than honest if I didn't admit to you that I also wondered if there was a connection between the demons that Tychon thought were pursuing him and those reputed to have stolen the shroud. So you can't tell me where these fiends went, or who the courier was, or why the relic was stolen or who stole it?"

"I wish I could. I would already have told the emperor."

"Tychon was not the most honest of servants. I would hate to think he became involved in anything illegal. And I would not want anyone to suspect me of wrongdoing because of the actions of a thieving servant."

"I can assure you, Antonina, I never suspected you of anything."

"What a bad liar you are, Felix. Do you want me to arrange for that horse now? There is still time to slip out of the city before the sun rises. I would hate for you to be arrested. Anastasia is upset as it is with her sister's death. I will send some of my servants as an armed escort, for your safety."

Felix got to his feet. If he took her offer, would he make it as far as the city gates? He doubted it. "I appreciate your concern for myself and Anastasia, however my investigation isn't done yet."

Whether Antonina would have called her guards to stop him from leaving, Felix never knew. At that moment Fate intervened, in the form of an ape bounding into the room.

No, a demon, shouting weird incantations, waving a necklace in one hand, a wet sack in the other.

Antonina screamed for her guards.

The creature scuttled toward the painted empress. "I command you, Theodora, in the name of all the frogs of Heqt, to step down and obey!" it cried.

The invader stopped dead, its nose practically touching Theodora's garments. The thing's fish-like mouth puffed in and out, revealing jagged teeth. A finger poked at the painted plaster. There was nothing in the least magickal about the next words to issue from the puckered mouth.

Dedi pivoted and sprinted out of the room, straight past the sword-wielding guard who rushed in.

"Never mind that one!" Antonina shrieked. "It's this man who attacked me!"

Felix had taken a step toward the door.

The guard raised his sword and rushed forward.

And crashed to the floor.

Felix stumbled over the prone body. Slipping and skittering, almost losing his balance, he flung himself into the hallway and stumbled after the nightmarish creature, whatever it was.

He didn't pause to scrape the squashed frogs from the slippery soles of his boots.

Frogs!

The demonic creature had emptied frogs out of its sack, before chanting incantations at Theodora's picture.

In his excitement, Felix hadn't put things together instantly. Racing through the darkened back garden he realized he was on the heels of whoever, or whatever, had invaded the empress' mausoleum.

The guard slumped beside the back gate looked up groggily, as if drugged, as Felix pounded past and into the street.

He had been steadily gaining on his prey as they fled Antonina's property. Now it took him only a few more strides to catch up. He grabbed the back of the small figure's tunic and pulled it to the pavement.

Half afraid he might find himself face to face with a demon, he forced the thing to face him.

"Dedi!" He recognized Theodora's Egyptian magician from performances at court. "You have some questions to answer. You're coming with me."

"Where are we going?" gasped the little man.

That was a good question. But there wasn't time to waste. Antonina's guards would be after them soon. What choice did he have but to trust Anastasia, for better or for worse?

Felix yanked Dedi to his feet and began dragging him along the street. "We're going to see a bear-keeper."

DAY EIGHT

Chapter Fifty-three

Maria flung a bucketful of dead rats over the railing into the bear pit. The bear reared up on its hind legs and batted at the falling rodents, its monstrous head looming so near Felix felt the animal's humid breath. He could make out a crescent shaped white patch on the creature's chest.

The pit looked dangerously shallow. Felix glanced nervously toward the gate at the top of the ramp descending into the well-like concrete hole, reassuring himself it was securely chained shut.

"Hercules does love his rats." Maria was a ponderous ruin of a woman, her face wattled and wrinkled as if it had come partly loose from her skull. She had succeeded her long dead husband as bear-keeper. "Now then, sirs, since I have served Hercules, how may I serve you?"

"We need a place to stay for a while," Felix told her.

Maria examined him suspiciously. "Is that so? I wouldn't think this would be a suitable place to stay for a gentleman such as yourself, sir. As for your servant…" She peered at the magician with a mixture of distaste and horror.

"We both need lodgings." He handed her the copper ring. "Anastasia said if I showed you this ring, you would assist us."

Again Felix was beginning to have his doubts about this arrangement. Even if the old woman were trustworthy, what about all the people in the Hippodrome he had asked directions from? Would they remember him asking the whereabouts of Maria the bear-keeper if questioned?

Maria drew the ring up close to her eyes. "Praise be! I always told the dear little sisters they could count on Maria, but now they are of high rank I never imagined any of them would ever need the help of a poor woman like me." She wiped at the tears suddenly running down her wrinkled cheeks. "To think, little Anastasia remembers old Maria. A fine lady like her and the sister of an empress."

Remembered you when you could be of some use, Felix almost said, then chided himself for being unfair to Anastasia. Maria appeared to be genuinely moved. Nothing in her demeanor suggested that Anastasia had sent Felix into a trap.

"Come along then." Maria turned and waddled away. "You can stay with me for as long as you wish."

Felix followed, Dedi at his heels.

The clammy air was disturbed by the occasional freezing draught slithering along the concrete floor.

He expected Antonina's guards to suddenly come running into the subbasement. After all, Antonina's house was practically next to the Hippodrome. The sun had long since risen. The guards must be scouring the area.

They passed several pits similar to that occupied by Hercules. He heard a cacophony of scrabbling, roars, hisses, grunts, growls. At one point he shuddered at what sounded like the dolorous cry of a distressed infant. Animal odors rose from the pits, each different yet equally foul. Who could say what beasts were confined in those noisome holes?

The trio passed by a wall into which were built cages with iron bars. Grotesque shadows shifted in the dark corners of the barred dens. Felix made no attempt to look inside. He knew there was nothing here but the common animals which regularly performed or were displayed at the Hippodrome.

After what felt like a long time but probably wasn't, Maria said, "Here we are."

Where they were appeared to be a heap of planks, bricks, broken masonry, and even pieces of carts piled in a corner of the subbasement. Maria invited them to step through the doorway that opened, incongruously, into the pile.

Felix hesitated. For no reason he could name he had a terrible premonition.

Something was waiting inside for him.

Antonina's guards? Excubitors? Porphyrius' murderous Blues? Or something much worse?

He clutched at the chains around his neck. His fingers brushed past the cross and touched the amulet Anastasia had given him. The irrationality of his reaction shamed him, brought him back to his senses.

Inside Maria's home a clay lamp burned atop a table made from an overturned crate. The body of a chariot served as a couch. The walls were draped with ragged, stained hangings.

Before Felix could assimilate all the details, Maria ushered them through another opening and into a smaller chamber, similarly lit by a guttering flame.

"Make yourselves comfortable," she told the pair, with no hint of irony. "I will be back soon with something to eat."

Felix blinked in the shifting light and fingered his amulet.

He glanced around and abruptly realized he was staring into two black, bottomless vortexes. The eyes in the stern face of the Christian's crucified god.

His fingers left the amulet for the cross.

Chapter Fifty-four

As the day passed the icon's baleful stare never wavered.

Or at any rate Felix hoped and believed the day was passing. How much time had gonne by he couldn't say. Now it seemed an eternity, now only a few heartbeats.

As a young soldier he had often waited for battle, sometimes in the darkness of a tent, other times in the open under night skies. Now he felt the same unbearable tension, every muscle in his body, every thought, screaming to get on with the fight, to be done with it, to feel the sweet relief of victory or perhaps to feel nothing at all ever again. But at least to have it over.

The future was always more frightening than the present. The present you grappled with as best you could. The future was a mocking, unreachable phantom.

But this waiting was worse because Felix did not know what it was he waited for. What sort of fight? Or would he have any chance to fight?

Felix tried not to stare at the icon, an image of Christ painted on a plank by an amateur hand. It had been half consumed by fire. The face wore a pointed beard, as black as the charred edges of the plank. The thin-lipped mouth evidenced cruelty and the enormous eyes were demonic in the flickering lamplight. Anastasia insisted her god looked into men's souls. This god seemed to be skewering Felix's soul. His head pounded.

"It's such a comfort to me," came Maria's voice from the doorway. "It reminds me that He is forever looking after us."

The bear-keeper had brought bread, cheese, and olives, along with a jug of wine. Felix thanked her. Perhaps if he got something into his stomach his headache would go away. Was it from being kicked or from the sleeping potion Antonina had slipped him?

"I found the icon shamefully abandoned in the ruins of a burnt house." Maria tapped the dented jug from which she had poured wine into a pair of mismatched ceramic cups. "The same place I found this jug."

"The authorities tend to frown on upon theft," Felix noted

"Theft? Rescuing useful items, you mean. Anyway, Hercules loves taking walks with me and no one seems to care if we pick up an item or two along the way."

"You take a bear out into the streets?"

"On a chain, naturally."

Recalling the animal cages they had passed, Felix supposed Hercules could use the exercise. "Apes," he said. The story of the watchman at Theodora's mausoleum had come into his thoughts. "Do you have apes?"

"We had an ape, but it escaped. Don't look so alarmed. That was years ago. The ape's long dead by now, or else married a rich woman and became a senator." She gave a hearty guffaw.

In speaking to her, Felix noticed the colorful wall hanging behind her shoulder. It showed several angels in flight. "Did you find that in a burnt-out building as well?"

"Oh, no. My girls sent that to me. The sisters, you know. They have never forgotten their old friend Maria. I refused to let them be put out on the street. Imagine the cruelty of the Greens, refusing to help the family of their own bear-keeper after he died so untimely. The Blues will show they are better than that, I said. And so we did. Not that we were not benefited. The girls turned out to be splendid performers."

Indeed, their performances were the subject of a thousand salacious rumors, some of which might even be true, Felix thought.

"They often sent me gifts," Maria continued. "Alas, poor Theodora has left us already."

"Maybe not," muttered Dedi, who had been keeping silent.

Maria glanced at him with grim disapproval before turning her attention back to Felix. "I am happy to find you so much better. When I looked in before you were dozing and muttering about strange events. I fear you may have a demon inside you, sir, contending for your soul. I have been praying and I am sure you are doing the same."

Felix grunted in a noncommittal manner.

Maria smiled at the icon. "You could not have come to a better refuge, unless it were the Great Church. Our Lord will surely expel any evil creatures that dare to come within His sight." She frowned at Dedi again. "I will leave you and your servant alone for now. If you should kill any rats, I collect them for Hercules, so throw them into the box beside the outer door." She lumbered away.

Felix squeezed his eyes shut. When he opened them the icon was still glaring at him. Or was it glaring at an evil creature inside him? "Did I doze off?" he asked Dedi.

"Yes. Probably you are still feeling the effects of whatever Antonina put you to sleep with. She could as easily have put you to sleep forever. You've been lucky."

"Lucky. That's my name, isn't it?"

Or was he only slow-witted? Maybe he should have taken Antonina's offer. He'd have been safely away from Constantinople. Dedi was right, if she had wanted to kill him he'd already be dead. What would be the point of ordering her servants to kill him before they reached the city gates when it could have been done in private at her house?

Well, Felix was often a step behind. But it didn't matter so long as you kept going. If your opponent stopped before the end of the race, you'd end up ahead. Still, Felix wished his head would stop pounding. Would Julius Caesar have crossed the Rubicon if he'd had a bad headache that day?

"Don't excite yourself," Dedi said. "Whatever vile potion Antonina's given you will take hold of your thoughts if you let them get out of control."

"You know a lot about such potions?"

"I studied much ancient lore when I lived in Egypt. How do you think I pass by guards as though I were invisible? A bit of powder in their wine, or tossed into the air and they are oblivious to the world."

"Do you have a powder that will tell me what to do next instead of sitting here, rotting away in this dark hole while half the city is hunting me?"

"I have explained how I shall bring Theodora back to save us."

"It seems to me you've already failed twice. An Egyptian amulet and frogs! Why frogs?"

"Because frogs are sacred to the frog-headed goddess Heqt, who represents resurrection. Just as scarabs are involved with resurrection."

"But they didn't work to resurrect the empress."

Dedi's mouth puffed in and out in annoyance. "It is more efficacious to place the scarab directly on the body, which I could not do. Also, I stood on a frog. Since they were sacred in Egypt at one time that was a capital crime. I hope I have not offended the goddess."

Felix shook his head. "I'd hate to be hanged for a frog. I saved your life, Dedi. The least you can do is tell me the truth even if nobody else will!"

"You saved me? It was I who burst in just as Antonina was about to finish you off."

"What are you talking about? She was offering me a way out of the city. And where would you have gone to hide, if not for me? You'd be in the dungeons by now."

Dedi patted the small satchel attached to his belt. "I was about to use the invisibility dust I keep here, but there wasn't enough for two."

"I thought you said it was your sleeping potions that made you seem invisible to guards." The self-styled magician had been making a living for years entertaining Theodora with his inventions and wild tales. "Look," Felix said wearily. "Tell me honestly what you saw that night in the mausoleum. Did demons run out of the church?"

"Yes. I did see those two demons fleeing from the church. I thought I had conjured them myself, by mistake."

"And then?"

Dedi turned his palms up. "And then...nothing. I saw demons racing off into the night. That's all."

Felix could see he was lying. But there was no use arguing and possibly antagonizing one of the few allies he had left.

Dedi reached up and rapped at the icon's nose. "Never mind these Christian tall tales. If the old woman senses demons around us it is because I have been summoning them from the underworld. The door has opened. The demons are here. Now I need only to command them to bring Theodora back up into the land of the living."

"Only..."

"It is not much, compared to what I've already accomplished. We must wait until dark. Then...then I will complete the task I have begun. I have everything I need in my satchel. In a few hours Theodora will rise to serve us."

Felix looked at the crooked little creature with whom he was temporarily trapped in this subterranean cell. Did Dedi actually believe the foolishness he was spouting? Or did he only want to believe? Was he as mad as the Jingler? Were old Maria or Anastasia any less mad for believing their prayers to an invisible god might somehow be effective?

But what could Felix do? His home was under surveillance. He couldn't stride out into the center of the Mese and defeat an army of guards and gangs of Blues single handed. If he fled the city then he would never dare to return. And was Dedi trustworthy? Better have him intent on reanimating Theodora than weighing whether to betray Felix to the emperor.

So let Dedi play his game. At least it would pass the time. And it would keep Dedi in his sight. And who knows, maybe it would work.

Felix couldn't help feeling that if his future depended on Dedi's magick, he didn't have much of a future.

Chapter Fifty-five

"Here she comes! Hide the buckets!" a tall excubitor shouted from the alley gate to a colleague lounging by the back entrance to Felix's house.

Anastasia gave the man announcing her arrival a haughty look as he opened the gate for her. "Impertinent fool!" she muttered as she passed. She noticed that the guard with witty remarks wasn't one of those with burns from the hot coals.

She crossed the courtyard in haste and paused when the guard at the door barred her way.

"You can't enter without permission."

"And whose orders might this be?"

"Mine," came the reply from the hall. "I will however make an exception for the sister of the late empress. You may come in and tell me why you are here."

It was Narses. The guard stepped aside and Anastasia crossed the threshold.

"Come into Felix's study. He should be back soon." Narses smiled grimly. "Like a bird to its nest."

"Lamb to the slaughter, you mean," snapped Anastasia.

Narses shrugged. "Those who plot against the emperor must take their chances."

"Why would you think Felix was plotting against Justinian?"

"We have received convincing information. What business do you have at the traitor's house?"

"It is a personal matter."

"Indeed?" Narses looked politely unconvinced.

"I do not see why I should be questioned by a palace function-ary, but since you ask, I have come for certain of my possessions."

Narses openly sneered at her. "Are all your servants intoxicated or run away like the brave former excubitor captain that you must fetch your belongings yourself? I fear I find that highly unlikely."

"Which is of no concern to me. You would not wish Justinian to hear you prevented me from taking my own property, Narses?"

The eunuch's thin lips curved into a baleful smile. "You may be able to rely on your family ties to protect you from harm but dalliances with those who plot against Justinian will cost you any influence at court. Since Felix's treachery has been discovered and his fate sealed, why not help yourself by assisting us? Where can we find him?"

"Betrayal doesn't amuse me."

"Think of it as cutting short the period of terror and misery the poor man must be suffering. A mercy, one might say."

"Felix is not seeking to overthrow Justinian."

Narses shrugged again. "If you insist. Cupid has much to answer for, it seems."

"What can you know of love, you loathsome creature? Get out of my way!"

Narses stood back with an exaggerated low bow and sweeping gesture of one arm. As Anastasia strode past and down the hall, his eyes—the black, expressionless eyes of a carrion bird—fixed their longing gaze on her back.

Anastasia went into Felix's room and sat down on the bed. Out of Narses' sight she allowed her hands to shake. She had expected, wrongly, that the guard at the house would be reduced by now. It would have been possible to take sufficient clothing and anything else that might be useful for Felix under pretext of retrieving her own belongings. With the disgusting eunuch on the scene that wasn't going to work. Luckily, she had brought money with her, concealed in a pouch hanging under her tunic. She would take that to Felix at Maria's and beg him to flee. What choice did he have? And now she would have to evade whoever Narses sent to follow her.

Narses had come after her and stood in the doorway, watching.

She placed several jars of cosmetics, a hand mirror, and a silver comb in a sheet pulled from the bed. "You see, Narses? This is all I came for, although I am sure your suspicious mind sees it as disposing of incriminating evidence."

"Why dispose of the evidence? The entire palace knows the former captain of excubitors is your lover. At least your current—"

She pulled an alabaster jar from the bundle she had made and drew her hand back.

Narses flinched.

Rather than throwing the jar, Anastasia laughed at him and left.

As she entered the Mese, she saw a familiar figure walking in her direction. It was Anatolius, the lawyer she had arranged to free Felix from the dungeons. After she had cleared the way with Justinian, she had sent a senator she knew to Anatolius. Was he hurrying to Felix's house? "What a wonderful surprise, meeting you like this," she exclaimed loudly as he approached, for the benefit of whoever was following her.

Anatolius gave her a look of bewilderment as she half dragged him down the wide street.

"I'm not in need of any…uh…services right now," he stammered, peering at her.

"Don't you remember me? From the palace? We have so much to talk about! But first, I wish to choose a new lamp. You know how careless servants can be, and here is just the place to find one."

The shop was a cave filled with flickering light from lamps of clay, bronze, silver, gold, alabaster. Some small enough to carry in one's hand, others as big as cauldrons. Lamps hung from the ceiling by chains and stood on tripods and thin marble pedestals.

Anastasia propelled Anatolius to the rear of the shop where a lamp modeled on the Great Church, covered with a glowing perforated dome, sat on a table against a wall from which elaborately worked hanging lamps sprouted like a form of fabulous fungi.

"Thank heavens I saw you, Anatolius." Next to the Great Church was an Egyptian artifact made of silver to a design that would bring a blush to many. She pretended to examine it. "Narses is waiting in ambush in Felix's house."

"You're Anastasia," Anatolius said. "Theodora's sister. I've seen you at a distance with Justinian and Theodora but we've never met. How did you recognize me?"

"Oh really! When you worked for the emperor, all the young ladies knew about his handsome young secretary. You were pointed out to me. We'll have to get to know one another better soon. But right now, it's fortunate I did recognize you."

She pointed to a pottery lamp decorated with a wreath and inscribed with a wish Fortuna would light its owner's days. "Perhaps an omen? You were walking right into their clutches."

"I was alert for such a trap and would just have strolled past if need be. I am aware Felix has got himself into a great deal of trouble. May I assume you know where Felix can be found? Tell him he must come to my house, as soon as possible, no matter what. It is urgent."

Chapter Fifty-six

Dedi and Felix crossed the moonlit race track toward the spina. Felix half-expected to be greeted by the sight of the hanged man still dangling from the bronze serpents, the man without a face. Some whispered the emperor was a demon, that he'd been seen stalking around the palace late at night and he'd had no face.

Now the emperor was stalking Felix or rather having him stalked.

The shadows cast by sculptures and jutting pieces of architecture were so blackly featureless, every time he walked out of moonlight into their darkness he felt as if he were stepping into a pit. It felt like a dream, considering that he was here to observe Dedi bring back Theodora.

Which was impossible. Wasn't it?

But then it was impossible that Felix had become involved with Theodora's sister. Impossible that at any instant he might be seized and end his life screaming for mercy in the dungeons.

On the other hand, it was very possible that if he let Dedi out of his sight he'd run straight to the emperor or Narses in order to save himself by betraying Felix's whereabouts. What choice did Felix have but to go along with him? Besides, he couldn't bear to have the fiendish icon staring into his soul any longer. Its angry stare was like having skin ripped off by imperial torturers.

"This is madness," Felix growled.

Dedi waved his hand dismissively. "Do you think I cannot accomplish what I say?"

"She's dead, you fool! Your humors are deranged!"

Dedi shook his head in vigorous denial. "You'll see! You'll see! If I could control the demon that was posing as a servant to Antonina, I can control Theodora, too."

"Servant posing as a demon?"

"Tychon. I followed him from the mausoleum to Antonina's house the night the shroud was stolen. Later I put him under my power."

So, Felix thought, there is a connection between the shroud and Antonina's servant. No wonder she wanted Felix out of the city.

"You didn't tell me anything about following demons that night."

Dedi frowned. "Didn't I?"

"No. Your boastfulness has betrayed you."

"I didn't mean to mislead you."

"Nobody does. That's why I'm totally lost."

"You'll feel better when you see Theodora return."

"I'd much rather not see her, if I had any choice. And why the race track? You used every coin I had to bribe the guard to let us in. What if he recognized me? We might find ourselves surrounded by armed men before we're much older!"

Or was that Dedi's hope? Felix wondered.

"Maria told us he was the man to bribe," Dedi said, "that he was honest. He wouldn't talk. No one will think anything of another request."

True enough, Felix had to admit. He wished the curse tablets he'd paid to have buried at the turns of the track had actually influenced the outcome of the races, or even one race. Then he wouldn't have found himself in this dilemma because he would not have gambling debts.

"Couldn't you summon her in a less public place?"

"No. We're here because I need a place where thousands have died. It makes the magick more powerful." Dedi's crooked teeth glinted as he gave a malicious grin. "And where else in Constantinople have as many died as here during the riots?"

Felix had fought the mobs back then, under the command of Belisarius. That had been an exciting time. He had not been involved in the massacre, thank Mithra. "You're right. It was nothing but slaughter, trained armed men against a rabble. You weren't in the city then. It took days to bury the dead."

The only sound was the faint crunch of their feet on packed sand.

Dedi came to a halt. Felix noticed uncomfortably the entwined bronze serpents looming above them, silhouetted against the gray sky. This was where the latest death had taken place.

"Now attend, and make sure you keep silent," Dedi ordered.

He produced a necklace from his garment and laid it into a shallow hole he scooped out. "Stand back!"

Felix needed no urging. He took a few steps back and cast another uneasy look around. The bone white moon stared down. He could almost see the hanged man in the empty air beneath the serpents. The sound of Dedi pushing sand back over the necklace became the creak of twisting rope.

He looked into the stands. Inky shadows concealed most of the surrounding tiers of seating. He shifted from foot to foot, hoping whatever Dedi had to do could be done quickly and they could leave.

But what if Theodora suddenly appeared in the imperial box?

True, the Egyptian was deranged and yet…

Dedi finished scraping sand back and began to mutter, "May the blood of Isis—"

"Isis? What? Isis isn't—"

"Fool! I'm not talking about that Isis! You must be quiet! First, a protective ritual. When powerful magick is involved, demons are not far off, waiting for their chance."

Dedi returned to his task. "May the blood of Isis guard us from harm in this and all our doings."

Clouds sailed across the staring moon and a chilly wind stirred Felix's hair. From where had it come? Hadn't the air been noticeably still earlier?

"…and by the words of power of the frog-headed goddess, I command you, Theodora, to come to me and do my bidding."

Dedi spat three times onto the little mound marking the grave of the necklace and, raising his arms to the moon, burst into a rolling cadence in his native tongue.

It sounded hideously loud in the dead quiet.

Felix would have found the scene Dedi presented, his fierce face above the short body, addressing invisible gods in the skies in a shrill voice, comical under better circumstances. The wind was getting stronger and blowing some of the sand off the tiny heap by which Dedi stood. The clouds skittering across the moon made the light waver and the shadows lying across the Hippodrome squirm.

He could hear a rustling from the tiers of seats behind him.

Turning his head slowly he saw a shape rise and begin to step down.

Then more shapes. Animated shadows. Leaping and striding about.

Demons! The Hippodrome was filling with demons! The stands were alive with demons!

Cursing his imagination he forced himself to look away. But the effort did not free him from the nightmare, because he immediately saw, at the end of the track where the starting gates were located, a lone figure. Floating toward him, through bands of moonlight and darkness.

No, not floating, running.

A woman.

For a heartbeat Felix could see the cruel scimitar of Theodora's smile, before he fought through the fog of horror engulfing him. "Anastasia!"

Dedi wailed in terror. "You've interrupted me! I warned you! The demons will descend upon us!"

"They're already here," Felix shouted back, grabbing Anastasia's arm and turning to flee.

"Them?" She slapped his hand off her arm. "What are you seeing? You mean those beggars in the seats? A few always manage to get in here at night to sleep. Never mind them. I've got a message for you."

Dedi moaned. "I should never have stood on those frogs!"

Anastasia put her face close to his. He felt her warm breath as she whispered. "Anatolius says you must meet him at his house. It is urgent."

She had no time to say anything further before a contingent of armed men poured out onto the track, their raised lances and swords flashing coldly in the stark moonlight.

Chapter Fifty-seven

At least Felix had a destination. Not that reaching Anatolius' house would be easy. Once he managed to get to the stables beneath the track he found his path blocked repeatedly by pursuers. How many were there? It seemed as if Narses had sent a whole army after him. At Anastasia's urging he had bolted instantly. He knew the guards wouldn't touch her and as for Dedi, he was a magician. Let him take care of himself.

Fortunately he was familiar with even the most obscure recesses of the Hippodrome's understructure, having utilized those dark and deserted places for confidential meetings with charioteers and fellow gamblers.

He had managed to elude the hunters so far, but could not shake them off entirely.

Could they hear his pounding footsteps echoing in the stillness? If he stopped and kept quiet they would catch up.

He'd stolen a lantern. The light from the holes in the lid flung patterns against rough brick walls and a low concrete ceiling. At some point, without noticing, he had left the subbasements of the Hippodrome and entered the chaos of cellars, cisterns, and ruins beneath Constantinople. Was it any wonder the demons Dedi had conjured joined in the chase?

No, he told himself, the scurrying he heard was nothing but rats.

As he descended further into the underworld the darkness enclosing him seemed to call to some inner darkness. All of his fears rose up and filled his mind, a sickly haze over a dismal swamp.

More scuffling, louder this time.

"Rats," he muttered. "Only rats."

He looked back over his shoulder.

There! In the shadows!

The rat was man-sized and had extremely long limbs, spider-like, and a coat of black fur.

Mithra! A demon! Felix whirled and raced away.

He had completely forgotten the pursuing guards. Behind him he could hear the loud click of sharp claws on concrete as the thing came after him, never gaining but always on the point of being close enough to leap forward and grab him.

Wild-eyed, Felix raced down a passageway, rounded a corner, and plunged across a cavernous space half filled by piles of rubble, its ceiling vanished into darkness overhead. The shadows on the walls, writhing in the light from Felix's swinging lantern, were huge bat-like creatures with squirming snake hair.

He flung himself down a set of mossy stairs. The drip of water plopping into the black mirror of a cistern below turned suddenly into the sound of regular breathing. He approached the cistern cautiously.

The huge head of a magnificent cat had emerged from the sty-gian depths and beckoned him with an immense paw, its breathing magnified by the walls of the vast chamber. Tattered strips of cloth, the wrappings of a mummy, hung from the gesturing paw.

"Come, Felix, I have been waiting for you for so long." The cat thing spoke in a woman's voice.

Felix pivoted and ran back up the stairway, slipping on the moss, while the cat roared its disappointment.

Demons! Dedi had loosed them on the city, he thought. When he emerged would he find a slaughter in progress in street, alley, and forum? Would misbegotten shapes be feasting on flesh while monstrous beings soared in flocks above the Great Church and the Hippodrome?

He paused, standing among rubble, panting, to listen for sounds of pursuit.

Nothing but his own labored breathing.

Had Antonina poisoned him after all? Had he died and gone to the underworld? He trudging wearily through a series of linked rooms containing only dust.

The flame in the lantern began to gutter, the oil nearly gone. When the lantern went out, he would be lost in impenetrable darkness with no means of escape. "And not a chance to climb the seven-runged ladder to heaven," he murmured, his Mithran beliefs crowding out everything that Anastasia had tried to teach him.

And there, as if conjured up by the thought, stood a ladder outlined by a rainbow, reaching toward the ceiling.

He began to climb. Or was he dreaming? Or dead? The more he climbed, the longer the ladder seemed to become. Halfway up, holding on grimly with one hand, he batted away a flying monster blessed with large teeth and a small body that whirred up from the darkness below.

Finally he reached a trapdoor.

Pushing it open, he looked cautiously out.

He had arrived in a torch-lit courtyard over which loomed the walls of the Hippodrome, but as far as he could see there were only the usual beggars and whores on the street.

Then again, they could be demons in disguise, he thought, levering himself into the open air.

The star-pocked night sky dazzled him after the inky depths. It drove ideas of demons from his mind. Perhaps they had been partly the result of Antonina's potion or the knock he'd taken on his head? As for his pursuers, he must have lost them underground.

He began to walk toward Anatolius' house.

Chapter Fifty-eight

Felix waited impatiently beside the desk in Anatolius' office. Why was Anatolius being so mysterious? Had he made a discovery about the theft of the shroud? Felix hoped so. He had had to slip past several patrols to reach Anatolius' house. How much longer would be able to elude the grasp of the authorities, not to mention the Blues?

The damned skull in the mosaic desk top kept grinning at him. At least the icon in Maria's hideaway hadn't grinned. He pushed an unpleasant-looking legal paper over the horrid visage.

As he looked up an ill-clad man shuffled in, leaning on a staff. His sandals slapped the floor as he approached. "Captain Felix, I am pleased to make your acquaintance."

"Mithra! John!"

"Not so loud, Felix. You'll alert the servants. I've kept on my travel disguise so they don't recognize me. They think I'm from a country monastery, come to consult Anatolius about a property dispute."

"You're risking your neck, John. What do you think will happen if Justinian's spies catch you?"

"I'm more worried about what Cornelia will say when I get back."

"If you get back."

"I thought it too dangerous to send a letter and I couldn't trust a messenger."

"It's to do with the shroud?"

John sat on one side of the desk and Felix on the other. "Yes. I understand from Anatolius you have made progress in your investigation, but time is running out."

"I have formed suspicions. Too many. I sense I'm on the verge of a solution though. Don't tell me you've deduced from our visit to the church what I haven't been able to find out after running around the city for a week?"

"Not at all. I was presented with new information you couldn't have discovered."

"Aboard a ship?"

"Let me explain quickly. As far as I can tell I managed to get into the city without being recognized, but nothing is ever certain here. This is what happened. Almost as soon as the *Leviathan* sailed, a well-dressed traveler drew my attention because of his secretive behavior and apparent special relationship with the captain. At one point Peter was pushed overboard—he was fished out safely—and I suspected this traveler was the culprit, because it happened not long after Peter had been in the captain's cabin where the stranger was lodging."

"There was something in the cabin the rascal didn't want anyone to see?"

"That's right. Taking advantage of the absence of most of the crew ashore at the next port, I searched the cabin and found a soft package carrying the imperial seal. Although my inspection of the package was interrupted, I assume it was what the traveler feared Peter might have noticed, for he, the traveler, sought to silence me with a garrotte."

Felix stared at John in amazement. He noticed for the first time the necklace of purpled flesh around John's neck, a fainter copy of the deadly necklace worn by the dead courier in Felix's courtyard. "Was it a matter of the traveler hiding something or had Justinian ordered him to make sure you never made it into exile?"

"The former, I believe. He didn't take into account that I was a military man once. I managed to throw him off and get a glimpse of his face. However, I couldn't prevent him fleeing the ship with the package."

"Mithra!" Felix cursed.

"The ship's captain, who had not been paid in advance for his favored passenger's voyage, was only too happy to identify him, although at no little expense to me. His name is Karpos, and he's an aide to Belisarius. He did not reveal his business to the captain and the captain did not enquire, but given he was traveling on a boat wallowing from port to port around the coastline, it seems obvious he left the city in haste, taking the first available ship. You recall we sailed the morning after the relic was stolen and a piece of cloth would make for a small, soft package. An aide to Belisarius would doubtless possess an imperial seal in order to facilitate transportation of official documents. No doubt he thought the captain's cabin was a safer place to leave it than carrying it around on his person."

"Belisarius is involved in this business?"

"It points that way. I overheard crew members speak of the delights to be experienced when the ship arrives in Italy and calls at Crotone. Belisarius is currently campaigning in that area."

Felix nodded thoughtfully. If Belisarius was involved then doubtless Antonina was involved, as he had suspected, and it seems likely her servant Tychon had been assisting her.

"Witnesses to the theft at the church reported seeing demons, you'll recall," John went on, "and according to Hypatia visions could be created by inhaling a mixture of incense and mandrake. She tells me the latter is also known as Circe's plant."

"She's not the only person we know who is well versed in herbal lore," Felix observed with a frown.

"Indeed. The instant I learned the identity of our mysterious traveler, I recalled common talk about Antonina's entanglement with Karpos, the young man who had accompanied her back from Italy. She's as notorious for her infidelities as for her potions."

"It's no secret she came to Constantinople to convince Justinian to give Belisarius more financial support but was thwarted by Theodora's death. Could it be…?"

"A relic as precious as the Virgin's shroud would be worth a large sum, particularly if held for ransom, or perhaps it would attract loyalty from certain people. Some might even imagine it does possess magickal powers which would aid Belisarius."

"It's certainly possible," Felix replied.

"Antonina is a ruthless woman, but I cannot think how she would have the gall to steal one of the city's holies relics. Nor do I think Karpos would have taken part in the robbery himself. She's not likely to admit anything, but the weight of circumstantial evidence may be enough to bring about some sort of resolution."

"Well…"

John stood. "I must take ship and catch up with the *Leviathan* now." He pulled a folded sheet of parchment from his robes and handed it to Felix. "I have written this information down and added to matters to which you can attest it makes a strong case against Belisarius for someone who is looking to make a case against him."

"And I know exactly who that is."

Chapter Fifty-nine

"So, my great bear, you will have your command." Anastasia gave Felix a kiss he did not return with his customary ardor.

He had asked her to walk in the garden, away from the prying eyes and ears of the servants. They stopped in front of a huge rose bush. The roses, nodding as bees came and went, and the buds fallen to the path, enveloped them in sweet perfume. Sunlight slanting through the flowers lent a blush to Anastasia's features. She glowed with the impossible beauty of things forbidden.

"Yes, I will be leading troops in Italy when Germanus takes over the campaign, which is sure to happen. He grinned like a wolf when he read John's letter. I could practically see blood dripping from his jaws."

Anastasia made a face. "What an image!" She regarded him through narrowed eyes. "What is troubling you, Felix? Shouldn't we be celebrating?"

Felix found himself gazing over her shoulder into the roses and forced himself to look into her perfect, aristocratic face. "We can't continue, Anastasia. It won't work."

She looked at him as if she hadn't heard correctly. What was going on behind the mask she seemed to draw suddenly over her emotions? Felix couldn't guess. Then she laughed lightly, as a lady might laugh at an inept and slightly inappropriate joke from the lips of a callow young courtier. "What can you possibly mean by 'it won't work'? The events of the past days have upset your humors. I can understand that. We can soon put that right."

She laid a hand on his arm. He did not react. It took all his willpower.

"I am only a soldier, Anastasia, and you are the sister of an empress."

"Only a soldier? A general, you mean! What more fitting partner for a general than a member of the imperial family?"

"As a general under the command of Germanus I will occupy a lesser position than I do now as excubitor captain. For myself, I do not care. I would return to battle as a common foot soldier if necessary."

"And how long would a man of your ability remain a foot soldier or a common general?"

"You are ambitious, Anastasia. I am not for the kind of rank you envisage. You see me in charge of the Army of the East when Germanus succeeds Justinian and perhaps later my succeeding Germanus. You see yourself as empress, like your sister."

"Have I given you that impression? You're being unfair."

"I'm a simple man. I've always felt out of place at the palace. That is your world."

"You know I spend as little time at the palace as possible. I will travel to Italy with you."

"And we will be like Belisarius and Antonina. I don't want that."

"You think she rules him. Is that what you mean?" Her face was redder than could be accounted for by the reflection of the roses.

"Since you insist of putting it into words, yes."

Felix saw her stiffen.

"You think I've been using you?" she said. "You think I'm nothing but a whore?"

"I didn't say that. I don't think it. I don't regret our time together."

"A fine way you have of showing it!"

"Besides, you are much younger than me."

"Not that much younger."

"Enough so that I will be an old man before you are ready to settle for an old man."

Her eyes glistened. "People who are in love don't fear the future, Felix."

"Are you in love with me?"

"You doubt it? What have I done to make you doubt it? Why do you think I agreed to share your bed?"

Felix's hand went to his beard. "I wish I knew, Anastasia. I think you like exciting tales but I am not a very exciting man, however much you want to make me one."

Anastasia blinked until she had squeezed out a few teardrops, which ran down her flaming red cheeks. "You have thought out your whole case against me, haven't you? Now that you have what you want, I have no use to use. Why didn't you send your lawyer friend over to prosecute me?"

"I…I'm sorry…"

Her hand tightened on his arm and she leaned toward him. "You're out of sorts. We'll talk again tomorrow. You can't make a decision like this so quickly. You took me by surprise."

"No, Anastasia, I have thought about—"

She put her lips against his cheek. "Come with me to our bed, my big naughty bear."

He pried her hand off his arm and stepped away.

It made him ache to look at her. To never touch her again… He felt a breathless emptiness rise up inside him, as if he were about to step off a precipice.

"No," he said. "It is over."

Her eyes flashed. Before he could react she raked his face with her fingernails. He could feel the hot blood blossoming and running down his cheek as she spun around and walked away.

Epilogue

A rutted path led from John's villa to a wide field overlooking the Aegean. The waters were so bright and blue they might have been glazed, the color of a ceramic serving bowl at a palace banquet. Grazing sheep made John think of clouds drifting above the towers and domes of Constantinople.

Sheep! John hadn't realized that he owned so many sheep.

There was a small ruined temple in the field. The pillars and part of the roof remained but any representation of the deity it had sheltered—perhaps Demeter, who had been popular in the region—was missing.

John and Anatolius sat on a bench inside in the shade, near where the statue of the deity had once stood.

"You're a true soldier of Mithra, Anatolius, visiting a man in imperial disfavor."

His companion waved a hand. "I had business in Athens, an excellent excuse to visit in person. And if I decide to take a short tour while in Greece, well, why not? I don't think Justinian is hiding behind any of those bushes, and as for his spies, you haven't seen any strangers on the estate, have you?"

"No."

"If any do suddenly appear, we'll see them coming across the field and deal with them. We could stampede the sheep and crush them to death…though I see you still carry a blade. And wisely, in my opinion. So we don't need to worry about spies. I hope you and your family are prospering in your new lives?"

"It's a little too early to tell."

"It's very different from the city, isn't it?" Anatolius sounded almost wistful. "I would write a poem about your bucolic retreat but Felix, in sending his good wishes, made it plain I am not to descend to poetry as he put it. Alas, the muse's whisperings fall upon deaf military ears. So instead, a description of how events have unfolded."

Anatolius began with an account of everything that had befallen Felix with occasional refreshment from a jug of wine at their feet as the heat increased with the advancing day.

John stared out over the dazzling sunlit water as he listened.

"Felix and I have deduced," Anatolius said, "pooling what we had learned with what Anastasia gleaned from her friendship with Antonina, that Porphyrius the charioteer had long been involved in smuggling. Felix confessed he had been forced into assisting Porphyrius due to his debts."

"Debts are more deadly than a Persian sword, especially for a captain of excubitors," John observed.

"Indeed. But Porphyrius was clever, he kept his involvement in relic smuggling well concealed. Remember, Felix's contact was the Jingler. Felix didn't realize he was actually working for the charioteer. The murdered courier, Martinus, had become entangled for the same reasons as Felix. He was one of those foolish young fellows who get into debt by gambling on the racing. When I spoke to his widow, she told me in passing about their missing servant. Given his master's participation and admittedly drawing my bow at a venture, I suspect this unfortunate fellow was also involved in the matter and was the man Felix saw hanged in the Hippodrome."

"And his execution was either to punish him for some infraction or more likely to demonstrate to Felix that Porphyrius would not hesitate to carry out his threats if the piece of shroud was not returned?"

Anatolius nodded and took another sip of wine. "Of course, there is nothing to connect Porphyrius directly with the missing relic except Felix's account of their uncivilized meeting in the Hippodrome."

He paused. "By the way, I notice you have not yet restocked that foul Egyptian wine you favor. I'm happy to say."

"A consignment is on the way."

"Then I'll bring my own next time I visit. Let me see. I believe Martinus' servant must have been one of the thieves who fled the Church of the Holy Apostles with the shroud. He would have taken it directly to his master for delivery to Felix. The other thief was, it seems, Antonina's servant Tychon. We know that because Dedi, who was trying to reanimate Theodora from her sarcophagus at the time of the theft, followed one of these so-called demons back to Antonina's house. He told Felix all about his forays into magick."

"I'm surprised Dedi didn't sail immediately for Egypt as soon as Theodora died. He has enemies at court and no protectoress now."

"He's nothing if not inventive. Having failed to bring his former employer back, I gather from Felix he's taken up residence under the Hippodrome, making a dishonest living by selling curse tablets to faction members."

John gave a thin smile and said nothing.

Anatolius paused to collect his thoughts, watching his horse crop grass not far off, and then went on to tell John that he had deduced that Antonina's servant Tychon would have been known to the missing courtier Martinus because he was also a former Blue, as Antonina had mentioned to Anastasia. "And his task was to steal from Antonina's workshop the incense and mandrake causing those at the church to have visions of demons," he continued. "He was suspected of pilfering and died when he threw himself over the seawall as a result of Antonina drugging wine to which, as it turned out, he had been helping himself."

"It's a complicated affair, Anatolius. You and Felix make a good investigative team. From what you say, presumably Porphyrius didn't find out about Tychon's involvement, or he might well have suffered the same fate as Martinus' servant."

"That's what I think. After all it was the Jingler who was responsible for the details of the smuggling, so Porphyrius did not know every person involved, which added to his own safety.

"I base my speculation, admitting it is something a lawyer should never do, on the fact Felix told me he could never discover the Jingler's superior because the Jingler claimed his instructions came from an anonymous party. But when he mentioned Porphyrius to him he became agitated, and what strikes me is that the Jingler's death was unusual in a city where the typical method of settling disputes is a knife in the ribs. Quicker and simpler by far than creeping up on a man with a coil of rope over your shoulder."

"Then again it may have been suicide, but two private hangings in one set of rogues is not met often in my experience," John observed.

"At least some good has come of the poor man's death. It transpires the Jingler owned the tenement in which he lived and once sold the proceeds by direction of his will are to be used to found a home for lock-makers' orphans. Though I do wonder how many lock-makers' orphans there can be, perhaps he thought such charity was the key to heaven."

The two men fell silent. The scene stretching before them—the sheep, the sea, bees buzzing around clumps of wild flowers, a few olive trees—was almost too peaceful and transparent. There were no hidden mysteries here as there always were in the noisy, teeming crowds of Constantinople. Anatolius' words about devious dealings might have emanated from another world.

Eventually Anatolius sighed. "So I think it is safe to conclude that Porphyrius planned to steal the Virgin's shroud as part of his smuggling activities. He recruited accomplices he knew as gamblers or former Blues, while keeping his own distance. The Jingler acted as a go-between, coordinating those involved. Certain Blues helped Porphyrius to enforce his will when necessary since they are always eager for mayhem."

"And Belisarius' aide Karpos?"

"He was not involved with the smuggling operation. He had only arrived in Constantinople with Antonina a few weeks before and had hardly emerged from her house, even to attend functions at the palace, whereas Felix had on several earlier occasions taken packages from Martinus to pass along via his excubitors. Karpos, spending so much time at Antonina's house, somehow learned that Antonina's servant Tychon had been recruited into the plot to steal the relic, perhaps by overhearing a revealing comment or Tychon might have become intoxicated and talked too much.

"As I see it, Karpos discovered when Martinus was due to deliver the package containing the relic to Felix and either followed him or lay in wait. He strangled him, heaved the body over the wall into Felix's courtyard, and made off with the shroud. Naturally Porphyrius had no idea who stole it and did everything he could to retrieve it."

John considered the situation. "It was a master stroke on Karpos' part. Felix, a man well-known as a supporter of Germanus, was left with a corpse on his hands. Not only would Felix be destroyed but Germanus' reputation was bound to be sullied by association."

Anatolius nodded. "The urban watch arrived to search Felix's house only hours after the courier's murder, almost certainly sent there anonymously by Karpos. The relic is extremely valuable. Murder to obtain it would be nothing compared to how it could be used—sold to raise the funds Belisarius hoped Antonina could arrange or perhaps held to ransom it to the church authorities. Perhaps it could offer Belisarius divine aid in his military campaign…and so being a cautious man, Karpos left on the next boat for Italy, taking the shroud with him. The *Leviathan* being a coastal trader it would have been a slow voyage but he and the relic were at least safely away from the city. And where is Karpos now? Presumably he waited for the next ship onward to Italy, the relic still in his possession."

John said he thought the story seemed complete enough, but not entirely satisfying. Karpos, the man responsible for Martinus' murder and John's attempted murder, was free and beyond reach.

The Jingler and Martinus' servant must have been hanged by one or more anonymous Blues at the order of Porphyrius who, if he was not entirely above suspicion, was certainly for all practical purposes above the law.

"As so often happens," Anatolius pointed out. "Still, if the relic is as powerful as it's believed to be, it may bring its own punishment to those who misuse it. It may also have protected the *Leviathan* from sinking."

"A nun who was traveling on board prayed constantly to her god and to the mother of god. Her prayers didn't have very far to travel," John said. "Here's Cornelia," he added as she came across the grass, stepping out of the sunshine into the shady temple to sit beside him.

"What are you smiling about, Anatolius?" she asked.

"It's this. The shroud has been returned anonymously to the Church of the Holy Apostles enclosed in a beautiful box of polished wood which Anastasia recognized as a possession of Antonina's. It appears that the shroud is larger and whiter than when it was stolen."

Cornelia chuckled. "I see. A miracle, no doubt."

"Basilius and the emperor were pleased to be able to tell the populace the relic has been recovered."

"And what about Felix?"

"The information John gave him provided a weapon for Germanus to use against Belisarius, who is to be recalled."

"So Felix has been given his command now?" John asked.

"He's been promised one. The fact that most would consider a generalship a demotion from serving as excubitor captain is also convenient for Justinian, who has been embarrassed by this affair. Felix has freed himself of debt. Porphyrius helped arrange for their forgiveness in return for Felix keeping silent about the old charioteer's activities. Now Felix is in favor, he dare not threaten his life. Of course there are always accidents…but Felix has also finally given up drinking to excess and gambling."

"Again," Cornelia said with a smile.

"So far he has kept it up. And he's given up Anastasia as well."

"You mean she left him?" Cornelia said.

"Not at all. He parted with her. His own doing, it seems."

"A wise move," John put in.

"She also failed to convert him to Christianity," Anatolius said.

Cornelia frowned. "She must be furious. Do you think she is going to cause him trouble?"

Anatolius chuckled. "Not at all. She's off on a new adventure. Attached herself to a poet named Florus. He's penning an epic ode, as he calls it, about her." He stood. "Unfortunately I must leave now."

"You will not stay for a meal at least?" Cornelia asked. "We have fresh-caught fish. Peter proposes to grill it."

"I'm tempted, but it would be wise not to stay too long. One last thing, John. Felix told me someone had damaged the mosaic in your study. In fact, completely removed it and taken it away. Probably a petty bit of vandalism by one of your enemies." He frowned. "And yet, if someone was able to make the mosaic girl repeat the conversations you've had in that room…"

"That sort of hatred…it's a good reason to be gone from that place, John," Cornelia said, a quiver in her voice.

"I shall keep in touch, John, one way or another," Anatolius said.

"Mithra guard you," John responded.

Anatolius waved as his horse cantered away.

John gazed out over the sea. Its brilliance made him blink. He felt Cornelia's hand on his arm and turning, saw she was looking at him with concern.

"Don't worry," he said, "I'll get used to this new life in time. We are together here. That is the important thing."

Afterword

According to the fifth-century Euthymian History attributed to Cyril of Scythopolis, the Virgin's shroud was transferred in the mid-400s from the Holy Land to the Church of the Virgin in Blachernae in Constantinople. Procopius' On Buildings, written in praise of Justinian's public works, refers to it as the Virgin's robe, but we have taken advantage of our literary license to follow Cyril's statement.

Glossary

ATRIUM
Central area of a Roman house, open to the sky, provided light to rooms opening from it, and held an IMPLUVIUM, a shallow pool under the roof opening to catch rainwater for household use.

BLUES
See FACTIONS.

CITY PREFECT
High-ranking urban official whose duties included keeping public order.

CONCRETE
Roman concrete consisted of lime, volcanic ash, and pieces of rock.

CURSE TABLETS
Rolled-up sheets of thin lead inscribed with vindictive magickal imprecations, believed to cause harm to those named in them.

ECHO
In Greek mythology, a nymph who pined away until only her voice remained.

EXCUBITORS
GREAT PALACE guards.

FACTIONS
Supporters of either the BLUES or the GREENS, taking their names from the racing colors of the faction they favored; great rivals with their own seating sections at the Hippodrome; and the common brawls between them occasionally escalated into city-wide riots.

GREAT CHURCH
Colloquial name for the Church of the Holy Wisdom (Hagia Sophia).

GREAT PALACE
Located in southeastern Constantinople, not one building but many, set amid trees and gardens with barracks for the EXCUBITORS, ceremonial rooms, meeting halls, the imperial family's living quarters, churches, and housing for court officials, ambassadors, and various other dignitaries.

GREENS
See FACTIONS.

HALL OF THE NINETEEN COUCHES
Located on the grounds of the GREAT PALACE, the hall for ceremonial banquets.

IMPLUVIUM
See ATRIUM.

KNUCKLEBONES
Popular pastime resembling a game of dice.

MESE
Main thoroughfare of Constantinople, enriched with columns, arches, statuary depicting secular, military, imperial, and religious subjects, fountains, religious establishments, monuments, emporiums, public baths, and private dwellings—a perfect mirror of the heavily populated and densely built city it traversed.

MITHRA
Sun god who slew the Great Bull, from whose body all animal and vegetable life sprang; usually depicted wearing a tunic and Phrygian cap, his cloak flying out behind him, in the act of slaying the Great Bull. He was also known as Mithras. His worship spread throughout the Roman empire via followers in various branches of the military.

SILENTIARY
Court official whose duties were similar to those of an usher.

TESSERAE
Small cubes, usually of stone or glass, used to create mosaics.

To receive a free catalog of Poisoned Pen Press titles, please contact us in one of the following ways:

Phone: 1-800-421-3976
Facsimile: 1-480-949-1707
Email: info@poisonedpenpress.com
Website: www.poisonedpenpress.com

Poisoned Pen Press
6962 E. First Ave. Ste 103
Scottsdale, AZ 85251